THE SERPENT'S EGG

For Jamie, the first reader, and for G. and K.,
for whom I wanted to write this book
twenty years ago.

A Saratime Book

Published by Saratime Publishing Inc.
363 Churchill Avenue North
Ottawa, Ontario
Canada K1Z 5C4

www.theserpentsegg.com

Copyright © 2001, J. FitzGerald McCurdy

Map and Serpent's Egg art copyright © 2001, Saratime Publishing Inc.
Muffy animation copyright © 2001, Saratime Publishing Inc.

National Library of Canada Cataloguing in Publication Data
McCurdy, J. FitzGerald (Joan FitzGerald)
The serpent's egg / J. FitzGerald McCurdy.—1st ed., Sept.2001

ISBN 0-9688713-0-5 (hardcover)
ISBN 0-9688713-2-1 (trade pb.)

I. Title
PS8575.C87S47 2001   jC813'.6   C2001-900852-X
PZ7.M1394Se 2001

Manufactured in Canada

First Hardcover Edition: September 2001
First Trade Edition: November 2002
10 9 8 7 6 5 4 3 2

J. FitzGerald McCurdy

THE SERPENT'S EGG

SARATIME PUBLISHING INC. • OTTAWA, CANADA

TABLE OF CONTENTS

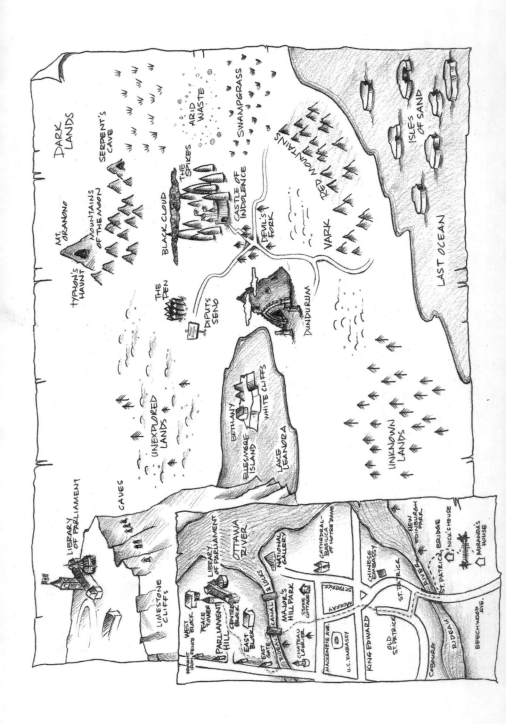

CHAPTER ONE

HATE

orth of Ottawa, deep in the Gatineau Hills, a tremor shook the still night air. One of the hills rippled and blurred as if a sudden breeze had disturbed its reflection in a pond. For an instant, the hill disappeared, replaced by space that was blacker than the landscape. Suddenly, the tip of a sharp stake pierced the blackness, splitting the air. A hot wind issued from the slit, carrying with it the sickening sweet odour of rotting flesh.

The stake prodded the tear, opening a jagged seam. Abruptly, the stake was withdrawn and, for a moment, the only sound was the flapping of the tattered opening as the heat escaped. Then, wicked fangs bit into the tear, and knifelike claws pulled it apart, stretching it as Taog wormed through the opening and dropped to the ground. In one of her right hands, she clutched the black iron stake with a human skull stuck near the pointed end.

The huge creature hacked at the rip with the spiked end of her stake, before reaching inside and pulling out four of her servants—lesser beings, but each more terrible than all the nightmares ever dreamed, and more deadly than anything that had walked the Earth for a thousand years.

When the fourth creature landed on the frozen surface, Taog swung the iron stake, smashing the limbs and snouts of other foul things that attempted to escape from the stinking black hole. *GET BACK!* She screamed into their hate-crazed minds. *IT IS NOT TIME!* She would let them taste freedom soon—as soon as she eliminated the human who had the power to force her back inside the Place with No Name.

Quick as thought, Taog pulled the sides of the opening together and ran her stake along the jagged seam, fusing the edges with liquid fire, and shutting off the shrill screams of those still trapped in the black chasm. But she could not shut out the smell. It stayed on her like rancid perfume—the stench of death.

The creature raised her head. The hill rose before her, solid and impenetrable. She swiveled her long neck, sniffing the air for danger. Satisfied that they were alone, she bit into the side of her thick protruding tongue and chewed on it until she tasted blood. Then, hissing with pleasure, she raised her arms. Four clawed hands tightened about the iron stake. She fixed her gaze on the human head skewered near the sharpest end. The ghastly eye sockets of the skull instantly burst into two blazing red fireballs that spread from the grotesque severed head along Taog's arms, down her body, and up her neck, illuminating the drops of blood dribbling in slow motion from her swollen tongue.

Pointing the stake at the frozen ground, Taog brought it down hard, driving it through the snow and into the earth below. Red flames flared out along the ground in a wide circle and for a moment, as the fire engulfed her, Taog glowed like a human torch. Abruptly, the flames sizzled and sputtered out.

The creature yanked the stake out of the ground. The snow had melted away, and steam rose from the scorched and blackened earth. The sharp smell of burnt soil mingled with the creature's foulness. But what a feeling! She opened her mouth and hissed again, white fangs black with blood. She was free at last! And, after a little killing spree, her powers would be stronger than ever!

Taog glanced at her four servants. She needed them for the task at hand. Crouching to conceal their size, they could go places where she could not—as long as their hoods were up, and they kept their eyes and limbs hidden. But she towered over them by at least five feet. Her body was as black as midnight, coated with armour-like scales. Her feet and the hands on each of her four arms ended in razor-sharp claws. Over her massive shoulders she wore a long black cloak with a loose-fitting hood. Under the cloak, around her middle, was a knotted belt of writhing, flexing serpents whose venom could kill a Vark Giant in seconds. Sticking out from under the shapeless hood was a tangle of matted wet black hair. Human skulls dangled from the creature's ears and around her thick neck she wore her favourite necklace of shriveled corpses. And burning with a fierce glow in the blackness under her hood were two red eyes—Demon's eyes.

The Demon smiled as her red eyes caressed her favourite servants. The four creatures responded as if they had been physically touched. Their massive forms lurched toward their Mistress, drawn like lumps of iron to a magnet.

Taog looked at them fondly. Her beautiful, perfect slaves were bonded to her for all time. She was their creator, and they existed at her pleasure. They were her assassins. They killed for her because the Demon's entire purpose was death. She drew power from the blood of each victim sacrificed to her. And she had been deprived of human blood for a millennium.

Like the Demon, the THUGS were immortal. Well, almost immortal. They could not die except by her hand. That's what she had told them, and they believed her. They stood ten feet tall, and did not know fear. They carried out her orders quickly and brutally. They never spoke. They never thought. They never failed. They were fiends who cared about nothing, except killing.

Thinking about killing and blood sent a thrill along Taog's scaly hide. But her eyes smoldered with hatred. For a thousand years she had been imprisoned in the Place with No Name—a disgusting cavity populated by her creatures and filled with the stink of dead things—things she had had to kill over the years. She hated those who had tricked her . . . no, trapped her, and sent her reeling into that Hell. During those years, her hatred grew until it ate her up and took away her name, and she became Hate. But she was free now! Blood pulsed through her veins as she thought about her enemies and what she had in store for them.

First, she would punish the Dwarves, the filthy sweating hole dwellers. Thinking of the treacherous Dwarves drove her into a frenzy. She raised her claws and scored the air in front of her again and again, hissing and squealing with rage. The other four creatures shrunk away from their Mistress and watched her warily. They looked like giant statues in their black cloaks, except for the chunks of red fire glowing from eyes that were not human.

When the fury left her, the Demon took a moment to picture the thousands of Dwarf bodies littering the streets of their squalid cities. And the blood! Rivers of blood shed for her, feeding her, fuelling her power! She closed her eyes and swayed back and forth in ecstasy, her gross tongue beating violently against the blackness beneath her hood.

After she had rid the world of the Dwarves, she'd deal with her worst Enemy: the despised Elves, a worthless race of treehuggers. No, she mustn't underestimate this Enemy. They might like trees, but they possessed awesome powers. Hate, the demon once known as Taog, smiled wickedly in the darkness. She had defeated the Elven magic. She was free, wasn't she?

When her enemies had driven her into the Place with No Name and used a formidable power to seal it, they thought they had shut her away for all time. Hate had waited a thousand years to escape from her prison, knowing that the deep binding spells woven into the invisible fabric of that black nameless pit could not hold forever. No magic was that powerful. Those who had created the Place with No Name were probably dead. She wouldn't be surprised if the wretched lot that followed had forgotten about her. Well, good! The creature laughed aloud, a horrible sound that cut into the silence like a saw hacking through bone. When the ground was red with their own blood, they would know her.

For seven hundred years, Hate had prowled through the Place with No Name, hunting for its boundaries. But the magic was potent, and the creature found only an endless black nothingness. Three hundred years ago, when the spells began to erode, she found the ends of her empty dimension. She studied the phenomenon— testing it, and calculating distances and locations in relation to the world she had known. Day by day, the magic that held the bleak void together faded, as if the sun were bleeding the colour from its pitch-black threads.

So, Hate watched and waited, knowing that every hour brought her closer to freedom. Moments ago, she had launched herself at the barrier, and had felt it stretch, as if she had run into an elastic wall. Finally, using her stake, she had poked a hole in a small section of the shield. Now she was free! Now her enemies would pay for what they had done to her. And soon, very soon, she would return and then, the hundreds and thousands of evil, demented creatures still trapped in the darkness would pour out and infect the earth like a virus.

But, now that she was free, she must make sure that the power used by her enemies to seal the Place with No Name could not be used against her ever again.

The thought of gaining freedom only to have it snatched away drove the Demon mad. She would never forget the terrible power that had defeated her. Even now, after a thousand years, the fear caught and held her in its iron grip as though it had happened yesterday. Hate shrieked and stabbed the ground with her stake, again and again, until her fear died. *NEVER! NEVER GO BACK!*

Suddenly the creature laughed. What was wrong with her? The only threat to her freedom was a girl. A nobody. A stupid human girl. By the time Hate's enemies realized that the shield enclosing the Place with No Name had been breached, the girl would be history.

That's why Hate had brought the THUGS.

And if they were good THUGS and did what they had to do with the girl, Hate would reward them. Yes! She'd give them a mountain filled with Dwarves and an entire Island of Elves to kill.

The Demon motioned to them now and they came to her quickly. She opened her arms wide and wrapped her huge cloak about them, drawing them close. The serpents around her middle writhed and hissed loudly as the THUGS pressed against their Mistress, but they would not harm her followers. They knew the difference.

Hate pointed the black stake toward the south, and planted her orders in the THUGS' brains. *FIND THE GIRL AND KILL HER!* She pushed the THUGS away. *GO! NOW!* she ordered, without speaking. *I WILL BE NEAR.*

The THUGS could do many things, but they could not fly. Only Hate could do that. After all, Power had its little perks. Her long tongue slid over her thick lips as she tasted victory. Soon! After the THUGS finished their dirty business, the world would belong to her. Soon, every creature on earth would be made to suffer a million zillion times worse than she had suffered. Yes! Nothing could stop her because, before another day had passed, the girl who might have saved the world would be dead.

The Demon froze for an instant, her long wide cloak spread out about her like a giant wing. She watched until the THUGS melted into the trees. Then, she rose slowly into the air and shot through the sky toward Canada's Capital—a black meteor bringing death and destruction.

CHAPTER TWO

SOMEONE ELSE'S DREAM

iranda D'arte woke up early on Friday morning. She was sitting up in bed, the sound of her pounding heart loud in the pre-dawn silence. Forcing herself to breathe slowly, she lay on her back and stared through the overhead skylight, trying to remember the dream that had awakened her. It was still dark and, while the few stars she could see seemed brighter, more defined, than usual, there was nothing to suggest that Hate the Demon was already streaking across the early morning sky toward Ottawa, to find her and kill her.

There had been something—a bloodcurdling terror—inches behind Miranda in the dream. It was a monstrous thing, so evil that she knew her mind would snap if she dared look over her shoulder. She remembered throwing, or dropping, a shiny object on the ground as she ran blindly, lungs bursting, knowing that it was only a matter of seconds before she felt the terror's sharp claws ripping through her spine.

Miranda scrunched her eyes shut, reliving the unbearable panic and wondering why she kept having the same scary dream night after night. What did it mean? Why couldn't she remember more than the running and the fear?

"Maybe I'm going crazy," she groaned. "What if I've got a brain tumour? Or Alzheimer's?"

She turned on the bedside lamp, got out of bed, and walked to the bathroom. Her green-eyed image stared at her from the mirror over the sink—a tall, slim girl with a boyish figure and an oval face framed by short blonde hair. A few freckles dotted her nose, but more would come when summer finally arrived. After feeling her head and examining it in the mirror, she dressed quickly and went in search of her mother who, being an early riser, was sure to be working in her office even though it was only five-thirty a.m.

Her mother looked up from the computer as Miranda entered the room. She took one look at the dark circles under her daughter's eyes and rested her hands on the keyboard. "Do you want to tell me about it?"

Miranda sighed loudly, eyeing the stack of reference books occupying the armchair, near the window. The overstuffed chair pulled out into a narrow spare bed for the rare overnight guest. She placed the books on the floor, plopped into the chair, and dangled her long legs over one of the arms.

"I had that horrible nightmare again," she said. "It seems so real, but when I wake up I can't remember any of the details."

Her mother listened without interrupting while Miranda told her about the thing chasing her. "I don't know what it is, I only know that it's going to kill me. All I can do is run and run until I feel my chest's going to burst." She pressed her fist against her chest as if the pain had suddenly struck again. "What's even worse is that I know it's going to catch me no matter how fast I run, but if I stop, I'll die for sure. I know it's just a dream, but it's real when I'm having it. When I wake up, I can't breathe, my heart's pumping like I've just run a marathon." She looked at her mother, helplessly. "Why is this happening to me? Is there insanity in our family?"

Her mother thought for a minute before grinning. "I think one of my aunts used to run through the village scantily dressed, and there was Uncle Elinvar who planted clothespins, thinking they'd grow into clotheslines. Loads of eccentricity, but no insanity." Noting her daughter's stern expression, she turned off the computer and walked around the desk to perch on the free arm of Miranda's chair, her smile now a look of concern.

"I'm sorry. I know it's not a laughing matter," she said, taking Miranda's hand. "But believe me. You are *not* crazy."

"How do you know?" protested Miranda, freeing her hand from her mother's grasp. "You're my mother. You'd think I'm sane no matter what."

Her mother stood and folded her arms, frowning at the younger image of herself. "Darling, I'm also the only psychiatrist in this house, and don't you forget it. And, despite the fact that you're my daughter, I've been trained to spot abnormal behaviour." She sat again and reached out to brush Miranda's hair off her forehead, chuckling softly. "I'd soon know if you were insane." Abruptly, she turned serious again. "You asked me why it's happening to you. I wish I knew, but I don't. Unless it's not *your* dream."

"What are you talking about?" asked Miranda, looking at her mother as if *she* were crazy. "If it's not mine, then whose dream is it?" She snorted rudely.

"I know that you're the one dreaming, but what if the dream is something that actually happened to someone else?"

"Mom!" Miranda was quickly losing patience. "You're not making any sense."

"It's one of my pet theories," said her mother excitedly, jumping to her feet and pacing back and forth between her desk and Miranda's chair. "OK. My grandparents had my parents. My parents had me. Your dad and I had you, right?"

"Yeah, so?"

"So, there's obviously something of each of them in us?"

"I guess," said Miranda, wondering where her mother was going with this.

"We inherit all sorts of things from our ancestors, like the colour of our hair or the way we look. But we also inherit bits and pieces of their memories. Imagine all of the memories of all of our ancestors." Dr. D'arte paused for a second and stared at Miranda. "What if, a long time ago, one of your ancestors, either on your father's side or mine, was running away from something and somehow what happened to her is being replayed in your nightmare."

"Could that really happen?" asked Miranda, shifting about in the chair, suddenly interested in her mother's theory. "I could inherit someone else's memories?"

"Why not?" said Dr. D'arte. "Look, I don't know if that's what's happening to you, but it's something to think about."

During the drive to school, Miranda thought about her ancestors. What did she know about them? Exactly nothing, except that her father and grandparents were dead. How did they die? Her mother rarely talked about them. Where were they from? What happened to them? Was her mother hiding something? *Is the dream about Mom?* she wondered.

"What?" asked her mother, breaking into Miranda's thoughts.

The girl jumped and looked about, surprised that they were already stopping in front of her school. "I was thinking about Dad," she said.

"Thinking what?" Dr. D'arte asked quietly.

For as long as Miranda could remember, there had only been the two of them. She suddenly realized that she missed not having more family. "Just stuff—like where he came from and how he died." She glanced at her mother. "Mom, I want to know about him."

For a second, Dr. D'arte's hands tightened on the steering wheel, but then she reached out and patted Miranda's knee. "I've been expecting this for a long time. Of course you want to know. I hope you haven't been afraid to ask."

Miranda shrugged. "Sort of. I didn't want to make you sad."

"We'll talk after school. OK?" Her mother tried to smile. "Right now, if you don't get a move on, you're going to be in Mr. Little's bad books."

Miranda rolled her eyes. Everything she did upset the grade four homeroom teacher. "It doesn't matter if I'm late or not, he'd still hate me," she said, giving her mother a quick hug and hopping out of the car.

The older woman watched her daughter wave at her best friends, Nick and Arabella, who waited near the student entrance. She frowned as the three friends talked together excitedly. They were so different from each other. Nicholas Hall lived in the house behind the D'arte's, and was two years older and two grades higher than Miranda. He was a tall, athletic boy, with a head of unruly dark-brown hair that he was forever brushing out of his pale blue eyes— a habit that drove his parents and teachers wild. He and Miranda had been friends since early childhood.

Both of them were heads taller than Arabella Winn, a dark-skinned, wiry dynamo, whose friends called her "Bell." Through the car window, Dr. D'arte noticed the small patch of white in the girl's short black hair, over her right eye, and smiled. For some unknown reason, the white patch bothered Arabella's mother, who kept pressuring her daughter to dye it to match the rest of her hair. But Bell liked it the way it was and refused to change it to suit anyone.

Dr. D'arte remained sitting in the car, staring after Miranda long after the girl and her friends had disappeared inside the school. Her usually calm, smiling face was lined with worry. She thought about Miranda's recurring nightmare. If someone from the past were trying to contact the child, that meant. . . . She shook her head. "Surely it couldn't have anything to do with . . . ?" She didn't realize that she was speaking aloud. "No! That's impossible." But she wondered why Miranda suddenly wanted to know about her father.

"Oh, dear Heaven!" she whispered, her green eyes misting over. "Let it be a coincidence. Don't let them find us."

CHAPTER THREE

STUBBY

r. Little glared at the grade four students and felt like throwing up. He hated the way they looked at him as if he had something stuck between his teeth. He ached to tell them how much he despised them. But no, that went against school policy. If he were running the country, he'd bring back the strap, and lots of other things too—like hangings, public floggings, and truant officers.

Once, before he came to teach at Hopewell Elementary School, Mr. Little had been happy and content, or so he kept telling himself. Now, though, he could barely remember those feelings. *How did I end up with this diapered bunch of snot-nosed brats?* he asked himself a million times a day. The truth was that Mr. Little ended up teaching grade four because his former job, teaching grade nine, caused him to have a total nervous breakdown. Unlike Miranda, her teacher really was crazy, but like most intelligent nut cases, he hid it so well that no one ever suspected how seriously *off* he was.

Ironically, Mr. Little was a small man, shorter than some of his students. He made the taller ones stoop in class so he wouldn't have to look up at them. Every morning, before leaving his apartment on

Prince of Wales Drive, he slicked down his frizzy salt and pepper hair with a handful of watermelon-scented mousse. During the day, clumps of hair gradually became unglued and shot up like bristly weeds sprouting out of his head. In September, just before the start of school, he bought one brown suit which he wore every day, except on parent/teacher days. Then he dressed to impress the parents. Every chance he got, he spent smoking outside the fire exit doors.

The teacher knew that the grade fours hated him and called him "Stubby" behind his back, but he didn't care. He didn't care because the parents of these monsters thought he was the cat's whiskers. They adored him. They trusted him. Like a chameleon, Mr. Little became a different person when parents and other teachers were around.

As he stared about the classroom, his eyes fell on Miranda and he felt the hairs on the back of his neck stand on end. There was something about that particular girl that made him self-conscious. He felt sweat forming on his palms and he knew if he spoke, his voice would be high and squeaky. The D'arte brat had a nasty way of looking at him with those clear green eyes, as if she were peering into his mind—reading his thoughts. Stubby hated her for that.

And he hated that friend of hers. Arabella! A stupid name for a stupid girl. *Rude, ugly, little monster, too*, he thought, and then smiled slyly. *I'll have some very interesting things to say to her mother and father.* He took a few moments to think up some nasty lies to report to the unsuspecting parents. *Believe me, Mr. and Mrs. Winn, she can't* help *stealing, but she's been much better since we started working with her after school.* Even better: *I'm sorry about the weekly detentions, but we can't have the grade fours using language like that around the younger students.* "Yes," he whispered, "that should get the little wastrel grounded for a few months." He grabbed his newspaper and held it up in front of his face to hide his spiteful sneer.

When he had composed himself, he laid the newspaper on the

desk and peered about to see if he could catch the brats whispering. Miranda was looking at him now, and he quickly dropped his eyes to the assignments the students had passed in at the start of class. He picked up the stack of papers and began counting them, annoyed that he let the D'arte girl get under his skin. One missing. He counted them again. Still, one missing. "They think they're so clever," he muttered to himself. "But they can't fool me."

"STOP FIDGETING!" he yelled. Why couldn't they sit still for five seconds? If he had his way, every one of them would be on *Ritalin*.

Because it was the last day of school before Spring Break, by two-thirty p.m. the students were so unruly that Mr. Little was ready to pull his hair out. Instead, he held up the assignments and glared from one mean little face to another.

"I'm missing a paper." He tapped his long, nicotine-stained fingernails on the desk and stared hard at Miranda, willing her to be the culprit. "If you passed in your assignment, raise your hand."

The teacher looked for the delinquent who hadn't raised his or her hand. He finally noticed that the entire class was staring at the student who occupied the desk in the last row behind William Potts.

"GO TO THE CORNER, WILLY!" he roared.

"W-Why?" stammered the bewildered Potts boy.

"Because I said so," snapped the teacher. "Now we'll see who's hiding from me," he said, as William Potts crawled among the desks to the front of the room and slumped on the floor in the corner opposite the door. Mr. Little stared at the red-haired girl who hadn't passed in her assignment, disappointed that it wasn't Miranda or that friend of hers.

"Where's your homework, Penelope?" Stubby was actually quite fond of Penelope St. John (pronounced "Sen Gen," if you please). She lived with her father and stepmother. Mrs. St. John was wife number five.

The St. Johns were rich—very rich—the kind of people Stubby

envied because they could buy anything they wanted. They also gave excellent Christmas presents. Last year he got a gold Swiss watch that must have cost a year's salary, and a huge box of white chocolate-covered caramel toffee, which he loved sucking on in front of the class. It made him happy when the brats drooled.

Penelope smiled shyly. "I did my homework, Sir. I really did. But I lost it."

"Tsk, tsk!" clucked Mr. Little. "How could you *lose* your homework?" He raised his eyebrows and tapped his long yellow fingernails faster.

Arabella blew a wisp of white hair out of her eye, rolled her pen off the desk, and bent over to retrieve it. "I wonder what excuse she'll use this time?" she whispered, grinning up at Miranda. "My brother really did get abducted by aliens, and they took my homework, too." She mimicked Penelope, as she fumbled for the pen and sat up.

Miranda quickly looked away to keep from snorting out loud.

Penelope gave an exaggerated sigh. "Sir, you're not going to believe what happened, but my little toy poodle . . ."

"Oh, no!" whispered Arabella, trying not to move her lips. "Not another Muffy story."

Miranda groaned. "Remember when Muffy ate two pounds of butter and twenty-four popovers?"

"Yeah," whispered her friend. "She had to go out every fifteen minutes."

". . . for a week," finished Miranda, feeling her ribs hurt from trying not to laugh.

Arabella giggled. "And they live on the twenty-ninth floor."

Miranda clapped her hand over her mouth and looked at the ceiling, feeling the teacher's eyes suddenly shift in her direction.

"BE QUIET!" Stubby screamed at the two offenders. "One more peep out of either of you and you'll be sorry."

He glared at the bold-faced girls, wishing he could flog them in front of the entire school, but having to be satisfied with pounding his fists on his desk and hurling several pieces of chalk at them. Then he nodded at Penelope and smiled encouragingly. "Don't mind them, my dear, please continue."

Penelope's face turned redder than her hair as she tried to avoid meeting the eyes of her classmates, which were glued on her. She knew they wouldn't believe her no matter what she said, but then, they weren't the ones she had to sell the story to.

"I finished my assignment last night," she began breathlessly, keeping her eyes on the teacher. "But, Muffy raced into the study, snatched it out of my hand, and ran and hid under the armoire in the living room."

She held her breath waiting to see if Stubby was buying her story, ignoring the loud snigger from one of her classmates. She was relieved when he smiled at her and nodded.

"My brother, Tyler, tried to get my homework away from her, but she wouldn't drop it." She thought for a second. "Tyler thinks it's a psychological thing because Muff's never had puppies, but—"

"Yes, yes! Spare us Tyler's thoughts and just stick to the story," Mr. Little interrupted crossly. Then he looked at the expensive Swiss watch on his wrist and his tone became butter. "Perhaps you can tell us about Tyler another time."

"OK," shrugged Penelope. "Well, we tried everything to get her out from under the armoire. Tyler even went and got a steak, her favourite treat, from the fridge, but nothing worked. Whenever we'd reach under the armoire, Muffy'd growl at us. You should have seen her growling with my homework sticking out of her mouth." She let her eyes roam about the classroom for a second. Then she yelled, "'GRWOORF'—"

"Penelope—" warned the teacher.

"Sorry, but that's what she sounded like," she said, smiling sweetly. "So, finally, Tyler got his hockey gloves and tried to reach under and grab the papers, but Muffs was so fierce, she attacked the gloves. You wouldn't believe how vicious she was. Even Tyler, who's not afraid of anything, was terrified."

Arabella rolled her eyes and whispered to Miranda. "How fierce can an inch-long dog be?"

Penelope gave her a scorching look before continuing.

"Then I got this great idea. I got my violin case and slid it under the armoire from the side, and pushed it against Muffs until she had no more room left and had to get out."

"Where are you going with this story?" Mr. Little asked, totally bewildered.

"I'm just getting to the worst part," said Penelope, knowing that the other kids were all ears now. "As Muffy sped out from under the armoire, Tyler made a grab for the papers, but the little rascal dashed between his legs and ran off so fast, we couldn't catch her. Then, we searched the house but we couldn't find Muffs or my homework anywhere."

"You lost the dog, too?" asked the teacher, incredulously.

"No," said Penelope, triumphantly. "Later, when Tyler was going to bed, he lifted up the toilet seat and saw this big wad of toilet paper. So he flushed the toilet. But it wasn't toilet paper—"

"—IT WAS MUFFY!" shouted the entire class.

One boy laughed so hard he fell off his seat. Infuriated, Stubby flew out of his chair, grabbed a large dictionary and threw it at him. Still not satisfied, the teacher gave him a month's detentions and sent him scurrying to the corner next to William Potts.

"Yes," said Penelope, when things had quieted down. "What happened was Muffy jumped up on the toilet and fell in. And the seat fell down, trapping her. Lucky for us, she yelped just as she got flushed down the toilet. Tyler started yelling like crazy, and we could hear Muffy's little 'woofs' in the pipes. She was stuck between the basement and the ground floor. The plumber came and he had to shut off the water and rip up the floor. Then he had to take apart the pipes. We finally got Muffy out, but the poor baby was icky and cold and wet. I had to give her a bath. The little pet shivered and whimpered all night. We never found my homework, but we saved my Muffsey Wuffsey."

For once, Mr. Little was speechless. He finally found his voice. "My, my! Oh, my! My, my, my! What a terrible thing. I hope your little Muffsey Wuffsey—er—dog is all right?" He slapped himself hard on the leg for making a stupid blunder like that in front of the class. He glared at the brats until their giggles turned to nervous coughs.

"She's okay now," said Penelope, looking as innocent as an angel. "But thanks for asking. The plumber's coming back today to see if my homework's stuck in the toilet pipes, so maybe—"

"No," said the teacher quickly. "I think not." Then he smiled wickedly, anticipating the looks of disbelief that were about to appear on the faces of the other grade fours. "Don't worry about your assignment, my dear. Just make sure you get it in on the first day after Spring Break."

He almost giggled out loud as the brats exchanged looks and their mouths formed the words, "Not fair!"

Arabella whispered through gritted teeth. "She's such a liar."

Miranda wondered about Penelope's story. She could tell that nobody, except Stubby, believed her. Then she shrugged and whispered. "Maybe it's true."

Arabella looked at her friend as if aliens had performed weird experiments on *her*. "Humph!"

When the buzzer sounded at three p.m., Miranda and Arabella joined the tail end of the line of grade fours swarming out of the classroom. Just as they were about to exit, Mr. Little stepped in front of them, closing the door and blocking it with his body. When he noticed that the D'arte girl wasn't stooping, his face turned purple and he shook with rage. *Dare to disobey me, will you? I'll make you pay!* He looked up at her and took a quick step closer. Miranda, thinking he was going to hit her, stumbled backwards in shock, nearly knocking Arabella down.

"I hope you've made some exciting plans for the holidays?" he asked, controlling his anger as his voice dripped syrup.

"Yeah, we're going skiing," Arabella piped up, before she felt Miranda's elbow in her ribs.

"How nice," said Mr. Little. "I hope you'll have a lot of fun skiing. . . ."

The girls looked at each other incredulously, and then stared at the teacher suspiciously. He had never shown any interest in them before, so why the sudden change? They found out when Stubby suddenly leaned forward until his face was inches from their own, and the sweet voice turned to acid.

". . . AND COPYING THE TELEPHONE DIRECTORY!"

The girls fell back, arms up to protect their faces from the spittle flying off the teacher's lips. For a second, they were too stunned to speak. Arabella untangled her tongue first.

"You're not serious?" she cried.

"That's not fair," protested Miranda, her green eyes flashing angrily.

"I saw the pair of you chitchatting. And after I warned you. I explicitly told you that if I heard so much as a peep out of you, you'd be sorry." He stepped aside and opened the door. "Have fun! I know you'll be thinking of me over the holidays," he jeered, pushing the girls into the corridor and slamming the door.

Arabella stomped her feet on the floor, her face etched with fury. "No way!" she fumed. "I'm not doing it."

When her friend didn't respond, Arabella turned to her. Miranda was as still as a stone, staring at the classroom door as if by staring, she were about to blast it from its hinges. A shiver ran down Arabella's back and she grabbed Miranda's arm and shook her.

"Mir, what are you doing?"

Miranda jumped at the touch. She shook her head and turned away from the door. "Thinking," she said, her voice just above a whisper. "Listen! You were just saying that you're not doing the assignment. But that's crazy." She took her friend by the arm and led her toward the lockers. "There's something seriously wrong with all of this."

"There's something wrong all right," agreed Arabella. "He's wrong if he thinks I'm going to copy the phone book."

"That's not what I meant," said Miranda, growing impatient. "We shouldn't be upset about whether or not we're going to do the assignment. We should be wondering why he'd give us an assignment like that in the first place. It's all wrong."

"Give it up, Mir," laughed Arabella. "You're starting to sound like your mother."

"I don't care," snapped Miranda, opening her locker and shoving books and binders into her backpack. "Anyway, Mom's smart and I know what she's going to say about this."

"Whatever," said Arabella. "Let's just get out of here and forget about him." She gripped Miranda by the elbow and pulled her quickly along the corridor toward the student exit.

Miranda stopped suddenly, jolting Arabella off her feet. "You haven't noticed that he's getting worse?"

Her friend sighed, and rolled her eyes toward the ceiling. "What do you want me to say? It's Stubby. He's the same as always—mean and stupid."

"You're wrong," said Miranda. "He really does hate us, you know."

"What are you talking about?" asked Arabella, tossing her head impatiently. "He hates everybody."

"No, he hates us—you and me," answered Miranda. "I noticed the way he looks at us in class. And just now, when he blocked the door . . . he was using every bit of self-control he had to keep from punching me."

"You don't know that," said Arabella.

"Yes I do," said Miranda. "But don't ask me how I know." Finally she shrugged. "You're right. Let's get out of here. At least we won't have to look at his ugly face for a whole week."

"Or listen to any more of Penelope's stupid lies," said Arabella.

"Or stoop," added Miranda, suddenly breaking into a grin.

At the other end of the hall, Mr. Little stared after the girls, fists clenched so tightly his knuckles were white. "That D'arte girl is a trouble maker," he muttered. "I'm going to have to do something about her. And soon." He quietly pulled the classroom door shut and skulked toward the girls' washroom. Inside, he produced a black felt marker from his jacket pocket and, shaking with silent glee, scrawled on the outside of one of the stall doors:

**MIRANDA D'ARTE THINKS SHE'S SMART.
BUT SHE LOOKS AND SMELLS
LIKE A BIG FAT F'ARTE.**

Still grinning, he poked his head from the washroom door, peered up and down the corridor and moved toward the fire exit, stained fingers groping for a cigarette.

Outside the school, Miranda tilted her face toward the sky and stuck out her tongue to catch the wet snowflakes that were coming down heavily. "Please keep snowing," she begged.

"Yes," shouted Arabella. "We want snow! Snow! Snow!"

The sound of a car horn tooting made the girls jump. Miranda saw her mother's blue station wagon parked on the street. She hitched up her backpack and raced Arabella toward the waiting vehicle. They piled into the back seat and Dr. D'arte eased the car away from the curb into the traffic.

Because the teacher had kept them after class, the other students had already left and the school grounds were deserted. Once they were settled in the station wagon, it never occurred to the girls to look back toward the school. But if they had, they might have caught a glimpse of their teacher sneaking out the fire exit door at the side of the school to meet a huge, black-cloaked figure, whose face was hidden beneath a loose-fitting hood. They might have seen Mr. Little pointing toward the car, or caught a glimpse of two glowing red eyes staring after them from the blackness under the stranger's hood.

CHAPTER FOUR

UNWANTED VISITORS

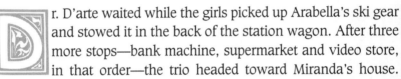r. D'arte waited while the girls picked up Arabella's ski gear and stowed it in the back of the station wagon. After three more stops—bank machine, supermarket and video store, in that order—the trio headed toward Miranda's house. During the drive, Arabella told the Doctor about Stubby's weird behaviour. Miranda pressed her head against the back seat, wondering when she'd get a chance to talk to her mother about her family.

"I don't care if I get expelled," said Arabella. "I'm not doing his stupid assignment."

"It won't come to that," said Dr. D'arte. "How can you get expelled for failing to copy the telephone book? It's absurd."

Miranda leaned forward, trying to catch her mother's eye in the rear view mirror. "If Bell's not doing it, I'm not either."

Dr. D'arte briefly locked eyes with her daughter. "The whole thing is so bizarre," she said. "Why on earth would he give you an assignment like that? It doesn't make sense."

"Oh, it makes sense alright," said Arabella. "He does it because he knows our parents won't believe us. At least mine won't."

"So, I don't have to do it?" persisted Miranda.

"Of course not," said her mother crossly. "When we get back from skiing, I intend to have a talk with that ridiculous little man." She laughed at the unintended pun.

Miranda giggled. "He didn't say it had to be the Ottawa phone book. We could find a place with a population of fifty, and copy that phone book." She nudged her friend. "He'd go ballistic."

"That's an idea," said her mother, joining in her daughter's laughter.

"You do it if you want," said Arabella, crossing her arms and wearing one of her looks. "I said I'm not doing the assignment."

Miranda felt like arguing with her friend. She hated it when Arabella got stubborn. Instead, she grinned. "You're such a typical Taurus." But she ducked down quickly as the other girl tried to bash her on the head with her backpack.

"I'd rather be a Taurus than a Scorpio," said Arabella. "Especially after I read your horoscope."

"What did it say?" asked Miranda.

Arabella shook her head. "Believe me, you don't want to know."

"Come on," said Miranda. "You know I don't believe that stuff."

"Yeah, right!"

"Seriously! Tell me what it said."

"I don't remember exactly, but it was bad. I mean really bad."

Miranda laughed easily, despite the sudden chill that entered the station wagon and wrapped about her.

It was after six p.m. and already dark when they finally got to Miranda's house. Dr. D'arte and Arabella lugged the groceries to the kitchen while Miranda dug the junk mail out of the mailbox and dumped it on the hall table, absent-mindedly flipping through the circulars.

"What's this?" she said, as a thin gauzy envelope slipped out from among the pile. "Somebody must have dropped it off by hand. No stamp, no address, and what are these strange lines?"

$+ \text{⫴} \text{⫼} + \text{⫿} \text{⊥} +$

The envelope was thin as silk and made of a pale gray paper. On the back was a raised gold seal, in the shape of an oval. It looked like an egg with an "S" in the centre. There was a mark over the "S" but Miranda couldn't make it out. Stuck to the seal was a large feather, black, tipped with gold.

Removing the feather, she held the envelope up to the light but, despite the fact that she could see through it and the paper inside it, she couldn't see any writing.

"Hey, Mom! This is so amazing. Can I open it?" she called, waving the envelope at her mother, who was busily packing provisions for their ski trip.

"Go ahead. It's probably a new gimmick to get us to read more junk mail."

"I don't think so," said Miranda, squeezing the envelope to feel its contents. "If it's advertising, surely they'd want us to be able to read it."

"It's from a secret admirer," said Arabella, dropping a box of cereal on the kitchen table and coming to look at the strange envelope. She poked Miranda in the ribs and giggled. "A marriage proposal from Miles Trent."

"You wish," said Miranda.

"Who's Miles Trent?" asked Dr. D'arte, her ears perking up.

"Nobody," said Miranda.

"Just this dreamy guy in sixth grade," answered Arabella. "All the girls think he's so hot." She grinned mischievously. "Don't they, Mir?"

Miranda glared at her friend. "Shut up, Bell."

"Open it," urged Arabella.

"There's nothing inside but a blank sheet of paper," said Miranda, but she reached for the letter opener and tried to slide it under the flap. Finally she dropped the letter opener and stared at the letter. "That's so weird."

"What?"

"I can't get it open."

"Here, let me try."

"OK, but don't damage the seal. I want it."

Arabella took the envelope and, using her fingernails, picked at the paper around the gold seal. "What *is* this stuff?" she grunted, pressing her nails into the paper as hard as she could. But even using all of her strength, she couldn't pierce the thin envelope.

Miranda stared at the letter, shivering slightly as icy fingers walked up her spine. Questions raced through her mind. What was it? Where did it come from? Who put it in the mailbox? Why? Was it important?

The letter was very important, but since neither she nor Arabella could read the lines on the envelope or manage to open it and, since they lived in a relatively safe world, there was no way Miranda could have known that it contained an urgent message. For one clear second, she had an image of something huge and evil breathing on the back of her neck. But then it was gone, the picture driven out of her mind by the sound of the telephone ringing.

She raced to get the phone, automatically folding the envelope over the golden seal and slipping it and the feather into one of the wide pockets on the legs of her jeans.

"So, was it a marriage proposal from Miles what's-his-name?" asked her mother, tapping Miranda on the head as she stepped over the girl and continued down the hall toward her office.

Miranda put her hand over the mouthpiece. "I don't think so," she said crossly to Dr. D'arte's back.

"Are you still there?" asked Nicholas on the other end of the phone. "If you are, I'm just leaving with my skis. I'll be over in a few minutes."

After she hung up, Miranda stomped into the kitchen and glared at Arabella. "Just shut up about Miles Trent."

"Well, you don't have to bite my head off," snapped Arabella.

"I'll do worse than that if you don't put a lid on it. I barely know the guy and you're acting like he's my best friend or something,"

"Or something," said Arabella, giggling. "I saw you talking to him in the cafeteria yesterday."

"Yeah? So?" said Miranda. "And now you got me marrying him. Duh!" She turned her back and opened the fridge.

Arabella knew it wasn't like Miranda to get upset over a bit of teasing. She watched her friend banging bottles around as she pretended to hunt for something on the shelves. *No*, she thought. *There's something else going on around here and I'm going to get to the bottom of it*. "I'm sorry, Mir," she said. "I know you don't like Miles Trent."

Miranda stopped rooting through the fridge, straightened up and rested her head against the freezer. "I know," she said. Then she closed the door and looked at Arabella. Grins spread slowly across their faces, growing broader until the girls were doubled over with laughter. "HE'S SUCH A JERK," they shouted at the same time.

Arabella decided this would be a good time to tackle Miranda and find out what was going on. But, at that moment, the doorbell rang.

"It's Nick," said Miranda, grabbing her jacket and heading toward the door. "He's bringing his ski stuff."

Outside, the girls pelted Nicholas with snowballs while he fastened his skis to the rack on the station wagon roof. Back in the house, they talked excitedly about their ski trip.

Every year, over Spring Break, for as long as Miranda could remember, her mother rented a ski chalet in the Laurentian Mountains, north of Montreal. Dr. D'arte was planning to leave at six a.m. for the long drive, so the three companions ordered a pizza and settled on the sofa in the den to watch a movie.

Miranda had just flicked the "play" button on the remote, when the doorbell rang again. "I'll get it," she yelled, for the benefit of her mother, pressing "pause" and jumping to her feet.

It was Penelope St. John, wearing a fuchsia neon ski jacket and carrying skis, a duffle bag, and Muffy, wearing fuchsia neon fur and a thin rhinestone collar.

Miranda stared at her in disbelief, too stunned to speak. Penelope didn't seem to notice anything unusual. "Isn't it great, your mom asking me to come skiing with you?" She dropped Muffy in the hall. "We're going to have the funnest time."

The toy poodle took one look at her new surroundings and raced through the house, barking, growling and snapping at the sofa, coffee table, TV and everything else in its path. Miranda gaped at the garishly coloured animal and babbled. "Muffy . . . what have you done to Muffy?"

"You're sooo funny," giggled Penelope, handing Miranda her skis and duffle bag. "Isn't she gorgeous? Same colour as my new jacket."

"Mom!" Miranda shouted crossly, dumping the skis and luggage on the floor and making a beeline down the hall to her mother's office. She almost tripped over a pink blur that sped out of the office and zoomed under the nearest chair.

Dr. D'arte was on her knees mopping up Muffy pee from the carpet. She looked up at the sound of the office door closing. "Don't look at me like that. You invited her."

"That's a lie," said Miranda. "She said *you* asked her to come with us."

Dr. D'arte dropped the soggy paper towel in a garbage bag and gave Miranda one of her impatient looks. "Penelope called this morning and asked what time she should show up. I thought you had arranged it with her." She shook her head in exasperation. "I don't like being manipulated, but it's too late now to do anything about it."

"It's not too late," cried Miranda. "You don't know her. She'll ruin everything. Tell her to go home."

Her mother put her hands on her hips and glared at Miranda.

"I'll do no such thing. We're stuck with her, so let's make the best of it."

Miranda shook her head sullenly. "I hate her. She's such a liar."

Dr. D'arte sighed. "Don't worry. I intend to get to the bottom of this. I will not be lied to." She glared at the wet spot on the carpet. "And what was that—that—flaming pink thing that did this to my carpet?"

"That was Muffy," said Miranda, smirking as she turned to leave the room. "But don't worry, Mom," she added. "You'll like her. As you said, 'we're stuck with them.' But, hey, it's only for a week."

CHAPTER FIVE

MORE UNWANTED VISITORS

t was close to midnight when things finally quieted down in the D'arte house. Penelope went off to bed, sticking Miranda with the task of walking Muffy.

"See what she's like? Too tired thinking up lies to walk her own dog," Miranda complained to Nicholas, waving the plastic bag her mother had pressed into her hand. "For the dog, dear," Dr. D'arte had said, unable to hide the grin that quickly became a chuckle.

"Give her a chance, Mir," said the boy, stopping beside a large snowbank. "I know her brother and, from what he tells me, all they do in that house is talk about money. Their mother ran away with a rapper when Tyler was five and I think they've been brought up by a bunch of nannies. Mr. St. John's been married five or six times since. So it figures Penelope's pretty screwed up. She probably doesn't have many friends."

"I'll tell you why!" snapped Miranda, annoyed with Nicholas for not agreeing with her and with herself for hating Penelope. "One, she's a liar. Two, she's always sucking up to the teacher. Three, she's a braggart. Four, she never thinks of anybody but herself. Shall I go on?" She kicked the snowbank hard.

Nicholas shrugged. "Chill, Mir. You're not joined at the neck or anything, so just ignore her. Anyway, she probably doesn't even know how to ski. We'll stick her with the schuss boomers and only have to see her at night."

Miranda grinned. "You're right. But it still makes me boil." She looked down at Muffy who was standing on her hind legs, front paws scratching at the girl's jeans.

"She's cold, but I'm afraid to touch her in case she bites me for saying mean things about Penelope." Laughing, she picked up the dog and turned back toward the house. "Don't worry, Nick. I'll be cool. It'll serve Mom right if she has to babysit Penelope and Muffy the whole time."

Back home, she dropped the poodle in her mother's office. Growling happily, Muffy jumped onto the chair bed, bit the duvet and pulled the bedclothes off Penelope. The girl giggled, scooped up the wriggling creature, and planted a kiss on its thin, rubbery lips. "Mommy's little cutesy wootsey," she cooed.

Miranda gave her a look that was meant to cause serious injury, and slammed the door on Penelope's "Nighty night! Sleep tight!"

When Miranda finally dragged herself up the stairs, she found Arabella already asleep in the spare twin bed in her room. Fully dressed, she flopped onto the covers but, tired as she was, sleep would not come. Suddenly she remembered the strange letter. What had she done with it? She got out of bed and crept downstairs but, after searching through the mail on the hall table without finding the letter, she finally gave up.

Back in her room, as she stepped out of her jeans, something sharp pricked her leg. It was the black feather that had been stuck to the letter. She removed it and the envelope from her pocket. She pulled on a pair of boxer shorts and a t-shirt and, with the bedside light on, lay on her back tracing the curious lines with the gold-tipped feather.

Again, she tried and failed to open the envelope. She stared at the golden seal and idly pressed her thumb into the cool, waxy substance. To her surprise, the flap of the envelope lifted. She practically shot off the bed, quickly removing the thin sheet of paper before closing the flap and pressing the seal to reopen the envelope.

Eager to share her discovery, Miranda glanced at Arabella. What she saw made her laugh. The girl was curled up on her side, snoring softly and completely cocooned in the duvet. The only signs that the lump in the twin bed was human were the tip of her nose and her toes sticking out from the snug bundle.

Deciding that the news would keep until morning, Miranda unfolded the letter. More lines. "What's going on?" she whispered, hoping that by staring at the writing, the lines would mysteriously form known words.

(encoded cipher text)

* to decipher Miranda's letter, see the alphabet at the back of the book.

Suddenly, her eyes widened. "You dummy!" she said, hopping out of bed and racing to her computer. Within minutes she had logged on to the Internet and was searching for *languages*. She grinned when *Klingon* appeared, bookmarking the site to check it out later. Finding nothing that looked like the lines on her envelope, she searched again under *alphabets*. Still nothing. She typed in *ancient alphabet* and punched the search key. Bingo! She found it on the second hit. Ogham—the ancient alphabet of the Celts. Excited, she hunted for the lines that matched the ones on the envelope. The lines spelled *MIRANDA*. The letter had been left for her.

Why? Who was using an ancient alphabet to write to her? She was sure that none of her friends had ever heard of Ogham. So, if it weren't a friend, who was it?

"There's only one way to find out," she mumbled, spreading the letter on top of the envelope. She tackled the first grouping of lines, comparing each mark with the Ogham alphabet displayed on her computer screen. *P - R - I - - A - T - E*. One letter was missing. She scanned the key beside each Ogham letter. The ancient alphabet contained only twenty-one letters, and "J," "K," "V," "W," and "X" were not included in it. "Never mind," she muttered, going on to the next group of lines which spelled *AND*. By the time she had deciphered the third grouping, Miranda felt sleep stealing over her. Running her fingers through her short hair, she forced her eyes open and printed *CONFIDENTIAL* above the corresponding lines on the letter. The missing letter in the first group of lines must be "V". She read, "PRIVATE AND CONFIDENTIAL."

She sped through the next groupings, recognizing her own name from the lines on the envelope. *DEAR MIRANDA*. She printed *YOU* above the first word of the body of the letter. Then *ARE*, and *IN*. Next came *GRA - E*. And *DANGER*. Quickly, she wrote "V" over the blank in the fourth word. Now the sentence read, "YOU ARE IN GRAVE DANGER."

She saw the cloaked monster reaching for her, its sharp talons glinting in the moonlight. She felt the grip on her shoulder—felt the claws pressing deep into her skin. The shock coursed through her body like glass shattering, jolting her awake. She lifted her head, hands flying out to fight off the creature. Her neck felt stiff and her heart was racing a mile a minute. For a second, she didn't know where she was. Then she realized that she had fallen asleep at her computer. But who had turned out the light? She twisted her shoulders as her hands closed about two strong wrists.

A frantic "Shhh!" sounded close to her ears and, as her eyes adjusted to the darkness, she recognized Arabella leaning over her. She almost choked with relief.

"Bell! What—?"

"Be quiet!" whispered the other girl, tightening her hold on Miranda's shoulders.

At that moment, the moon appeared from behind a cloud and in the pale light Miranda saw that her friend's normally dark face was almost gray with terror. She tried to get up, but Arabella's trembling hands held her in a sitting position. The girl put her head close to Miranda's ear.

"Don't talk," she whispered, her voice thin and shaky. "There's something outside."

Miranda tilted her head, one ear tuned to the partly open window, straining to catch the sound that had frightened the other girl. She was just about to give up when she heard it—a sharp crunching. Someone or something was in the backyard breaking through the crusty surface of the snow. Quickly, she pushed Arabella's hands away and slid out of the chair.

"Stay here and keep down," she whispered. "I'm going to look."

Slowly, heart in her throat, Miranda crept toward the window, careful to keep to the side where the open drapes concealed her. Reaching the wall, she froze for a second, working up the courage to look outside. Then she inched the drapes away from the window frame, and peered into the moonlit yard.

The creature was so still that, at first, Miranda thought it was one of the huge trees along the fence behind the garden. When it suddenly moved, she almost died of fright. The intruder was a monstrous black shape, and Miranda knew, instinctively, that it was a thing of evil. She watched, holding her breath, as the creature moved slowly through the shadows of the trees toward the house. It stopped just below her window, its head only a few feet from the sill. If it reached up, it could get its hand under the open window.

The creature's massive size turned Miranda to ice. She gripped the curtains so tightly her short fingernails tore through the fabric. Her eyes were glued to the black shape below. Then, abruptly, the Monster tilted its head toward the window, and Miranda looked into two glowing red eyes.

She jumped back as if she had been stung, and collapsed on the floor, hugging herself and rocking back and forth, terrified out of her mind. Arabella crawled across the carpet and huddled next to her friend, crying silently.

Except for the recurring nightmare, Miranda had never come face to face with sheer terror. Her whole being screamed at her to run, to get away as fast as she could. But she was too scared to move. And then, with a shock that hit her like an iron fist, she knew that the creature outside was there because of her and it was going to kill her if it found her. Instead of running, she began to shiver so violently that Arabella gripped her arms to keep her still.

Suddenly, they heard the familiar sound of a car door slamming and a dull "THWACK" as old Mrs. Medley's newspaper hit her front door. Then a dog barked. Miranda recognized the source of the bark. It was Montague, Nicholas's black lab who followed the same routine every morning at three a.m. when the neighbours' papers were delivered.

Still trembling, Miranda stood and peered warily into the darkness. There were now two of the creatures, their hulking forms motionless among the trees against the picket fence that separated her backyard from Nicholas's. She saw something black move through the white snow near the boy's house. It was the dog, advancing guardedly toward the danger that lurked on the other side of the fence.

No, Monty! she screamed silently. *Go back!* But the courageous Labrador Retriever ranged back and forth across the snow coming closer and closer to the trees. Just short of the fence the dog stopped, glaring into the shadows and growling from deep in his throat.

As one unit, the two black creatures reacted instantly, springing toward the dog so swiftly, Miranda gasped. They tore at the wooden pickets as if they were made of paper. Montague crouched low and snarled savagely. Miranda knew she couldn't bear it if the creatures reached the animal. She pushed the window all the way up and opened her mouth to scream at the dog or the Monsters, but at that moment, lights went on in Nicholas's house, then in the house next door. More lights appeared.

Neighbours looked out of their windows to see what was making the racket. Nicholas opened his back door and whistled. At the familiar command, Montague turned and trotted reluctantly toward his young master, peering back into the shadows as he went. The boy spoke to the dog, but the words were muffled and then he followed Montague inside the house and slammed the door. Lights went out, and darkness fell upon the neighbourhood again. The creatures moved like shadows through the trees and disappeared around the side of the house. Miranda quickly closed the window and ducked back down. Tears of relief streamed down her cheeks.

"What—?" whispered Arabella, gripping her friend's arm.

"I think they're gone, but wait," said Miranda, straining for the sound of the creatures outside her window.

"They? There's more than one?" Arabella's eyes were all whites in the moonlight.

"Shhh!" warned Miranda. She glanced at the illuminated face of the clock on her bedside table, watching the second hand crawl through its cycle. When five minutes had passed, she nudged Arabella. "It's OK now, but be quiet," she whispered.

"How many of those things were out there?"

"I saw two," answered Miranda, getting up and scanning the white surface beneath the window and along the line of trees near the fence. Then she moved toward a chair and began pulling on pants and a heavy sweater. Arabella scrabbled across the floor, perched on the edge of the bed, and started to cry again.

"Mir, I'm scared."

Miranda slipped her feet into a pair of boots and sat on the edge of the bed beside her friend. She pulled Arabella close and whispered in her ear. "Me, too. But get dressed. We've got to wake up Mom and Penelope and get out of here."

Arabella nodded and sniffled as she started pulling on her clothes. When they were ready to go, Miranda whispered. "Follow me. Don't talk and don't turn on the lights."

With Arabella clinging to her shoulder, Miranda led the way along the black hall. At the top of the stairs, she stopped and whispered. "When we get downstairs, you wake up Penelope and keep Muffy quiet while I get Mom."

"No! Let's stay together," said Arabella.

"Bell, we don't have time. We've got to get away." Miranda moved down the stairs easily in the darkness. She felt Arabella's hand trembling on her shoulder. Outside her mother's office, Miranda turned to her friend. "I'll be right back."

"Don't leave me alone," cried Arabella, grabbing Miranda's arm and gripping it so tightly the girl almost cried out.

"Please, do what I say," whispered Miranda. "We've got to hurry. Go inside and lock the door. I'll be back in a second." She opened the door and pushed the still protesting Arabella inside, waiting until she heard the click of the lock before continuing along the hall to her mother's bedroom at the back of the house.

Slowly, she turned the doorknob and peered into the darkness. The drapes were closed and the room was as black as ink. Miranda crept across the floor to her mother's bed, whispering desperately. "Mom! Wake up!" She reached out to shake her mother's shoulder and her heart stopped when her hands touched the bedcovers and the pillow. The bed was empty.

Miranda turned back toward the door in a panic, stifling the scream that was growing inside her. Suddenly, a huge black shape loomed up in the corner near the closet on her right and moved swiftly toward the bedroom door to cut off her escape. The girl saw the door outlined in the faint moonlight from the hall and then she saw the creature. One of them was in the house! What had they done to her mother?

The black shadow closed the door and moved toward the girl. Fear drove Miranda wild. She cried out, skidding backwards toward the French doors that opened onto the terrace. As she raised her hands to fight for her life, her eyes darted about the room for a weapon. A heavy cast iron floor lamp stood beside her mother's reading chair. Quickly, Miranda reached out to the side and groped for the lamp, her eyes never leaving the advancing form, whose face was lost in the blackness of its clothing. She whimpered softly as her hand touched and then closed about the lamp.

"I will not hurt you." The sudden sound of the creature's deep voice startled Miranda. She stumbled backwards, falling on her butt on the carpet. The lamp crashed to the floor, crushing the delicate shade and smashing the light bulb. Miranda was sobbing now, but even as she struggled to her feet, the figure extended one hand toward her. Miranda caught the glint from a large ring on one of the creature's fingers before she heard the voice again.

"Believe me. I am here to help you."

Quickly, Miranda scrabbled to her feet, backing away from the outstretched hand. She stopped crying and squinted fearfully into the blackness that was the stranger's face, expecting at any moment to see the creature's horrible red eyes fastened on her. But she saw nothing. A part of her desperately wanted to believe that the creature had come to help, but a tiny voice inside wondered what the chances were of three cloaked figures showing up at her house on the same night. *No chance*, she thought.

"Listen to me," said the voice. "You are in terrible danger. Those things outside will be back."

The thought of the creatures returning to finish her off was too much for Miranda. She turned and ran blindly toward the terrace doors, certain that the huge figure would be upon her in a flash. But the stranger remained motionless.

Miranda clawed at the drapes, pushing them aside as her hand found and gripped the doorknob. She turned the knob and pulled inward at the same time. A loud sob burst from her throat. The door was locked and the key was gone. Then, powerful hands gripped her arms from behind, pinning them against her side. In the next instant, she was lifted into the air and swung back into the middle of the room.

"Running will not stop them," said the stranger, his voice cold with anger.

Miranda struggled, but the strong hands held her so tightly she might have been an ant caught in crazy glue. "What do you want?" she cried finally.

"What I want, girl, is to keep you alive. Now, I will release you if you promise to remain silent and listen to what I have to say."

Miranda nodded, too weak to speak. The fear that had been driving her was gone, leaving her drained and spent. The creature's voice suddenly thawed.

"I will take that as your word," he said, removing his hands from her upper arms and taking a long step back.

Miranda crossed her arms and rubbed her aching muscles, convinced that she could feel indentations where the stranger's fingers had dug into her flesh. She turned toward him. "Who are you and what do you want?" she repeated, backing toward the bedroom door, and wondering what was waiting for her on the other side.

The creature didn't answer. He moved to the heavy floor-to-ceiling drapes that covered the entire wall in front of the terrace doors, and drew them apart. He peered into the backyard. "We are safe, at least for the moment," he said, letting the drapes fall back into place. Then he strode across the room and turned on the bedside lamp. "We can risk some light."

Miranda stared up at the man standing before her. He was the tallest person she had ever seen and, while he looked thin, her aching arms were proof of his strength. He wore a long, dark blue or black cloak that covered him from head to toe. As Miranda watched, he lifted one arm and pulled back the loose hood. His face was crisscrossed with deep lines, making him look like a woodcarving of an old, old man. His long black hair was tied back on his neck. Miranda could see streaks of white running through the black. His eyebrows were completely white, above a pair of eyes the blue-black colour of sapphires. Those eyes were on her now and Miranda squirmed under the stranger's hard, unblinking gaze.

"There was something outside, under my window," she mumbled, thinking of the hideous Monsters she had seen only moments ago. "They looked like you. I thought you were—"

"You were wrong," interrupted the stranger. "They look nothing like me. I am not one of the Demon's creatures."

"What—?" But Miranda was too stunned to continue. Her mind raced with images of Demons with red eyes, who were probably still outside, watching the house. Or were they, too, inside, waiting for her?

The stranger stooped and picked up a long wooden staff lying on the floor, before lowering his lanky form into Dr. D'arte's reading chair. He stretched his long legs out on the carpet, leaned his head back, and closed his eyes. He was much too large for the dainty piece of furniture and, if Miranda hadn't been so frightened, she would have giggled. One hand gripped the wooden staff, while the other rested on the arm of the chair. Miranda noticed the large oval ring on the middle finger of his right hand. It was gold, with a black "S" in the middle of a yellow stone. She knew she had seen something like it before, and recently, but couldn't remember where.

Feeling the girl's eyes on him, the man opened his own dark eyes and the pair stared at each other silently. He knew that Miranda was afraid of him. She is right to be afraid, he thought, bowing his head, suddenly saddened by the knowledge of what he had come here to do.

"Why are you here?" Miranda asked for the third time, surprised at the sad look that washed over the stranger's face.

The question seemed to startle the stranger. He shook his head, as if he had just awakened from a restless sleep, and looked at the pitiful human child.

"I came to find you, Miranda," he said quietly.

CHAPTER SIX

THE STRANGER

"Why are you looking for me?" Miranda's heart was pounding so hard she felt dizzy. She looked wildly about the room. "And where's my mother?"

She wanted to crawl into her mother's bed and hide under the covers, anything to feel safe. Instead, she hugged herself, hunched her shoulders, and stared at the strange man slumped in the small chair. Who was he? How could he possibly know her? She was only ten years old and had seldom been out of Ottawa, except to attend summer camp and to spend a week every spring at the ski chalet in the Laurentians. She didn't think she could ever forget meeting someone like him. Wearily, she slumped onto the edge of the bed.

"Even if I wanted to tell you where your mother is, I could not," said the dark stranger. "For one simple reason. I do not know. But she assured me that she would be safe where she was going."

For some strange reason she couldn't explain, Miranda believed him. "Why didn't she wait for me?" she asked, her eyes filling with tears.

The stranger cleared his throat. "Leaving you behind was, perhaps, the most difficult decision your mother ever made," he said. "But, in the end, she knew that it was the right decision. In fact, it was the only decision."

"But why? I don't understand any of this," cried Miranda, the tears shining in her eyes. "Will I ever see her again?"

"I would be lying to you if I said yes. But know that I will do everything in my power to see that you are reunited with her." He rose slowly out of the chair and moved toward the girl. "She trusted me to protect you. Now you must decide whether to believe me or not. And quickly! Because we must leave this place before Taog sends more of her creatures after you." He suddenly chuckled. "We have been talking for several minutes now, and you are still alive. Do you think that would be so if I had come here to kill you?"

It's true, Miranda thought bitterly. The stranger was strong and there was a ruthlessness about him that scared her. Yes, he could have killed her in a second if he had wanted to. For the first time in her life, she hated being ten years old and powerless. She ran her arm across her face wiping away the tears. It seemed that she didn't have much choice. She had to trust this stranger who broke into her house in the middle of the night. There was nobody else.

"Well, what is your answer?" he asked, and seemed satisfied when the girl nodded silently. But then he glared at her. "Now tell me why you remained here after I warned you to flee?"

Miranda stared at the man incredulously. "You warned me? How? When? I never saw you before in my life."

"Someone read my letter," the stranger insisted. "It is not where my friend, Charlemagne, left it."

"Charlemagne? Letter?" Miranda was puzzled. "I don't know anybody by that name or anything about a letter. What are you talking about?"

"Charlemagne would take great offence at being called a person," said the man, smiling at the thought. "He is an Eagle—a King of Eagles."

Miranda gulped. "Charlemagne's an Eagle? How—?"

"I will tell you about Charlemagne in due course. We were talking about the letter."

The girl flushed as she suddenly remembered the flimsy envelope with the strange Ogham line writing and the golden seal on the back. That's why the stranger's ring had looked familiar. "Oh!" she said finally. "*That* letter."

"So you *did* receive it," said the man triumphantly. "Then kindly explain to me why you did not heed my warning?"

"It was here when I got home from school. But I only figured out how to open it when I was going to bed and then I had to search for the proper alphabet. I was just starting to decipher it when I must have fallen asleep."

"Nonsense!" snapped the stranger. "What do you mean you had to decipher it?"

"I couldn't read it!"

The stranger looked at her as if she were a brainless twit. Miranda felt her face turn red. "At first I thought it was a joke. You know, just a lot of dumb lines."

"Those dumb lines, as you so colourfully put it, happen to be the oldest alphabet in this world," snapped the stranger.

"I know that now but it's not *our* alphabet."

The strange man rolled his eyes toward the ceiling. "But surely your mother . . . you did show the letter to your mother?"

"No," said Miranda. "Mom thought it was junk mail."

The stranger glowered at her but said nothing. Miranda waited a second before breaking the silence. "I stopped right after 'YOU ARE IN GRAVE DANGER.' What did the rest of it say?"

"Since you did not read it, what it says is irrelevant now," said the stranger crossly. "We must go immediately."

Miranda leapt to her feet. "Go? Go where?"

"There is only one place where you will be safe," he answered.

"And where's that?" demanded Miranda, her hands planted firmly on her hips.

The stranger's face darkened and Miranda moved to put the bed between them, in case he flew into a rage. But the big man only nodded, and began pacing back and forth in front of the drapes. "We do not have time to go into this now, but I will tell you one thing. You will die this night if we remain here. I mentioned Taog a moment ago. Do you know of her?"

Miranda shook her head, her face a blank. "Who or what is Taog?"

When the stranger sighed and gave her a black look, Miranda felt that he hated her for being stupid.

"Taog is an evil thing of great power, who now calls herself Hate."

"If that's true, why haven't I heard of her?" Miranda stared at him suspiciously.

The stranger sighed. "I am beginning to think there are a great many things you have not heard of," he said, his voice heavy with sarcasm. "Such as, who you are, for instance."

"What do you mean?" snapped Miranda. "I know who I am. What I don't know is who *you* are."

The man ignored her obvious question. "We are wasting time," he said. "Listen to me. The evil ones that were here tonight were sent by Hate—to destroy you."

Miranda felt like covering her ears with her hands. She didn't want to hear any more of this. Why would anybody want to hurt her? What had she ever done to make this Hate person so angry?

"What were those other things?" she asked, her voice quivering with fear.

But the man ignored her and seemed to be thinking. Then he looked at her and said. "They are called THUGS. They are Hate's servants, half-dead creatures she keeps alive to carry out her vile purpose."

"What is *she*?"

The stranger glared at the frightened girl. "She is evil personified—a Demon who escaped last night from the Place with No Name—a black universe into which she was driven a long time ago." He turned to her impatiently. "That is all we have time for. Now, hurry and get your things together."

Miranda glared back. "What does all this have to do with me?" she asked, staring at the drapes as if she could see through them into the darkness outside where the horrible black creatures might be lurking even now.

For the first time, the stranger's eyes softened. "Hate knows that you are the only person who has the power to send her and her creatures back to the Place with No Name. She sent the THUGS here to kill you. I came to try and prevent your untimely death." He reached out and took the girl's trembling hands. "I am sorry that I have frightened you," he said. "But I must make you understand that the Demon is your worst nightmare come true."

Miranda pulled her hands out of his firm grasp and wrapped her arms about herself. For a moment, the only sound in the room was the loud chattering of her teeth. Then, the door swung open and Arabella, with Penelope following, burst into the room. Penelope took one look at the tall, black-clad man and started screaming. All two pounds of poodle flew at the stranger, growling and snarling savagely. But, for perhaps the first time in the spoiled dog's life, things didn't go her way. The stranger pointed the long staff at the flying fuchsia terror, and froze Muffy in midair.

CHAPTER SEVEN
FLIGHT

"STOP THAT, AT ONCE!" thundered the stranger, glowering at Penelope, who stopped screaming as suddenly as if someone had duct-taped her mouth shut.

"I could have used a fireball, think about that," said the tall man.

Penelope obviously thought about it because she started sobbing loudly.

"And I will use one on you if you do not stop blubbering," he continued. "NOW!" He extended his right arm toward the terrified girl, who was trying to pull Muffy out of the air, without success. Finally, she gave up, sniffled once and draped her arms about the dog, burying her face in the poodle's stiff, bright fur.

Arabella thought about the story Penelope told at school yesterday, and suddenly wondered if it were true after all. She knew nobody would believe her if she ever told them about this.

The stranger walked around the poodle, staring at it as if he couldn't quite make out what it was or what it was supposed to do. "I have never seen such a creature," he said, stooping to peer under the suspended animal.

"It's a dog," said Miranda, wondering where the man had come from. "A poodle. She dyed it."

The stranger gave the dog's owner an evil look. Then he suddenly lost interest in Muffy and glared at Miranda. "What are they doing here?" he demanded.

"They're my friends. We're going skiing today—" She stopped and looked at him. "Oh! We're not going skiing, are we."

He shook his head. "I'm afraid not," he said, turning to the two girls. "Go home. If you leave now, you will be safe."

"No way!" snapped Arabella, walking past the stranger to Miranda's side. "What's going on, Mir? Who is this man? What were those things doing in the yard? Are they after you?"

"Thunder and lightning!" muttered the stranger. "Are all girls in this world so nosy?"

Before Miranda could answer her friend's questions, the man moved behind her so that he was facing Arabella. "Yes. Those things, as you call them, are looking for your friend here. If you want to help her, you will leave now. I am the only one who may be able to keep Miranda alive through this night. But, to do that, I must get her away from here immediately."

"Who are you?" demanded Arabella.

"I am Naim, one of the five Druids," he answered. "Now are you satisfied? Now will you leave us?"

Arabella looked at Miranda. "Mir, what's a Druid? I don't understand anything." She locked eyes with the stranger. "If Mir's going with you, then I'm going too."

"YOU ARE GOING HOME," he roared. "Now be off with you, before I lose my temper." He pointed at the fuchsia-coloured poodle. "And take that—that fluffy thing with you." He snapped his fingers and Muffy fell into Penelope's arms.

The little dog took one look at the big, fierce stranger and tried to dig its way into Penelope's chest. "What did that horrible man do to my little Muffsey?" sobbed Penelope, cuddling the wretched animal, her eyes shooting poison darts at the Druid.

"Go home, Bell," said Miranda gently. "Take Penelope. He's right. This has nothing to do with you, so please, just go. I don't want anything to happen to you." She hugged her friend and tried to smile, despite the tears building in her eyes. "I'll be OK. When I get back . . . from wherever . . . I'll tell you everything."

Arabella also started to cry, but she nodded as Penelope grabbed her by the arm and pulled her toward the door.

"I know when I'm not wanted," said Penelope. "Come on, Bell. Let's just go."

Arabella felt like kicking the girl, but she realized that Penelope hadn't seen the black creatures outside the house and couldn't know what sort of danger Miranda was in. *It's a good thing, too*, she thought, *or it would be all over the TV and in the newspapers in no time*.

When the two girls had gone, the Druid turned to Miranda. "Don't just stand there sniffling, girl. Hurry and get your things together." He sighed, and Miranda heard the weariness in his voice. "We have far to go this night."

Miranda wiped her eyes on the sleeve of her shirt, but she didn't budge.

"What now?" demanded the Druid. Then his voice became gentle. "Of course. Forgive me. You should be safe for the moment, but I will accompany you while you pack if that will comfort you."

Miranda nodded and led the way up the dark stairs to her room where she crammed some clothing into her backpack, along with soap, toothbrush and other things she might need, wherever they were going. The Druid stood at the window, peering into the night, his back to the room. He was so still that Miranda wondered if he had fallen asleep on his feet. But he surprised her.

"No, I am not sleeping," he answered her thoughts. "And I do not think you or I will rest or sleep easily for a long time."

Miranda bent and gathered the duvet from the floor, where Arabella must have kicked it when she heard the THUGS outside. It seemed like ages ago, but a quick glance at the clock told her that less than an hour had passed. She piled the bulky cover on top of the bed, wondering when she would see her mother or her home again.

The Druid thumped the floor with the end of his staff. "Come, girl. We have wasted enough time," he stormed.

"Where are we going?" asked Miranda, grabbing the backpack and heading for the door.

"We must find Parliament Hill," he answered. "Do you know of this place?"

"Of course," answered Miranda, looking over her shoulder at the Druid and wondering again where he came from. "Everyone knows Parliament Hill. But why are we going there?"

"Do you have to pester me with so many questions? Can you lead us there?"

Miranda nodded. "We can take the bus. If they're running at this hour."

The tall stranger looked at her curiously. "What is the 'bus'?"

"You're not serious?" said Miranda, grinning at the strange man. "Never mind. It's our public transportation system—what everybody rides on. You know—to get from one place to another."

"I do not know that word," said the Druid. "This is the first time I have set foot in the new world." Then he thought for a second. "No, we must not be seen. Hate has eyes everywhere."

"We can't walk," said Miranda. "It's too far, and it's cold outside."

The Druid looked at her. "We will walk," he said, the sound of his voice leaving no room for argument. "But we must keep away from the main roads."

Downstairs, Miranda slipped on her jacket and led the way into her mother's bedroom. Naim took a key from a pocket inside his cloak and unlocked the French doors, leaving the key in the lock as he followed Miranda onto the snow-covered terrace.

Miranda cut across the back yard, avoiding the deep imprints of the THUGS' feet in the snow. At the fence, she and the Druid tore away the pickets that Hate's slaves had smashed when they went after Nicholas's dog. They slipped through the opening into the boy's backyard.

Miranda paused, carefully scanning the darkness in case Montague had been let out again and hoping to spot the big dog before it saw them and started barking. There was no sign of him. Nicholas must have kept the animal in the house after the earlier barking episode. She shivered when she thought of how close dear old Monty had come to being ripped to pieces by the Demon's creatures.

Leaving Nicholas's property, they raced into New Edinburgh Park and followed the packed snow trail along the Rideau River toward Beechwood Avenue. When they reached the main street, Miranda stopped beside a cluster of young saplings and peered west across the bridge where Beechwood turned into St. Patrick Street. The way seemed clear enough, but she worried that they'd be seen crossing the open bridge. "There's no other way," she whispered, sensing the Druid's impatience.

"Then we must chance it," he said, giving her a gentle nudge. "Go now, and run as if death itself were snapping at your heels."

Miranda didn't need to be told. She took a deep breath, steeling herself for the mad dash, and ran as she had never run before, afraid to look left or right for fear of seeing the horrible black creatures, who surely must see them now. She almost laughed hysterically when they made it safely across the bridge, huddled behind a bus shelter, gasping for air, cold tears frozen on her eyelashes.

The Druid waited patiently for her, his breathing as regular as if he had been out for a leisurely stroll. Miranda wondered about this strange man, the fifth Druid. What had he said about the new world?

And what did he mean that she was the last one who could destroy the Demon? Either he was mistaken or she had misunderstood.

Then they were off again. Miranda led the way across St. Patrick Street toward a more secluded side street. Looking over her shoulder, she saw a lone car heading west on St. Patrick toward Parliament Hill. It careened from one lane to another. "A drunk driver," she muttered, squinting at the vehicle as it sped past. *That's funny. It looks like Nick's dad's car,* she thought, instantly forgetting about the car as she crossed Coburg and entered Old St. Patrick Street.

Miranda suddenly realized that she was utterly exhausted. She focused all of her thoughts and energy on taking one step and then another. She tried to fight off the doubting voices in her mind that said she should give up, or lie down in the snow and sleep. "No!" she whispered through gritted teeth. When she finally looked about to get her bearings, she was amazed that they were now following Murray Street and had completed over three-quarters of the distance from her house to their destination.

They had just crossed MacKenzie Avenue, beside the American Embassy, and entered Major's Hill Park when the Druid gripped Miranda's arm and pulled her to a sudden stop. "Listen!" he hissed, tilting his head to one side and straining to hear the sound that had set his nerve ends tingling.

Miranda froze, holding her breath. "What?" she whispered.

The Druid's only answer was to tighten his grip on her arm. The girl peered over the snow-covered surface of the park. Terror made her eyes play tricks on her, changing the motionless trees into writhing black shapes. Everywhere she looked, horrible creatures lurked just outside her vision. She squeezed her eyes shut and waited, listening intently. And then her blood ran colder than the snow under her feet as she felt another presence in the park. She turned to the Druid, her eyes as big as saucers.

"I know," he whispered urgently. "But it is not aware of us yet.

Walk quickly! Keep ahead of me, but close enough so that my size will shield you. Stay on the path until you reach the trees ahead. Now go!"

"What . . .?"

"Not now," hissed the Druid. "Go!"

Miranda forced herself not to run. She walked quickly along the hard-packed trail, eyes fixed straight ahead. The squeak of her boots on the snow sounded loud enough to be heard for blocks. Ahead, the trees seemed awfully far away. Too far. They'd never reach them before the creature spotted them. What if they got there and the thing was already there, hiding in the trees, waiting for them? *Stop thinking!* her mind screamed.

It seemed to take forever, but they finally reached the shelter of the trees. The Druid leaped off the path and hid behind a squat evergreen, pausing for a second before peering around the thick branches back along the path into Major's Hill Park. Miranda crouched down in the snow behind him, taking several deep breaths, before she, too, looked back the way they had come.

Seeing nothing moving on the white surface, Miranda glanced at the Druid. He was peering intently at a small stone structure near the street side of the park. Miranda knew the building. It was an old gardener's or maintenance cottage. She had seen it from the car window several times a week for as long as she could remember, but she had never really looked at it. At least she had never noticed the huge black chimney on the roof. *That's odd*, she thought. *It's almost bigger than the roof.* And then, the thing that was not a chimney moved.

"What is that?" she gasped, gripping the Druid's cloak and pointing toward the building, even as the monstrous shape disappeared below the roof on the far side of the stone structure. Miranda was shaking like a tree in a hurricane.

Naim turned and held the girl firmly by the shoulders. "Do not give up now," he said gently. "Tell me, how much farther is this place?"

"W-we're a-almost t-there," said Miranda, unable to control the chattering of her teeth.

"Then run, now, while she is out of sight," whispered the Druid, turning the girl away and pointing her through the trees.

"You said 'she'?" Miranda almost screamed. "That thing back there is the Demon?" She bent double, holding her arms tightly over her stomach, afraid that the sound of her retching would draw the Monster to her like a moth to a flame. She knew the Druid was watching her anxiously, but her fear drove away any embarrassment she might have felt vomiting in front of a stranger. Finally, she straightened. "I'm OK now," she said, scooping up a handful of snow to rinse her mouth.

"We must keep moving then. Come on. Hurry!" urged the Druid, looking over his shoulder.

Miranda felt as if her dream had become real as she led the way along the boundary of the park, running as if Dracula himself were behind her. Without stopping, she waved in the direction of Parliament Hill, where the Peace Tower reached toward the stars.

"Over there!" she shouted, the words clipped.

The park ended abruptly at the bottom of a steep hill where a series of locks separated the Rideau Canal from the Ottawa River. Miranda picked her way down the hill, hearing the sound of the Druid's boots breaking through the crusty snow behind her. They followed the frozen pathway along the east side of the locks until they came to a narrow, pedestrian bridge.

"We can cross here," Miranda breathed, her voice high with uncertainty as she looked at the thick ice coating the walkway. "Watch out. It's very slippery."

But they crossed the locks without incident, and continued along the opposite pathway until it ended at a flight of concrete steps that led up to street level. Miranda took the stairs two at a time and when she reached the top, she ran along Wellington Street toward the nearest entrance onto Parliament Hill.

"We made it," she gasped, stopping just inside the east gates, her heart racing like a revving motor. She slumped back against the wrought-iron fence that enclosed The Hill along Wellington Street, suddenly aware that nothing in her life would ever be the same.

CHAPTER EIGHT
PARLIAMENT HILL

he Druid took in his surroundings, staring in amazement at the three gracious buildings floodlit on the low hill before him. Stone towers and spires soared into the sky.

"What is this place?" he asked, unable to take his eyes off the magnificent neo-Gothic structures.

"It's where you said you wanted to go," said Miranda, a sinking feeling washing over her.

"I know it is Parliament Hill, but what *is* it?" he asked, deeply agitated.

"It's our Parliament Buildings, our government," answered Miranda, wondering what had upset the old Druid. "This is the East Block," she said, pointing at the nearest structure. "That's the West Block over there."

"And that one?" asked the Druid, nodding his head at the jewel of the Parliament Buildings, a massive structure that included the gigantic tower they had seen while crossing Major's Hill Park.

"That's the main building, the Centre Block," said Miranda, looking around nervously, anxious to be moving again.

"We're going there," said the Druid, striding purposely toward the Centre Block, Miranda running to keep up.

The massive Peace Tower formed part of the Centre Block. It loomed above the two travellers in the moonlight, as they mounted the steps to the building's main doors. Suddenly, the Druid stopped so abruptly that Miranda, close on his heels, walked into his back. But he didn't seem to notice. He was gazing in wonder at the heraldic carvings framing the arched entryway.

"Impossible!" he said, running his hand over the archivolt, ornate with coats of arms surrounded by delicately carved pine cones, flowers and leaves. His fingers traced the intricate designs on the stone lion standing guard on the left side of the entrance to the Centre Block.

"So the Dwarves were here!" He glared at Miranda. "Tell me, quickly, what you know of Gregor's people."

Miranda could only stare at him, speechlessly. When she finally found her voice, she stammered. "Gr-Gr-Gregor? I don't know any Gregor."

"You do not know what this is?" he said, pointing at the stonework, and looking as though he were about to strangle the bewildered girl. "This is the work of Dwarves, the finest stonework I have ever seen." He shook his head. "Bah! Your kind do not deserve to have this treasure, when you know nothing about it."

"D-Dwarves?" Miranda babbled, not believing her ears.

The look the Druid flashed her made her feel awkward and stupid, as though she had been caught doing something terribly wrong. Abruptly, he ignored her, turning his back and moving away from the entrance, down the steps, and closer to one of the floodlights. Miranda followed meekly, not daring to breathe lest she make him angry again.

Naim stuck the wooden staff into the snow and began searching through the inside pockets of his cloak. After a good deal of rooting, he finally produced a tattered scrap of parchment, which he quickly unfolded. But before he looked at the paper, he suddenly started and peered about.

Miranda jumped too, thinking the Demon was somewhere close

by. But after a second, the man shook his head and held the scrap of paper toward the light, squinting at the drawing, one long finger following the lines across the paper. Then he refolded it and replaced it in the depths of his cloak.

"The drawing shows a library," he said.

"The Library of Parliament," answered Miranda. "It's at the back. I don't know if there's a way in from there. In the daytime we could get there through here. . . ." She looked up the steps at the solid wooden doors. "But they're locked now, we'll never get inside."

Naim picked up the staff and walked under the archway to the main doors, his eyes studying the deep crevices and grooves in the aged wood. He pressed one hand flat against the cold surface. Miranda almost jumped out of her skin when one of the doors slowly opened. Before she knew what was happening, the Druid had slipped through the narrow opening, pulling her after him. The heavy door closed behind them.

It was black as tar inside the building and the damp and cold seeped through Miranda's clothing, setting her teeth chattering. All at once, a light flared up in front of her and the girl stared into the flame, spellbound. In his right hand, the Druid gripped the long staff, but in the middle of his left palm, a white flame grew brighter and brighter, lighting up the darkness. Miranda followed him up a flight of wide steps. When they reached the top, the Druid raised his arm, sending the brightness up and out in a wide circle.

They were in a great Hall. In the soft white light, the magnificent vaulted ceiling spread over them like a giant umbrella. Miranda saw the gables along the sides of the room with their richly carved bosses. The sight took her breath away, as it always did, and for a moment there were no horrors, no such things as Demons. For Miranda, more than any other building on Parliament Hill, the Centre Block was Canada. The tension left her neck and shoulders and, for the first time in many hours, she felt safe.

She even grinned with pride when she heard the Druid's breath quicken as he turned in a slow circle, stretching his arm high above his head. He passed the staff to Miranda and ran his free hand appreciatively over one of the black-green stone pillars that surrounded the room.

"Syenite!" he marveled. "Now I know for certain that my dear old friend, Gregor, has been in your world."

"Who is Gregor?" Miranda ventured, seeing that the Druid's face no longer wore its angry look.

"I have known all fifteen Gregors during my lifetime," the Druid answered. "But this," and he touched the syenite pillar again. "This is the work of Gregor the Fifteenth."

"But, who are they?" pressed Miranda.

"Dwarves, girl," he answered. "Kings of Dwarves. Have you not been listening?"

Miranda nodded dumbly, unable to think of a reply. She did not believe in Dwarves. And here was this strange Druid standing in the middle of Confederation Hall, in the middle of the night, telling her that Dwarves built her country's Parliament Buildings. It was too much to grasp all at once.

Naim shook himself, as though it made him sad to leave this place, and looked about once more, this time to find their direction. Miranda pointed toward a passage at the far end of the room.

"The Hall of Honours. It goes to the Library."

The Druid nodded. "Keep close to me, and be quiet." He reclaimed the Staff, and led the way across the great Hall. Miranda followed, the sound of their footsteps on the marble floor echoing dully through the empty chamber.

As they drew near, Miranda felt a cold draught seeping from the passage. She shivered uncontrollably as the chilly air went through her clothing and turned her skin to goosebumps. The Druid seemed not to notice the cold and dampness. At least he did not bother to pull his heavy cloak about him. When they reached the passage, he extended the arm holding the flame into the blackness and peered ahead. Miranda opened her mouth to ask what he was looking for, when he stepped into the Hall of Honours.

They had taken only a few steps when the Druid stopped so abruptly, Miranda's wet boots slid on the cold marble and she slipped to her knees, clutching frantically at the man's cloak. Naim didn't even look at her. Instead, he tilted his head, listening to the heavy silence, dark eyes trying to pierce the black shadows beyond the light in his hand. He had heard something—a sound that, for a second, made his flesh crawl. He should know that sound.

Miranda, watching him in the white light, reacted instantly, forgetting to whisper. "What—?" The sound was loud in the cavernous halls.

"Shhh!" warned the Druid.

For another moment, he stood as still as one of the Windsor green pillars. Miranda held her breath, staring at the dark places, but terrified of what she might find there. Finally, Naim breathed and touched Miranda's shoulder, smiling for the first time.

"I, too, have nightmares," he said. "I thought I detected another presence." He shrugged. "It is nothing, just my suspicious nature." Holding his cupped hand in front of him to light their way, he moved cautiously along the passage.

"Stay behind me," he ordered, but kindly.

Miranda meekly obeyed, sticking as close to him as his cloak, as they continued their slow but steady progress toward the double doors at the end of the corridor.

Then, without warning, the Druid stiffened, turning his head and looking over his shoulder. There, framed in the entrance from Confederation Hall into the Hall of Honours, like a hideous shadow, stood the towering, black shape of Hate, the Demon.

CHAPTER NINE

THE HELLHAGS

iranda froze, her green eyes riveted on the Demon. Out of the corner of her eye, she saw Naim raise the staff as his body pivoted to face the creature. Despite her fear, she stifled an insane urge to giggle hysterically. The Druid's weapon looked like a piece of kindling compared with the long, evil-looking stake aimed at them now.

Hate dwarfed the large entrance from Confederation Hall into the Hall of Honours, three clawed hands resting on the smooth surface of the pillars on either side of the opening. Her fourth hand gripped the cold iron stake. Miranda heard a terrible sound coming from the creature, shattering the heavy silence—a raucous hissing, as if a giant hand had stabbed deep into the heart of the building and its life force were pouring out through the rent. The sound made the girl's blood run cold.

"She is not aware of you yet," whispered the Druid. "Get behind me. Go quickly toward the Library. Hide yourself and wait for me there."

It took every ounce of Miranda's strength to muster enough courage to obey, when she wanted to run and scream, and run and scream. As she forced her trembling limbs to move away from Naim's protection, she wondered if her nightmare had become real. Near the Library doors, she slipped her slim body into a narrow space behind a pillar. Then she dared to peer back along the passage. One look and she knew beyond any doubt that they were going to die. Naim was the tallest man she had ever seen, but he looked small and scrawny next to the Monster waiting at the end of the passage.

Naim and the Demon faced each other—both so still that for a moment Miranda thought they had turned each other to stone. And then, as if the spell had suddenly broken, Naim moved gingerly away from the pillars into the centre of the passage, the magic white light in his palm growing brighter, casting a wider circle. Quickly, he looked back to where he knew Miranda had hidden herself near the Library doors.

About twelve feet from the Library of Parliament, between the Druid and the girl, was a large balcony, with a wrought-iron railing, overlooking the Hall of Honours. That's where the others waited.

Naim saw their eyes first—red eyes burning into him. One after another, they leaped over the iron railing, pale misshapen bodies landing hard on the marble floor and slinking through the shadows, mouths gaping wide. He counted eight of the creatures. Not THUGS.

They stopped suddenly, dropping back on their haunches as if in obedience to a command only they could hear. The leader, a large ugly brute, padded boldly into the outer rim of the light, its loathsome head jerking up and down like a rabid jackal. Naim's heart stopped when he recognized her.

He had fought her once, long ago, when the Dwarves and Elves went to war against the Demon and drove her into the Place with No Name. She and three others had almost succeeded in killing him then. Now there were eight. The realization that these vicious beasts had escaped from the nameless place stunned him. How many other evil creatures were free?

He stared at the twisted and malformed thing, his face mirroring his disgust. It had once been human, but now belonged to Hate—was Hate. As he watched, the creature flexed its forelimbs and sharp claws sprouted instantly from the knobby joints.

Naim locked eyes with the leader. "I know you," he taunted in a cold, hard voice. Oh, yes! He knew her all right. She was Slain, leader of the Hellhags—half-dead beings—vampire beasts, who sucked the blood of their victims and ate human flesh.

From her hiding place, Miranda watched the four-limbed creatures waiting motionless, like stone gargoyles. Red, unblinking eyes bored into the Druid and white froth drooled from their open mouths as if their teeth were already ripping into his flesh. And Naim would certainly die. Even if he managed to fight off the creatures, there was still Hate. The girl shuddered violently, trying to push her body into the smooth cold stone.

Naim ignored the Demon. He knew where she was and that was enough. He also knew that it made no difference to her whether the Hellhags finished him off or she did. It was the shedding of blood in her name that fed her power. He could sense her unmoving presence behind him, black and menacing, and he knew that she was smiling horribly.

Hate hissed with pleasure, savouring the man's fear, her long, protruding tongue lashing wildly from side to side. There was no escape, no magic strong enough to save him. He was cornered. In a few seconds the Hellhags would bring him down, finishing what they had failed to do the last time they met, and then they'd feast on fresh, warm human for the first time in a thousand years.

Naim's heart pounded against his ribcage as he desperately tried to think of a way to protect Miranda and live to remember it. But, if he were to die this night, he would not die needlessly. He exhaled slowly, hoping he had bought a few seconds to work out a plan.

Mistaking the Druid's sigh as a sign of weakness, the creatures suddenly rushed at him, toying with their prey like cats playing with a mouse. They charged into the circle of light but, at the last second, backed away. Their claws scraping along the marble floor sounded like giant nails on a blackboard.

Then, the Hellhags attacked in force.

It happened so swiftly, so horribly, that Miranda barely had time to react. Her hands were clenched so tightly, she didn't feel her fingernails cut into her palms. Hot tears, a mixture of weakness and despair, blinded her for an instant. Through misty eyes, she watched helplessly as the Druid was dragged down, and the Hellhags' sharp fangs closed on his living flesh. The white flame in his hand flared once, and died.

Despite the sudden blackness, Miranda squeezed her eyes shut and waited for the end to come—waited for the creatures to smell the blood on her palms and turn their hungry red eyes on her. It wouldn't be long now.

She felt the touch on her arm, then the iron grip dragging her out from where she had wedged her body into the narrow space between pillar and wall. *So this is how the dream ends*, she thought. She should have guessed—should have known.

"Quickly!" hissed a familiar voice in the darkness. "In a few seconds they will be on to us."

Miranda almost fainted with relief. "How—?" she started to speak, but a loud "Silence!" froze the words in her throat.

But, I saw you die, she thought, shuddering at the image of the creatures' long pointed fangs snapping at the fallen Druid. The grisly image broke up and scattered, as Naim shoved the terrified girl toward the beautiful wood and stained glass doors that opened into the Library of Parliament.

Suddenly, a red glow illuminated the passage. Miranda risked a quick glance over her shoulder. Silhouetted in the glow from the skull near the end of Hate's black stake, she saw the Hellhags, claws slashing, sharp teeth biting at the spot where the Druid had fallen only moments ago. They still didn't realize that he had escaped.

But Hate knew now. Raking her claws along the syenite pillars in rage, she raised her head, opened her huge mouth, and hissed—a high earsplitting sibilation that grew louder until the very foundations of the Centre Block shuddered and shifted. It went on and on, building higher and higher, pushing into the stone walls and rising upward. Wide cracks appeared in the masonry. Massive chunks of hand-carved, polished stone crashed to the floor below, squashing two Hellhags, whose limbs convulsed briefly and then went still. Behind the Demon, in Confederation Hall, the beautiful vaulted ceiling crumbled and fell, smashing on the marble floor with a deafening roar.

Miranda ran, nose bleeding from the stone-splintering hiss. She sobbed loudly, anger as white as the Druid's flame building inside her. This was her country—her home. Naim had said that she was the only one who could stop this Monster and she would, no matter what.

"This means war," she shouted through the noise. Then she skidded to a stop and turned toward the Demon, wanting the creature to see her, to know her. She raised her arm, and shook her fist in defiance.

Hate had been so intent on killing the Druid that she had not noticed the girl until now. The hissing stopped abruptly, turning into a harsh laugh at the brazenness of the child waving her puny fist from the opposite end of the passage. Who was she? What did the Druid want with her? Then she knew, and she felt the first faint stirrings of fear. This was the girl who had the power to destroy her. Her red eyes burned with rage as she suddenly realized that the THUGS had failed.

The Demon raised the stake, pointing the grotesque human head at the wretched girl. Red lightening exploded from the skull's eyes and streaked down the passage, straight at Miranda, who saw it coming but was unable to react. Then she was moving, yanked off her feet by Naim's firm grip on her arm, and flying sideways through the air.

The Demon-fire roared past her like a backdraft, singeing her hair and clothing, before blasting a syenite pillar from its mooring, and sending jagged chunks of green stone hurtling through the air. The force of the stone pieces slamming into the beautiful Library doors shattered the aged stained glass and ripped the sturdy wooden doors from their ancient hinges, splitting them apart as if they were made of cardboard. Shards of glass and sharp splinters of wood bombarded the fleeing companions as Naim dragged Miranda through the ruined doorway into the Library.

"Wait!" cried Miranda, struggling to free her arm from the Druid's grasp. She peered over her shoulder in time to see the Hellhags bounding toward them down the passage. For once in her life, she was glad that she had listened to the stories about the Great Fire that had destroyed the Centre Block in 1916. The Library was saved from the blaze by a pair of iron doors behind the stained glass doors. Miranda knew that those same doors were their only hope now.

"The fire doors!" she shouted, clawing frantically along the wall on one side of the opening and praying they hadn't been removed when the new stone building was constructed. The crunch of broken glass under her boots grated loudly in the dim light.

"Stand back," ordered the Druid, stretching his arms across the opening and pressing his hands against the cold metal, muttering words in a language Miranda did not recognize. He stepped back and the two massive iron doors rolled shut with a loud clang, repelling the horror advancing upon them like a landslide.

"It will not keep them out for long," he said, turning and moving deeper into the Library. "Follow me."

Floodlights on the ground outside the Library illuminated the steepled copper roof, allowing light to enter through the sixteen windows set in the gilded cupola of its lantern and through sixteen lower windows. Miranda knew there were more windows on the main level, but they were on the other side of the bookshelves. Although the light was dim on the Library floor, Miranda could easily follow the dark form of the Druid as he strode through the building, every now and then stopping to run his fingers over the sculpted masks and rosettes decorating the white pine paneling.

Suddenly Naim laughed. The rare sound startled Miranda. "I must be losing my skills," he said, shaking his head. "It was here all the time."

He pressed his hand against a small rosette in the lower right corner of a larger sculpture on one of the wooden bookshelves. Slowly, the shelf began to rotate out from the wall.

"There will be a flight of stone steps," he said, as something hit hard against the iron fire doors that he had only barred moments ago. "I must seal this gateway behind you. I may not be able to join you for some time."

"Don't leave me!" cried Miranda, clutching his cloak. "I can't—"

The Druid placed a hand on Miranda's shoulder and, leaning on the staff, bent down to look her in the face. "You can," he said gently, "and you must. I will be with you as soon as I can. Descend the steps and wait for me there." And with that, he pushed her through the opening and stepped aside.

Miranda just made it through the gap behind the bookshelf when she heard the sound of the heavy fire doors crashing apart. Slain, and the rest of the Hellhags that had escaped death from the crumbling masonry, tore through the doorway, bolting into the library, knocking over tables and desks, sending computers flying, and scattering rare books everywhere. Their spike-like claws left deep ugly gouges in the priceless parquet floor as they followed the Druid's scent, their shrieks high with hunger. The Druid touched another rosette and the bookshelf closed, leaving Miranda alone in the dark.

CHAPTER TEN

SLAIN

lain, the leader of the Hellhags, snarled and snapped her grotesque jaws at her companions. Whining, they fell back, giving way to the dominant creature who had once been a human woman but was now Hate's servant. In the confused black cauldron of her mind, the huge Hellhag knew she must kill this evil Druid now, tonight, or forfeit her own life. Hate, the Demon, did not tolerate failure. Slain looked at the five remaining Hellhags and saw the hatred in their eyes. Should she fail, they would be only too willing to carry out the punishment Hate prescribed.

Ahead, Naim faced her, his back against the massive wooden bookshelves along the outer wall. Slain howled once. At her signal, the other creatures broke away from their leader, bounding out to left and right to come at the man from both sides. Then the Hellhag pounced, knocking Naim to his knees, her claws slashing at the heavy cloak and slicing deep into the soft tissue of his left shoulder. But the man was quick and agile. He caught her by the neck and flung her away from him into the middle of the Library, his hands leaving dark purple marks on her bleached throat.

Slain felt the snap of bones breaking as she hit the base of a massive white marble statue that dominated the Library of Parliament.

Bright red spots of blood splattered against the pure white stone, but she did not know if it were her blood or the Druid's, from her claws. As she struggled to rise, she stared up at the statue, glowing opalescent in the pale light. It was a woman, young and proud and beautiful—Victoria, Canada's first queen, in the early days of her reign. Slain recoiled as though she had been struck blind, her red eyes burning in their sockets, the pain from her broken body was nothing compared with the pain she felt now. For, as she gazed at the glowing white marble figure, she saw herself, and she suddenly knew that she had once been a woman, young and beautiful, like the woman whose likeness seemed to be looking at her so sadly.

With a great effort, Slain pulled herself up on her two front limbs, but her hindquarters would not obey her command. Slowly, she dragged her broken body toward the Druid, lower back and hind legs leaving a smear of blood across the parquet floor.

Naim's strength was failing fast. Because of the ancient wood and stonework in the splendid library, he dared not use the staff to send the Druid-fire blasting into the Hellhags. The destruction to the building would be total, and he did not believe that the people in Miranda's world possessed the knowledge and skill to rebuild. Only the Dwarves built structures such as this.

Two Hellhags lay dead at his feet, their heads twisted at an obscene angle. That left three, four if he hadn't succeeded in killing Slain. As Naim weakened, the Hellhags grew stronger, drawing into themselves the spirits of their dead companions. Naim knew that he could not last much longer. He waited for the next lunge, wondering whether, this time, they would revert to their former tactic and attack as one unit. He might stand a chance if they came at him one on one, but he couldn't survive against the three creatures with their heightened strength.

Then he saw Slain. She stood on two front limbs, just beyond the others, red eyes burning into him. And then she attacked, hindquarters sliding along the floor. The Druid gasped at the suddenness of the charge. Her sharp claws slashed through the throat of the nearest Hellhag, who raged with hatred as blood spewed from the gaping wound. A minute later, the creature died horribly, drowning in a pool of its own blood, its body writhing and flopping on the floor like a fish, before going rigid.

The two remaining creatures turned instantly to see their despised leader crouched over the body of their dead companion. For a moment they were too stunned to react. They forgot about the Druid and ran in a frenzied circle around and around Slain and her victim. Then, as if they suddenly worked out the puzzle, they lunged at the doomed leader, great jaws snapping, wicked claws unsheathed.

Naim stared at Slain, shaking his head in disbelief. He would never know what made the big Hellhag turn against her own kind, but he knew that she had given him a few minutes and he would not waste that precious gift. With Hate nearby, waiting for the creatures to finish him off, he could not take the chance of reopening the hidden stairway. He must find another way out of the Library and make his way to Miranda through the maze of caves and connecting tunnels under Parliament Hill.

The Druid moved quickly away from the bookshelves then turned back and looked up. Above his head, against the wall of the circular building, were two additional galleries of books, accessible by a narrow catwalk on each level. He looked about for a way up, noting various passageways, but saw nothing that showed which one led up to the second and third galleries. He threw the staff up and over the railing, and then, calling on his remaining strength, he leaped into the air, strong hands gripping the solid wood and wrought-iron railing bordering the catwalk on the second level. Quickly, he hoisted himself up and over the railing, knowing that time was running out.

Naim leaned against the railing, holding one hand against the gash in his shoulder to stem the flow of blood. He risked a quick glance down into the middle of the library, in time to see the red fire dim and then die in Slain's eyes. But she had taken another Hellhag with her into death. That left one, and it now raised its ugly head, scanning the library for the Druid. The creature howled when it saw the human. It streaked after him, hurtling its body into the air again and again in an attempt to gain the catwalk.

Clutching his shoulder, Naim raced for the nearest exit, mounting the stairs to the upper gallery three at a time. He could hear the maddened creature skidding on the floor below and springing up the stairs in pursuit. On reaching the upper gallery, he climbed onto the top of one of the bookshelves and stretched until his hands grasped the frame of the nearest window. He pulled himself up onto the narrow sloped sill. He felt a pang of guilt as he smashed his elbow into the ancient glass panes, and slipped out onto the steep roof, the sound of the Hellhag's outrage pouring through the broken window into the still winter night.

Clinging to the arch of the flying buttress, Naim worked his way to the edge of the roof. He tossed the staff to the ground, and leaped after it, his weary body falling heavily on the soft cushion of snow, the blood from his wounds leaving a dark crimson stain.

CHAPTER ELEVEN

ALONE IN THE DARK

he last sounds Miranda heard, before the library shelf slid shut leaving her alone in total blackness, were the metallic crash of the heavy iron fire doors bursting apart and the bloodcurdling screams of the Hellhags as they streaked through the library. Then nothing. She did not obey the Druid's command to wait at the bottom of the stone stairway. Instead, she huddled on the top step, inches from the hidden panel and waited, wishing she had brought a flashlight and wondering what would become of her if Naim didn't make it.

What if he didn't escape the Hellhags? Without him, how could she destroy the Demon? She didn't have any magic powers and she certainly couldn't light a fire in her hand. What if he didn't come for her? How would she find her way out of this dark place? Would she ever see her mother again? Or her friends? She had never thought about danger or evil before. Of course, she knew there were bad people, or mean, nasty people, like Stubby, but the creatures who were hunting her were truly evil. Where did they come from? How did they get that way? What if they caught her and made her evil too? What if they said, be like us, or die? What would she do?

As the minutes turned into hours, Miranda grew more depressed. "He's not coming," she said. She suddenly remembered what Arabella had told her about her horoscope. Well, things couldn't get much worse than they already were. Just as she had decided to stay where she was until somebody found her, she heard a scraping sound coming from one of the tunnels below. Then voices. She strained her ears, listening intently. Was it the Druid? Or were the creatures coming for her? Did Naim tell them where to find her? No! She decided, realizing that she believed with all her heart that the Druid would never betray her.

Miranda waited, not daring to breathe as the scraping sound and the voices drew closer. She almost cried out when she recognized normal, human voices. But then she wondered what normal humans were doing under Parliament Hill in the middle of the night, and she remained silent.

"MIRANDAAAA!" She heard someone calling her name. They *were* looking for her. Then a flashlight shone up the stairs, into her eyes, blinding her.

"I'm here," she shouted, weak with relief, her hands shading her eyes. "Wait! I'm coming."

She stumbled down the steep stone steps, talking nonstop. "How did you find me? Is Naim with you? He told me to wait for him, and I did, but he never came back and I was afraid those things would. . . ." She stared at her rescuers. "What are you doing here?" she asked in astonishment, scarcely able to believe her eyes.

Nicholas brushed a clump of unruly chocolate-coloured hair out of his eyes and grinned. "Ask Bell. It was her idea."

Miranda looked at Arabella and laughed, the sound loud in the silent tunnel. She should have known that her short, stubborn friend would never obey the Druid and go home meekly, like Montague answering Nick's whistle. Miranda was so happy to see her friends that she had to sit on the bottom step and take a minute to make sure she wasn't dreaming.

"No way was I going to leave you alone with that man," said Arabella, smiling smugly. "But I knew it was no good arguing, so I pretended to go home. Instead, I went and got Nick."

"But how did you know I'd be down here?" asked Miranda.

Arabella grinned slyly. "I heard that Druid person say something about having to get to Parliament Hill."

"We didn't know where you'd be going on the Hill," said Nicholas. "So we figured we'd get here first, and follow you."

"But how?" repeated Miranda, noticing the guilty look that was spreading slowly over the boy's face.

"He stole his dad's car," snapped Penelope, moving into the light and glaring at Nicholas. "And he doesn't even have a driver's license."

Miranda grinned when she saw Muffy's little pointed fuchsia head sticking out of the front of Penelope's ski jacket, with a bootlace tied around her muzzle.

"Oh, shut up," said Arabella. "How else were we going to get here before Miranda?"

Miranda gaped at Nicholas. "I saw your car on St. Patrick Street. I thought it was a drunk driver. Was it really you?"

Nick nodded, looking more miserable by the second. "Dad's going to kill me when he finds out."

"At least you left a note," said Arabella, turning to Nicholas. "Tell her about the Library."

Nicholas shrugged. "There's not much to tell. I buried myself in a snow bank near the Centre Block. I almost died when the Druid suddenly walked toward me. At first I thought he spotted me. He went real still and stared at the snow bank."

"I remember that," said Miranda. "I didn't know what was going on."

"Anyway," continued Nicholas. "Talk about relief when he stopped about three feet away and pulled out a map or something." He looked at Miranda. "He asked you where the Library was."

"We tried to follow you into the Centre Block," Arabella cut in. "But we couldn't get the door open. Then Nick said his father had an old map that showed all the tunnels under The Hill and he knew a way into the Library. So we went around back and came through these amazing caves. It took ages, but here we are."

"My dad did this survey of the tunnels and caves a few years ago. I used to come with him sometimes. It's the same as the old map. I know the tunnels by heart."

"Would somebody kindly tell me what's going on?" said Penelope.

"Shut up, Penelope," said Arabella and Nicholas at the same time.

"Hey," said Miranda. "She's in this too. It's not fair to leave her out of it." She looked at the girl who made up the most incredible lies and thought how much more unbelievable the truth was. So she told her everything, starting with the black creatures outside the house and ending with the Druid pushing her through the opening behind the Library book stacks. In the beam from Nicholas's flashlight, Penelope paled as Miranda told her companions about Hate the Demon, and the other horrible creatures that had attacked them in the Hall of Honours.

"I want to go home," Penelope cried, when Miranda finally finished.

"You can't go home now," said Miranda sadly. "I wish you had listened to the Druid. But if those monsters could find me so easily, they already know who you are and where you live." She looked at her friends. "I'm sorry if I've put all of you in danger. The worst thing is I can't tell you what's going on because I don't know. I only know it has something to do with me."

"What are we going to do?" Penelope wailed, her voice rising in panic.

"The first thing we should do, is get out of here," suggested Nicholas.

"I hear you," said Arabella. "Come on, guys, let's go."

"I can't," said Miranda, not wanting to stay behind. "I have to wait for Naim."

"Mir, it's been hours since you went into the Centre Block," reasoned Arabella. "If he's not here by now, he's not coming."

"She's right," said Nicholas. "I read a lot of stuff about Druids—most of it pretty bad. They used to sacrifice people and all kinds of weird stuff. If I were you, I'd get as far away from him as I could."

"And good riddance," said Penelope. "I never trusted that horrible man."

Miranda's green eyes flashed in anger. "You don't understand anything," she said, her voice hard, tears of anger filling her eyes. Then she bowed her head and spoke in a whisper. "You weren't up there. You didn't see. . . . He saved my life." Lifting her head, she pointed up the stone stairway. "I have to wait. Go if you want. I'm staying."

"Wise girl," said the familiar, gruff voice of the Druid, as the man lurched into the light, leaning heavily on the strong wooden staff. He slumped down on the steps beside Miranda.

"I knew you'd come back!" she said, her eyes bright.

The Druid patted her hand but his eyes rested on Nicholas. "You should watch your tongue, young man. Or stick to subjects you know something about."

"I know about Druids," said Nicholas. "I dare you to deny that they sacrificed people?"

"Of course I deny it," said Naim, looking at the boy as if he were an idiot.

Nicholas clenched his fists. "I read—"

"I do not care what you have read," interrupted the Druid wearily. "You are wrong and I am right."

"Nick! Shut up!" cried Miranda, suddenly noticing the jagged rips in the Druid's black cloak, and the dark stain around his left shoulder. "You're hurt!" she cried, jumping to her feet and looking at her friends. "Help me! We have to get him to the hospital."

"No," said the Druid. "I just need to rest. Just let me rest."

Naim leaned back, his head resting against the stone foundation, eyes closed.

"What are you doing?" Miranda asked Nicholas, as the boy rooted in his backpack.

"Going to sleep," he answered, producing several thin, metallic blankets and tossing them to the girls. He shot an angry look at the Druid. "He's right, my foot." Then he turned to Miranda. "My Dad uses these when he's in the North. They don't look it, but they'll keep you warm." He wrapped himself in one of the blankets and lay down on the floor. "I've got a bad feeling about your Druid," he muttered.

"Just drop it, OK?" hissed Miranda.

"You're not going to bark, are you, Muffers Wuffers?" said Penelope, untying the bootlace from around the poodle's snout. Then she unzipped her ski jacket and the miniature dog jumped to the ground and disappeared in the darkness.

Miranda draped one of the space blankets over the Druid and curled up on the hard floor by his feet. Within minutes, the only sounds echoing through the tunnels under Parliament Hill were the shrill "Yap! Yap! Yap!" of the little dog, the scrabbling of rats, and the Druid's loud snores.

CHAPTER TWELVE
THE PORTAL

"here!" said the Druid, pointing the staff ahead where the passage ended in a wall of limestone.

Nicholas tugged Miranda's sleeve. "Where's he going?" he whispered, suspiciously. "There's nothing down there but a dead end."

"Leave it alone, Nick," Miranda snapped. "He knows what he's doing."

"You don't know that," answered Nicholas, stung by Miranda's abrupt tone. "But you'd probably jump off a cliff if your precious Druid told you to." He looked at her in disgust. "What's the use?" he said, striding ahead angrily.

"What's eating him?" asked Miranda, turning to Arabella.

"Give him some credit, Mir," said Arabella, coming to the boy's defence. "He knows these caves and tunnels like the back of his hand."

"I know," agreed Miranda. "But this isn't about caves and tunnels, or who's right or wrong, Bell. It's not a contest. I told Nick what happened in the Centre Block and I know he believes me. But he wasn't there . . . when the Demon and those other horrible creatures attacked us. He wants to help, but he doesn't want to

listen to Naim. And, he doesn't have a clue what we're up against."
She gripped Arabella's arm. "You saw those things outside my house.
You know that Naim's the only one who can help us. We have to
trust him, Bell."

"Maybe," said Arabella. "But you've got to wonder what's in it
for him."

Ahead, the Druid stopped at the end of the tunnel. It appeared
that Nicholas was right after all. It looked like a dead end.

"I hate to say 'I told you so,' but I told you so," said the boy,
folding his arms and gloating, as he leaned against the tunnel wall.

The Druid looked at him, scornfully. "You do not know everything,
my young friend."

"Maybe not," answered Nicholas boldly. "But you don't have to
be Einstein to see there's nothing there but a solid wall." Even before
the words were completely out of his mouth, the wall was gone.

"Whoa!" Nicholas shouted, stumbling back from the edge of the
sheer cliff that plunged down, thousands of feet, into a vast lake.
"This can't be real!" he said, peering over his shoulder into the dark
tunnel, and then looking back over the cliff at the lake, sparkling
sapphire blue in the bright sunlight. In the middle of the lake, he
saw an island gleaming like a clear emerald amidst the startling blue
water. He looked at the Druid, questioningly.

The tall man placed a hand on the boy's shoulder. "You were not
wrong," he said gently. "You saw a dead end, I saw past it."

"But why couldn't I see what you saw?" asked Nicholas, feeling
his whole world turn upside down.

The Druid thought for a moment. "Your race has always seen what
it wants to see, and no more," he said finally. Then he clapped the
boy on the shoulder and smiled. "But perhaps there's hope, after all."

"HELLO! ARE YOU ALL STUPID, OR WHAT?" screamed Penelope,
dropping Muffy on the limestone floor and stalking toward the edge
of the cliff. "I've seen this on TV. It's nothing but an illusion." She

turned and faced her companions, hands on her hips. "And I'll prove it." Before anyone could make a move, she turned and walked straight off the cliff. And dropped like a rock toward the distant lake, calling out, "MUFF-EEEEE!" as she fell.

For a moment, the three friends stared at each other, unable to take in what had just happened. Then Arabella burst into tears, and Muffy dashed to the cliff, peering over the edge and bouncing stiffly with each shrill bark. Miranda, afraid that the dog would bounce itself off the cliff, caught the poodle and held her, talking soothingly while trying to pet the frantic animal. But Muffy bared her tiny fangs and growled savagely, snapping at Miranda's hands, arms, belly and anything else within reach.

"CAN NO ONE CONTROL—THAT—THAT MINIATURE HELLHAG?" stormed the Druid, snatching Muffy out of Miranda's arms. He held the poodle in the air, in his right hand and, for a second, Miranda thought he was going to hurl it off the cliff after Penelope. But the Druid simply stared at the miniature animal, who squirmed and twisted and then, suddenly, went limp.

"What did you do to her?" demanded Arabella, glaring at the Druid.

"I did nothing," answered the Druid coldly, stuffing Muffy in a pocket inside his heavy cloak. "The dog will be fine."

"The question is, what are we going to do now?" said Nicholas.

"What are we going to tell Penelope's parents?" wailed Arabella, eyeing the Druid's cloak, still not convinced that Muffy was alive.

"The girl will be fine," said the Druid.

"Right!" snapped Arabella. "Like Muffy?"

Miranda watched the Druid. He was pale and she noticed that the dark bloodstain on his left shoulder had spread since she first saw it.

"BELL! PLEASE STOP ARGUING!" she shouted, startling her companions. Then she turned to Naim. "Tell us what's going on. What do we do now?"

"Yes, it is time I told you a story," said the Druid, easing his body down onto the stone floor, and resting his back against the limestone wall. Then he motioned for the others to join him.

"It all started with the Elves," he said, unaware of the young people staring at him in disbelief. "They came to this planet one hundred and sixty million years ago. From where, they have never revealed. And they brought magic with them." He paused for a second, before shaking his head. "No, that is untrue. They did not bring magic with them. They *were* magic."

Nicholas rolled his eyes. "Are you seriously saying that Elves are real?"

Naim looked at him and laughed, as if the boy had made a joke. "As real as Trolls and Dwarves. As real as you."

"Trolls! Dwarves!" Arabella snorted. "That's not possible."

"It is not only possible, it is true," the Druid replied calmly.

"Then how come we don't learn about the Elves in school?" persisted the stubborn girl. "The last Elf I read about was Rumpelstiltskin."

"Rumpelstiltskin was an evil Dwarf," corrected Nicholas.

"Actually, you're both wrong," said Miranda. "He was a 'little man'."

"Whatever," said Arabella.

"But Bell's right," continued Nicholas. "There's nothing about Elves in our history books."

"Well," said Miranda grinning to ease the tension. "Penelope believed in aliens. She told us once that her brother had been abducted. Next, she'll be saying the Elves kidnapped her."

At the mention of Penelope, Arabella started crying again.

"What's wrong with you?" said Nicholas. "You didn't even like her."

Miranda glared at Nicholas. She had known him all of her life and had never seen him act as rudely as he had with Naim and now with Bell. The boy met her eyes and quickly looked away.

The Druid placed his hand on Arabella's arm. "I do not lie," he said. "Your friend is fine." Then he chuckled. "Perhaps a bit wet, but she is alive and I will see that she is reunited with you soon."

He looked at the three children sitting on the hard stone floor. "Now, where was I?"

"You were about to explain," said Nicholas, "why we don't learn about Elves in school."

"Do you expect me to explain to you why your race does half the things it does?" answered the Druid. "Better you tell me."

Arabella shook her head. "I don't believe any of this."

"Whether you believe or not is unimportant," said the Druid. "But I will tell you one thing. Read your early books. Surely even your race retained some memory from the time before the Great Break."

"What's that?" asked Miranda. "I've never heard of the Great Break."

"Six thousand years ago, the Elves split the world into two parts—the old, where I come from, and the new, the world you know."

"This is crazy," scoffed Nicholas, shaking his head.

"Why did they split the world?" asked Miranda.

"Because the people in your world wanted it that way," answered the Druid.

"What's wrong with all of you?" cried Nicholas, jumping to his feet. "Don't tell me you believe this crap."

"Sit down, young man, or go home," said the Druid.

Nicholas was shaking with rage. "Don't tell me what to do."

"SIT DOWN, NICK!" shouted Miranda. "AND STOP INTERRUPTING."

The boy scowled at her, but he did as she said.

The Druid glared at the young companions, daring them to interrupt again. "I will now finish your history lesson," he said. "When the Elves first appeared on Earth, they took a vast barren area where nothing lived, and made it their own. Using their special skills, they turned the desert into a gigantic lake, and in the middle of the lake they created a huge island country which they named Ellesmere."

Nicholas gulped and waved his arm toward the cliff. "Down there, that little island. . . ."

The Druid nodded. "Yes, Nicholas. But it is not as small as it

84

looks from here. That is Ellesmere Island, home of the Elves. And the beautiful Capital City, Bethany."

"Is that where we're going?" asked Miranda.

"We'll get to that in a minute," answered the Druid. "My story is almost finished. The Elves lived on their Island and were happy there for thousands of years." He stopped and a shadow darkened his eyes.

"What happened next?" prompted Miranda, fascinated. From the moment she first read *The Lord of the Rings*, she had loved Elves. She did not need much urging to convince her that such creatures existed. After what she had already seen during the night, she was ready to believe that black was white.

The Druid bowed his head. "Then evil came," he said softly.

"What evil?" asked Arabella.

Naim didn't seem to hear her as he continued. "The Elves were always careful to work with Nature. They respected the other creatures who shared their world. Remember. A hundred and sixty million years ago the dinosaurs also roamed the Earth."

"Wait a minute," said Nicholas. "Everybody knows the dinosaurs were wiped out when an asteroid hit Earth. How could the Elves survive the blast or the nuclear winter that lasted for a thousand years?"

"That's a good question, Nicholas," said the Druid, watching the boy turn beet red at the unexpected praise. "All of the Elves who were away from Ellesmere Island perished when the asteroid struck," he explained. "But, did I not say that the Elves created their country with magic?"

"You mean they built a shield, or something?" asked Miranda.

"I do not know what sort of magic they used," answered the Druid. "But it was powerful enough and they survived both the impact and the long, sunless winter that followed." He winked at Nicholas. "But you are wrong about one thing, my smart friend."

"What?" asked Nicholas.

"I know for a fact that the dinosaurs were not wiped out."

"No way!" breathed Nicholas. "This is awesome!"

"So, what about this evil that came? Are we talking about dinosaurs, or what?" asked Arabella, not believing what she was hearing, but unable to resist listening.

"The dinosaurs were never evil, they were simply dinosaurs," Naim answered. "When the sun gradually emerged, and the Elves ventured out into the world again, they quickly became aware of an imbalance in Nature. Creatures that traditionally hunted for food were now killing for sport. The king, I think it was Aeron Lafalafal back then, sent out hundreds of Elven scouts to scour both their own country and the adjoining lands. The reports they sent back all said the same thing. There were no signs of unusual disturbances in Nature before the asteroid hit Earth. The Elven Erudicia, the most powerful Elders in the Council at Bethany, studied the reports and reached a terrifying conclusion. Since the imbalance was not present in Ellesmere, and since all life outside Ellesmere perished as a result of the asteroid collision, some new form of anti-life came into being as a result of the nuclear holocaust."

"What?" said Nicholas. "Now, you're saying that something actually evolved from nothing, or from the fallout, or what?"

"No," answered the Druid. "I am telling you what the Elves believed."

"Is that where Hate and the THUGS came from?" asked Miranda, turning white just thinking about the Demon.

"Nobody really knows where Hate, who called herself Taog back then, came from. There were no signs of such a creature on Earth before the impact. But she has certainly been here ever since. The Elves believe that she is the anti-life that evolved during the nuclear winter."

"If everything on the planet, except the Elves on Ellesmere, were wiped out, where did the Dwarves come from?" asked Nicholas.

Naim took a patient breath. "Probably from the same evolutionary process that produced you."

"What about the THUGS?" pressed Miranda.

"Hmm, yes, the THUGS," answered the Druid. "They started out as humans, but they would not accept the ultimate reality of human life." He stopped for a minute.

"Which is?" Arabella prompted.

"The ultimate reality?" said the Druid. "That all living things die, of course. You see, Hate promised everlasting life. The THUGS were once men who chose to live forever by giving themselves to the Demon."

"How can we destroy them if they can't die?" asked Miranda.

"Hate lied to them," answered the Druid. "They are already dead— the living dead. The Demon drained them, physically and spiritually. They do not have one single memory of who they once were. They might well live forever, but they will not know a second's worth of the experience because Hate remade them into herself."

"And those other things, the ones in the Hall of Honours?"

"The Hellhags," said Naim, sounding as though he had eaten something bad. "They're another matter. They were once female humans, but they have no memory of that, only a craving. And, because they crave what they were, they thirst for blood and devour human flesh in the mistaken belief that it will satisfy their craving." He exhaled slowly, remembering Slain. "Poor creatures. But make no mistake about it, they belong to the Demon."

He looked at the three young faces turned toward him, spellbound, devouring every word as if he were reciting a bedtime story. *What am I doing to them?* He wondered, not for the first time. The man sighed. He wanted to protect them, but in his heart and mind, he believed that they must understand the nature of evil if they were to fight it.

"A thousand years ago, the Elves decided to do away with Hate once and for all. They used their powers to create a parallel universe, a vast empty nothingness that they named the Place with No Name.

And then they forced Hate and the thousands of creatures she had poisoned into that place. To keep the Demon there, the Elves combined their magic with an ancient Earthly power to seal the boundaries of the prison." He looked meaningfully at Miranda. "I came to find you, because the Earthly power used to close off the place is eroding and, as you know, Hate and some of her creatures have already escaped into your world and mine."

"You're looking at me as though I'm supposed to know what you're talking about. I mean, you keep saying that I'm the only one who can destroy Hate," said Miranda. "Why me? And how do you expect me to fight a huge Monster like that?"

"That's what we are going to Bethany to discover," said the Druid.

CHAPTER THIRTEEN

THE HORN
OF DILEMMA

'd like to know how we're getting there?" asked Nicholas suspiciously, walking to the edge of the cliff and peering over.

"I'm afraid it's not 'we,' Nicholas," said the Druid. "You and Arabella must return to your homes now."

Nicholas stared at the Druid as if he didn't believe what he was hearing. "But, you just told us all that stuff about the Elves. I thought—" He turned and angrily kicked a loose chunk of limestone off the cliff. "And what about Penelope? You said we'd see her soon."

"And you shall. The girl is in the care of the Elves. As soon I reach Bethany, I will send her back to you."

Arabella joined Nicholas at the edge of the cliff. She put her hand on his arm. "I'm going with Miranda," she said, as she followed Nicholas's gaze down to Ellesmere Island, glistening like an emerald on a dark blue cloth.

"I'm going too," said Nicholas.

"Then that's settled," said Arabella, looking at the Druid. "And you can't stop us." She quickly backed away from the opening and out of the man's reach, just in case he lost his temper and decided to hurl her off the cliff.

But Naim threw back his head and laughed. "Young lady, I could stop you before you could say Arabella." Then he stopped laughing and looked at the couple as if he were peering deep into their hearts. Nodding once, he turned his back on them and walked stiffly toward Miranda. Towering over the girl, he said. "You are the one who has the most difficult journey in the days ahead. It is your decision. Do your friends travel with us?"

"I want them with me," she said, without hesitating. "But first I have to know if they'll be safe?"

The Druid turned away so quickly, Miranda was afraid she had made him angry. "I have a right to know if we could die," she said to his back.

The Druid lowered himself beside her and leaned back against the hard stone wall, unable to hide the flicker of pain that dulled his eyes or the way he favoured his left shoulder.

"You are asking me to look into the future and I have never sought power that terrible." He took one of her slender hands. "I would be lying if I told you that there was no danger ahead for you and your friends."

"I don't want to die," she managed in a small voice.

"Nor do I," said the Druid. "But, child, we may very well die, and we probably will fail. Surely after last night, you know that?"

"I know that I have to go with you," said Miranda. "I still don't know how I'm involved in any of this, but I will go to Bethany and hear what the Elves have to say. And I want my friends with me. When I know what we have to do to destroy Hate, or if we can destroy her, then Nick and Bell should be the ones who decide whether they stay or go home."

"Fairly said," nodded the Druid. Then he turned to the others. "I was against including you in this business, but you have already proven that you care for Miranda. Last night you stuck with her, and did not give up until you found her. That speaks well of your courage," he said. "And for having come this far, you deserve to see the most beautiful city on Earth."

"We're actually going to see the Elves," whispered Nicholas, grinning foolishly. He nudged Arabella and the grin turned into a burst of laughter. "And maybe some Dwarves and Trolls, too."

"Oh, shut up," snapped Arabella, jabbing her elbow into his ribs. Then she laughed too. "It would've made me crazy if Penelope got to see the Elves and we didn't."

"No kidding," said Nicholas.

Miranda hopped to her feet and joined her companions. "I'm glad you're coming," she said, throwing an arm about their shoulders. Then she looked at the Druid, sudden panic welling up inside her. "But no way am I jumping off that cliff to get there."

Naim chuckled as he reached up and removed a large horn from a row of pegs that were wedged into the stone wall above his head. He tried, but failed, to hide the look of pain that darkened his face as his injured shoulder took the weight of the instrument.

"Naim! Wait!" cried Miranda, rushing to his side and taking one end of the horn. The thing was heavy. She staggered, feeling her legs begin to buckle. It took all of her strength just to hold onto it.

"I've got it," said Nicholas, sliding his shoulder under the horn where Miranda's hands were locked around it.

The Druid nodded and gave them a tight smile. "Set it down over there," he said, tilting his head in the direction of the cliff.

Miranda kept one eye on the mouth of the cliff as she and Nicholas gently lowered their end of the horn until it rested on the cavern floor. Breathing heavily, she backed quickly away from the cliff edge. The three companions stared at the horn, each positive that it had not been on the wall only seconds ago. Surely they would have noticed it, especially since it was at least ten feet long. It was made of ivory, or horn, and Miranda wondered what sort of huge animal had once worn it.

"I wonder what your Elves killed to get *that*?" said Arabella, sarcastically.

"Young lady," said the Druid, coldly, "you have an annoying habit of making ridiculous comments about things of which you know nothing." He shook a long finger in the startled girl's face. "I would advise you to change your attitude of disrespect before we reach Bethany, or it will be the worse for you."

"What?" smirked Arabella. "Or the Elves will ground me?"

"Don't push your luck," whispered Miranda. "At least not until we get to Bethany."

But the Druid either did not hear Arabella's comments or he chose to ignore them. He turned toward the sunlit opening, his shoulders rising as he took a deep breath, holding one end of the horn steady with both hands. Standing sideways to the opening on the very lip of the precipice, so close that the wind threatened to suck him over the edge, he lifted the horn to his lips and blew. The others, expecting to hear a great blast issue from the bell of the horn resting on the limestone floor, were surprised when they heard nothing. The Druid stood his end of the huge horn against the wall and, pressing one hand tightly against his shoulder and muttering to himself in a strange language, paced back and forth along the cliff's edge, unaware of the youngsters watching him curiously.

"Did you hear anything?" Nicholas asked in a whisper.

"Maybe it's like a dog whistle, we can't hear it," said Miranda, wondering who or what had heard the silent call.

Thousands of feet down to the lake and another thousand feet below its sparkling surface, in the deepest and darkest waters, a hideous creature stirred in its sleep. It felt, which was its way of hearing, the vibrations as the Druid blew the great horn, and its body expanded in anger. Not the Druid's horn! The creature's horn!

Centuries ago, the Druid had hacked off and stolen one of the sharp keratin spikes protruding from a ridge along the creature's spine and had fashioned it into a horn to enslave the creature. In the hacking, the Druid had used the spike to stab deeply into the creature's flesh, nicking the black poison sac between its eyes, and releasing a trickle of poison into the creature's body. As the centuries passed, the poison mingled with the creature's life fluids, until it became a contaminated thing, poisoned in both mind and body.

Slowly, the creature opened its eyes—two enormous, protruding orbs, completely white, all irises without pupils, as if the eyes had been turned inside out. The creature, the oldest living thing in the lake, did not require sight to hunt and eat. Even now, it felt the minute vibrations of the large walleye, hiding among the rocks off to its right. For a minute, it pictured the hunt, the catch, the ripping, and then the taste of succulent flesh.

But it could not refuse the call of the Druid's horn. Not the Druid's horn! Its horn! The creature hated the Druid and had waited centuries to hurt him and take back its property. It might have to wait centuries more but, one day, it would trap the Druid, reclaim its horn, and then savour that one's aged living flesh.

It had lived in this world from the beginning, long before the dinosaurs, before the Elves came with their magic, before the Demon, before the Druid gave it the ridiculous name, Dilemma, when the world was fire and magma. It had evolved slowly over the centuries, from a creature of fire to a creature of the depths. It served only itself, eating Dwarves, Trolls, Elves and all other living things, without discrimination.

But the call of the horn could not be denied. The creature puffed its massive body until it was three times its size and then it belched, again and again and again. Slowly, sluggishly, it began to drift up, a thousand feet, to the surface of the lake, thoughts of feasting filling the creature with grisly delight. The cautious walleye took the opportunity to dart to another, safer area of the lake.

"Excuse me!" said Arabella. "What is that horn supposed to do?"

"Give it a rest, Bell," commanded Miranda. "You're making things worse."

Arabella reacted as if she had been slapped, falling silent, her face like stone.

"Hey! What the—?" cried Nicholas, stumbling backwards, as a large transparent bubble suddenly appeared and hovered at the edge of the cliff, followed by three others.

"It's our transportation," said the Druid, calmly.

Nicholas stared at the bubble. It looked so delicate, surely it would burst the minute he touched it. Then he turned to the Druid. "But, how—? What—?"

"Walk into it," said the Druid. "And remember, do not fight it. Breathe normally."

The boy hesitated, his eyes darting from the bubble to Naim and back again. Then he locked eyes with the Druid, nodded solemnly, and walked into the bubble. For a second, his eyes widened, and a look of sheer panic flashed across his face. Then he was gone, the bubble spinning away from the edge of the cliff and dropping toward the lake.

"Arabella, you are next," said the Druid. "Hurry, now. And remember to breathe."

But the girl didn't respond. She looked like a wax figure, her face a mask of fear. "I can't walk out there. I can't stand heights," she whispered, looking at Miranda wildly and pointing at the transparent bubble. "Mir, I'm sorry. I can't do this. I'll do anything, but please don't ask me to go into that thing."

Miranda went to her, realizing that Arabella's bad attitude was a cover for the terror she was feeling. "It's OK, Bell. Don't cry. It's OK. Nobody's going to ask you to do anything. You don't have to go."

Slowly, the hysterical girl calmed down. Sobbing quietly, she nodded. "I'm sorry. I'm such a coward."

"You're not a coward," said Miranda. "If you knew how scared I am, you'd laugh at yourself." She took Arabella by the shoulders. "And you don't have to be sorry. You're my friend. You'll always be my friend."

"Do you know how to find your way out of here?" asked the Druid.

"I think so," said Arabella, nodding miserably.

But the Druid gave her instructions and made her repeat them until he was satisfied that the girl would not wander under Parliament Hill until she died of hunger.

"What about the Demon?" cried Arabella. "What if she's waiting for me at my house?"

"The Demon has no interest in you now that we are leaving your country," answered the Druid.

The unhappy girl blinked back hot tears and, without looking back, entered the tunnel.

Miranda watched sadly as the light from Arabella's flashlight finally disappeared. The thought of losing Arabella hurt more than she could imagine. She felt sick. How could she go on without her? And what if Nicholas decided to abandon her, too? What would happen to her then? She started to follow Arabella, forgetting, for a second, all about the Demon and her evil plans for the human race.

"Come on, girl," said the Druid, interrupting her thoughts.

Miranda forced herself to stop. She turned to Naim and let him guide her toward the cliff. She didn't resist as he urged her, with words and a firm grip on her arm, to step into the transparent bubble. A voice inside her head screamed at her. *Don't do this! Turn back! It's not too late.*

She felt a cooling sensation as she was suctioned into the centre of the orb. It was like walking into raw egg whites. It was not an unpleasant feeling, until the liquid started to enter her nose, ears, and mouth. She held her breath and put up her hand to block her nose. She saw Naim mouthing words she couldn't hear while waving his arms frantically.

"BREATHE!" roared the Druid, watching helplessly, as the bubble began to move away from the cliff and descend toward the lake.

And then, without warning, something shot past him and flew through the air, landing with a soft "plop" on top of Miranda's bubble and sinking into the cool, glutinous substance.

Black spots formed in front of Miranda's eyes as she struggled to keep from drowning in the horrible jelly. Then, just as she felt the blackness overtake her, strong hands gripped her own hands, pulling them away from her face. She fought her attacker like a demon, as the thick goop entered her nostrils and filled her ears. Horrified, she felt the liquid slip down her throat and she surrendered to the blackness.

CHAPTER FOURTEEN

THE JAWS OF DEATH

hundred feet below the surface of the lake, the creature known as Dilemma waited, its bloated body quivering as it received the micro vibrations from the approaching sacs carrying the Druid and the other human cargo. The poison in its brain induced vivid images of limbs thrashing, teeth rending, red water churning.

High above the pristine waters of Lake Leanora, Miranda's brain told her that she was very much alive. The blackness into which she had fallen cleared. Relief rushed through her as she grasped the fact that she was actually breathing, not air but the clear clinging liquid that filled the bubble. Cautiously, she opened one eye, just a slit, and shuddered as the disgusting slime oozed into the opening, coating her eyeball. But, miraculously, she could see and what she saw, staring wide-eyed into her face, was her best friend, Bell. It was the most fantastic, wonderful sight in the world.

"What happened? How did you get here?" Miranda asked, but, while her lips moved, no sound followed. For a few seconds, the girls stared at each other, smiling, then grinning, and finally laughing like actors in a silent movie.

They were totally unprepared when the bubble hit the water with a dull splash and plunged beneath the surface of the lake. Horrified, the girls gripped each other, their mouths gaping wide in silent screams as the missile's momentum took it deeper and deeper.

"No!" Miranda refused to end up on the bottom of the Elven lake, after having come so far. If they could enter the bubble so easily, then, surely, they'd get out the same way. She wanted to kick herself for not having thought of it sooner. She looked at her friend, made a swimming motion with her hands, and pointed toward the surface, waiting until Arabella nodded that she understood. Then, on a silent count of three, the girls tried to swim their way out of the ball.

Suddenly, they felt the pull of gravity, similar to the heavy tugging sensation just before a high-speed elevator reaches its destination, that told them the bubble was slowing. For a long second, the bubble came to a full stop, suspended somewhere between the surface and the bottom of the lake, then, slowly, sluggishly, it began to rise. Hands over their hearts, both girls fell back in the jelly, numb with relief.

Movement in the water caught Miranda's eye and she peered below, thinking that the lake must be awfully deep to be so black down there. A brief flicker of fear gnawed at her mind. She felt something watching her, something hidden, waiting in the dark waters, just beyond her range of vision. Then she shrugged the feeling off and watched fascinated as a school of brilliant blue fish moved through the water, undulating as a unit, in a tight pattern. It reminded her of a huge blue cloud.

What's that? she thought, as the fish suddenly scattered out in all directions. She wondered what had frightened them, and then she knew and her heart stopped.

The creature coming at them fast was so loathsome that Miranda gagged, spewing out a great mouthful of goop only to breathe it back in again. It was a huge, bloated thing, huger than anything

Miranda had ever seen. A row of giant spikes stuck out along the creature's back, and a pair of wicked claws snapped at the water on either side of its swollen body. But it was the ghastly protruding eyes, all white—cold, dead, unseeing eyes, that made Miranda's blood curdle. Until the creature's lower jaw shot forward and it opened its cavern of a mouth revealing the double row of sharp yellow teeth, each one over a foot long.

The two friends clung to each other desperately, Arabella's head buried in Miranda's shoulder. But Miranda could not take her eyes off the creature. She watched, sick and fascinated at the same time, as it homed in on them, its horrible mouth open wide in hideous purpose.

The bubble bobbed to the surface of the lake, then settled like a sodden piece of flotsam, three quarters submerged.

"Oh, Naim!" cried Miranda, the despair more terrible than anything she could imagine. "Who's going to help you destroy Hate now?"

The creature felt the strong vibrations of terror coming from the two humans in the bubble and savoured the thrill that travelled along its spine. Now it was glad that it had not let its poison seep into the oosphere it had belched at the Druid's command. That would have made the prize inedible. The humans were close now, their fear scenting the water like the smell of blood. Dilemma opened its huge jaws and surged upward, scooping up the jelly sac in its monstrous maw as it broke the surface. For an instant, it hung in the air above the lake, then it whacked the water with its powerful tail and slipped back into the depths, its thoughts vivid images of feasting.

Hope flared for one crazy moment, as Miranda wondered if they could slip into the monster's stomach and, like Jonah and the whale, escape somehow. But the fragile spark died as teeth like jagged spikes closed over the bubble. Suddenly, Miranda saw the jelly sac slip away and she felt strong arms snatch her from the jaws of death and hoist her out of the cold water.

"GET OUT OF HERE, NOW!" roared the Druid, but even as he gave the command, the sleek trimaran was already on the move, planing swiftly across the water, driven by the wind in its taut white sail.

Miranda and Arabella huddled in the bow, coughing and vomiting long strands of clear slime into a pair of buckets, shivering in their wet clothes, their lips blue. They barely noticed their discomfort. Between barfs, they grinned foolishly at each other, deliriously happy just to be feeling anything.

"Thanks," That was all Miranda could manage before another retching fit racked her body.

"For what?"

"For making me breathe. If you hadn't pulled my hands away, I . . . anyway, thanks."

"When I looked back and saw that you were in trouble, I didn't even think about my fear of heights. I just knew I had to do something." Arabella suddenly shivered even more violently. "Did I really jump off that cliff into that horrible balloony thing? How could I have done that?"

Miranda grinned and patted Arabella's arm. "You did it, that's what counts." She wanted to say how horrible she felt as she had watched the other girl disappear down the tunnel. She wanted to share her own fear with her friend, but she knew that if she opened that floodgate, she'd drown for sure. Instead, she forced a smile. "Don't think about it anymore. It's over."

"You wish," said Arabella, her voice breaking as she pointed toward the stern.

Arabella was right. They were not out of danger yet. When the creature's tail slapped the surface of the lake, it struck with the force of a small meteor, sucking the lake away from the shores and forming a great wall of water that rapidly spread out from the epicentre in all directions, creating a powerful shock wave.

Looking back, Miranda saw the giant wave advancing upon

them like an avalanche. She saw the Druid standing in the stern, one hand resting on the shoulder of the helmsman for balance. She caught his eye and pointed behind him, yelling a warning at the same time. The warning sounded as a mere whisper against the awful roar of the advancing tidal wave. At least the Druid saw her finger pointing, because he nodded almost impatiently, but he did not look back.

What's wrong with them? Are they deaf? She glanced at the helmsman. He was a young man, maybe in his early twenties—as tall as the Druid, but more graceful. His long golden hair was tied back in a ponytail. Miranda studied his clean-shaven face, liking the calmness written there and then, suddenly, it dawned on her that this was an Elf, a magical being whose race came to Earth in the days of the dinosaurs.

As she stared, open-mouthed, the Elf looked up at Naim and grinned. Now the Druid glanced behind at the colossal mountain of water, and she saw his hand tighten its grip on the Elf's shoulder. But Miranda wasn't afraid now. She looked at the giant wave, more in awe than fear. Then she looked at the Elven helmsman again, a smile of happiness lighting up her face.

As if he felt the girl's eyes on him, he turned to her. For a second, Miranda's green eyes met the eyes of the young man and, with a shock that almost paralyzed her, she saw herself reflected in their clear green depths. She dropped her eyes, falling back into the cockpit as though she had been shot.

It can't be true, she thought, knowing with absolute certainty that it was the only thing that made sense of everything that had ever happened in her life. She looked around wildly, needing desperately to be alone—to think—to sort out and try to absorb the startling truth she had just discovered.

The great wave was cresting now, preparing to dash the small craft to smithereens. But, in the nick of time, the trimaran dodged the onslaught by slipping through a small opening at the base of a high white stone wall. The laughter of the Elven helmsman and the Druid drowned out the sound of the water crashing impotently against the barrier outside.

CHAPTER FIFTEEN

REUNION

"Let her sleep," said the voice, and the blessed silence settled over Miranda once again. She curled on her side and slept, a long dreamless sleep that eased her tired body and soothed her troubled mind. Hours passed and still she slept. Then a hand gently touched her shoulder and she was awake instantly, sitting bolt upright, eyes darting around the unfamiliar room to finally rest on Naim, who was leaning forward in a deep armchair beside her bed. He was dressed in his old worn cloak, but the rips and the dark bloodstain were gone.

"You have nothing to fear in this place," said the Druid softly. "It is perhaps the only safe place left in the world."

Miranda wondered how long he had been sitting beside her. He looked tired. The lines in his weathered face were deeper, making him look even older. "Your arm . . . Bell and Nicholas . . . are they. . . . ?"

"A mere scratch," he said, absentmindedly massaging his shoulder. "Your friends are here. All three of them. I have only just managed to keep them away." He flashed Miranda one of his rare grins and the girl felt the power of this man's smile. It was as if the sun had suddenly burst through the clouds after long days of rain. "They have very suspicious minds, especially the wiry one that reminds me of a terrier."

Miranda laughed, thinking that the description fit Arabella to a tee.

"How long have I been sleeping?" she asked, letting her eyes wander about the large bright room, with its four long windows. It was a beautiful, restful place, with gay watercolours on the pale golden walls, and delicate rugs, woven with designs of birds, flowers and animals, scattered about the wooden floor.

"It is early evening. You have slept around the clock, and then some," answered the Druid. "But now it is time to get up and ready yourself for the Council of Bethany."

"What exactly is this Council?" asked Miranda.

"I had better tell you so that you will not look like a complete fool in front of the King," answered the Druid in his usual gruff manner. "Pay attention. The King runs the country with the help and guidance of the Erudicia, twelve of the wisest Elves on Ellesmere. The Council includes the Erudicia, the King, and anyone else who may have an interest in the issue to be decided." His piercing eyes bored into the girl. "Does that answer your question?" he asked, rising quickly and striding across the room. He stopped at the door and listened for a second before turning the doorknob and pulling the door wide.

Nicholas and Arabella tumbled into the room, followed by Penelope clutching Muffy against her chest. The poodle took one look at the Druid and uttered a sharp yelp.

"Visit with your friends. I will return in one hour. Be ready," said Naim, closing the door on his way out.

"'Visit with your friends. I will return in one hour. Be ready,'" mimicked Arabella. "Can you believe that guy?"

"Hey, sleepyhead, how're you feeling?" asked Nicholas, flopping onto the bedside chair and running his hand through his dark hair. "We thought you were magicked into some kind of sleeping spell or something."

Arabella hopped onto the bed, brown eyes wide with excitement. "You've missed everything. Bethany's so amazing. And guess what?"

Miranda shrugged. "What?"

"Because you're so important, they've put us up in our own villa. We've got servants and everything. No parents to tell us what to do. It's so excellent."

"Are you serious?" Miranda was speechless.

"Yeah!" Arabella waved her arm about the room. "It's ours. We can stay up all night if we want to."

"That old Druid wouldn't let us see you," grumbled Nicholas. "He just sat in this chair, day and night, in a foul mood too." Then he brightened, leaning forward. "But Mir, you've got to see this place. I get to stay in barracks with the King's Riders." His face glowed with pride. "I met this one guy, Laury. He's an officer, a captain or something, and he's teaching me how to fight with a sword."

"All you guys ever think about is fighting," said Arabella. "What's so great about learning to use a sword?"

Nicholas shot her a look of contempt. "You wouldn't understand." Then he turned back to Miranda. "Nothing like this has ever happened to me before. It's the best. The only thing I haven't seen yet is a dinosaur. But Laury said they're very elusive."

Miranda couldn't believe her ears. "Listening to you guys, I feel I've been sleeping for a year instead of a day. You'll have to show me everything."

"I just want to know who's paying for this, because I'm not," said Penelope, squeezing Muffy. "I don't trust any of them and I wouldn't be surprised if they present us with a whopping bill, when we check out."

Her three companions looked at each other and burst out laughing.

"Penelope, this isn't a hotel," said Nicholas, shaking his head in disgust. "Do you have any idea what this is all about? Why we're even here?"

"I know as much as you do," she said.

"What do you know?" persisted Nicholas.

Miranda interrupted, before a full-scale war broke out. "Penelope, tell me what happened to you. The last I saw, you fell off that cliff."

Penelope paled and dropped onto the foot of the bed. "I thought for sure I was going to die," she said, trying to control the squirming poodle. "But after I fell like a brick, I suddenly floated down into the water, and a bunch of Elves pulled me out, muttering something about some sea monster. Then they brought me here." She put her hand over her heart. "But, I still get palpitations when I think of falling."

Muffy seized her opportunity and escaped, darting about the room, and then stopping dead and snarling shrilly at the gold lace curtains blowing gently in the breeze from an open window.

"It's all in your head," scoffed Arabella. "The Ministers examined you and said you were quote, 'as hale as a hare.'"

"What do they know?" snapped Penelope. "I bet I know more about herbal remedies than they do. Anyway, I don't trust their medicine any more than I trust them." She looked at Miranda. "My clothes are ruined and everything. Somebody's going to pay for this."

"Right, you could try suing the Elves," said Nicholas. "I can see it now. 'Your Honour, there really are Elves. I've seen them. In fact, I've even visited them in their country, which isn't on any maps. This magic Druid showed me the secret gateway that the Dwarves built under Parliament Hill.'"

Miranda laughed until her sides hurt. The way Nicholas put it made everything sound so ridiculous no one would ever believe it. And yet, every word was true. Penelope's face turned red, but she finally joined in the laughter.

"Tell me about these Ministers?" asked Miranda. "Are they a religious group, or with the government?"

"No, no!" said her companions with one voice, grinning smugly at Miranda's ignorance of things Elven.

"They've got nothing to do with politics or religion," said Arabella.

"Ministers look after the sick. Like Doctors."

"That's too simple," said Nicholas. "We don't have anything like Ministers in Canada. They're more than Doctors. First, they're way more advanced." He paused for a second, hunting for the proper description.

"They commune with Nature," said Arabella.

"Yeah, but there's more to it than that." Nicholas leaned forward, his eyes shining. "They really know what's wrong with you. It's like they're connected to Nature and Space. And they're scientists too. I mean . . . Oh, I don't know what I mean."

The next half hour was one of the happiest times for the companions. For the first time in their lives, they had real, exciting things to share with one another. No one mentioned movies, or TV, or school gossip. Even Penelope, during that brief period, forgot to talk about herself. It was as if they suddenly realized that they were indeed part of something bigger, and everything that came before was trite and meaningless.

Miranda suddenly jumped to her feet. "The Council! Naim'll be here for us any minute. I've got to get dressed."

"What do you mean 'us'? He's coming for you," said Nicholas angrily, looking down at his boots. "We're not invited."

"It's not fair," said Arabella. "We're in this too."

Miranda was stunned. "It must be a mistake," she reasoned.

"Just forget it. There's no mistake," said Nicholas.

"Who wants to sit through some horrible stuffy meeting anyway?" said Penelope. "Bor-ing!"

"He said it wasn't our concern," continued Nicholas, ignoring Penelope.

"Listen," said Miranda. "Let's meet here after the Council. I promise I'll tell you everything."

Before her friends left her room, Miranda stretched out her hand. "We're in this together."

Nicholas placed his hand on top of hers. Then Arabella and

Penelope followed suit. "TOGETHER!" they cried.

Alone at last, Miranda moved from window to window, looking at, but not seeing, the tall oak trees that rose up like sentinels about the villa, filtering the late afternoon sunlight to a soft glow. She wondered why her friends were barred from the Council. How could the Druid expect them to make the decision to accompany her if they didn't know what was going on? Maybe he just lied to get her here. No! He might have his own secrets, but, in her heart, she didn't believe the Druid would purposely lie. Then she felt something cold and wet on her bare feet.

"Ahhh!" Miranda jumped as her bare feet trod in a puddle. Muffy pee! She walked stiffly on her heels to the bathroom where she bathed quickly. Then she searched the bureau and closet for clean clothes. She found a pair of dark green pants, and a creamy, baggy sweater, knit of the finest thread she had ever seen. Finally, she pulled on a pair of soft brown leather boots.

She had just finished running a brush through her hair, when she heard a loud knocking from downstairs accompanied by the Druid's deep voice. "Hurry up, girl!"

A wave of dizziness washed over Miranda as she started down the stairs. She stumbled, catching the banister to keep from pitching headfirst to the floor below. The Druid raced up the steps and caught her arm. "What is it?" he asked, concern filling his eyes.

"I'm hungry," answered Miranda, suddenly realizing that she had eaten nothing since the pizza at her house. How long ago that was she had no idea anymore.

"Is that all?" The Druid looked at her as if mere hunger were a failing. "There will be food after the meeting. You will just have to restrain your appetite for another hour or two." He did not see the face Miranda made behind his back as she followed him down the stairs.

Naim quickly led the way out of the villa and across a grassy park toward a low white structure, nestled under a grove of tall oak trees. Miranda trotted beside him, so intent on taking in all the sights that she did not see the lean dark shadow dashing from tree to tree behind her. The sun had set, but she could see clearly in the waning twilight. She gazed about in wonder, breathing the fresh, oleander-scented, air and searching her mind for a word to describe the feeling that tugged at her heart. *Home!*

Evergreen, tall oak and maple, and oleander trees with pure white blooms stood guard over the flowering shrubs and the white and black swans gliding lazily in a small pond. A few plain, weathered wooden benches, tucked away in quiet nooks, looked as though they had always been there. The park was immaculate, yet Miranda saw no trash bins or other such signs of civilization.

Except for the Elves. A group of Elven boys and girls paused in their game of kick ball to stare at the slender, blonde girl, who appeared frail beside the familiar sight of the Druid. They waved and sounds of their laughter carried across the green carpet. Miranda flushed with pleasure and waved back, wishing for a second that she could join them and lose herself in the game. Then, with a start, she realized that, in addition to the ball players, every head in the park was turned in her direction. Self-consciously, she turned and hurried after the Druid.

"I'll come back here," she thought, as Naim pushed against the solid oak door and Miranda followed him into the Hall.

CHAPTER SIXTEEN

THE COUNCIL
OF BETHANY

iranda was surprised that the Council chamber was so large. From outside, the building had appeared too small to hold a room of this size. She cast a nervous glance around the long, rectangular table that dominated the chamber without marring its beauty. There must have been forty chairs placed around the table, but only fifteen, not counting the ones reserved for Miranda and the Druid, were occupied. She counted twelve men and women all dressed alike in white tunics and pants. They were obviously the Erudicia, the wisest Elves in the land.

Miranda recognized the young helmsman, who smiled at her as the Druid reached for her hand and led her to the head of the table where an elderly man sat waiting patiently. Flustered by the warmth in the young Elf's smile, she looked away and focused on the old man. Instinctively, she knew that this person, calmly watching his guests approach, was much more than he appeared. She staggered backwards as if she had walked into a wall as wave upon wave of sheer power emanated from the man.

"I also sense power in you," said the old man, turning a pair of unclouded green eyes on the girl.

Miranda couldn't find her voice. Under the man's clear gaze, she suddenly felt gauche and awkward. She wanted to crawl under one of the chairs and hide. But she managed to return his look. And then, she smiled, feeling safe for the first time since leaving her home, as she looked upon the gentlest, kindest face she had ever seen. So different from Naim's stern countenance.

The man's once golden hair, tied back in the Elven manner, was now almost white. A thin band of gold, inset with precious emeralds, encircled his head. As they approached, he rose—no traces of old age in his movements—and extended both arms toward the Druid.

"Welcome, Druid friend," said the old man, embracing Naim warmly. Then he took Miranda's hand. "I am Ruthar." He directed Miranda to a seat by his right side.

"It is *King* Ruthar to you," whispered the Druid sharply in her ear as he slipped into the vacant chair on the other side of Miranda.

Ruthar, King of the Elves, turned to the Erudicia and the others seated around the table.

"This is the girl, Miranda, who has come from the new world to help us destroy the Evil One."

"She's a child. Can't fight. Knows nothing. Useless," objected a harsh voice near the other end of the table. Miranda looked and gasped in wonder at the short stocky creature who was glaring at her, his long straggly beard quivering with anger.

"Patience, friend," said Ruthar, raising his hand. "You will have your say before this meeting is concluded." He turned to Miranda. "This is Gregor the Fifteenth, King of our friends, the Dwarf people."

Miranda looked at the surly Dwarf, who folded his arms and glared at her rudely. Despite his obvious dislike, she couldn't take her eyes off him or control the silly grin that spread across her face. The King of the Dwarves became increasingly agitated under the girl's gaze. His face turned purple, as he fidgeted and stomped his heavy boots on the wooden floor. Realizing, with a start, that she was the cause of his sudden angst, Miranda blushed and quickly looked away.

Ruthar named the others around the table. When they came to the Helmsman, the old King sighed. "And my disobedient son, Elester, named after our ancestor, the first earthly King, although I am sorry to say that his actions with the lake creature yesterday were anything but kingly."

Elester grinned at Miranda. "Father, I would not have allowed harm to come to the girl. It just seemed unfair to use our power against Dilemma, but I would have if I had thought she were in danger out there."

The Druid cleared his throat to ease the tension between father and son. It seemed to work, because the King ignored the young Elf. But then he turned back to Miranda. "My son, with the help of others,"—and he glared at the Druid, who tried to look innocent, but failed miserably—"my son and others taunt the lake creature, who is becoming a major nuisance to our waters." He sighed. "One of these days, I am going to have to do something quite drastic about the one they call Dilemma."

Miranda was amazed that Elester played games with the monster of the lake. *Don't Elves have any fear?* she wondered, reliving the few terrified seconds she had looked down the throat of the revolting creature.

The Druid jabbed his sharp elbow into her ribs. "Pay attention!"

". . . know how much you have been told," said King Ruthar. "But I will proceed as if you know nothing. Is that acceptable?"

Realizing that the King was speaking to her, Miranda nodded, feeling her face turn as red as a ripe tomato.

King Ruthar addressed the assembly. "Two nights ago, the Demon we once knew as Taog escaped from the Place with No Name. Since then, she has released many of the other evil beings who serve her, among them, the Hellhags. And more will follow.

Gregor's scouts sent word of a massive army of half-dead creatures marching through the Swampgrass, east of Dundurum. The Trolls of the Swampgrass, the Bog Trolls, have joined her ranks, but that does not come as a surprise. They are an old Enemy who will align with any power whose purpose is to destroy us."

"Three days. Demon'll be at our gates. Three days," said Gregor, stomping the floor for emphasis.

The King nodded. "That is why we are here tonight, my friend." He turned to Miranda. "This must be very frightening for someone who knows little of our world."

"I saw the Demon in my country," answered Miranda. "I saw what she can do."

The King of the Elves smiled. "You have known the Demon for a few hours and, yet, you know her better than we who have had tens of thousands of years to study the creature. Because her reach did not extend to Ellesmere Island, we ignored her. Foolishly, I might add. Then, over a thousand years ago, she gathered a great army of her poisoned creatures and led them across the land like locusts. Wherever they passed, they left only death and ashes. Entire civilizations were sacrificed to feed her bloodlust."

He sighed heavily. "Do you know what we did while the peoples around us were being systematically butchered in her name?"

Miranda shook her head.

"Nothing," continued the King. "We did nothing. Until one dark morning, the Demon and her walking dead stood on the borders of Gregor's kingdom, the last stronghold before Ellesmere. I am ashamed to say that we did not act until the Demon was practically on our doorstep."

The old King looked at the Dwarf. "Correct me if I am wrong, but I think it was Gregor the Twelfth who—"

"Fourteenth," snapped the Dwarf.

"Yes, it was Gregor the Fourteenth who came to ask us to stand with him against Hate's mighty forces of evil. But we knew, even with the Dwarves alongside us, that we could not win through physical combat. There were too few of us and too many of them." He paused for a moment and poured a glass of water from a silver pitcher on the table in front of him. Then he took a long sip and turned to Naim.

"Our race owes much to you, Druid friend, but I understand that even with your magic, we could not have held out indefinitely."

Naim nodded and mumbled something Miranda couldn't make out. Amused, she realized that he was embarrassed by such praise. She also wondered how old he was. If he fought the Demon, that would make him over a thousand years old. And that, she knew, was impossible.

"We had to put up a front to divert Hate from our real purpose—to buy time until we could find the power to drive her away for good. While our armies dwindled, we fashioned a prison—the Place with No Name—that was neither of this world nor out of it, but somewhere in between. The power we used to seal the edges of that terrible place came from a potent magic known as the Serpent's Egg.

"All of this took time, because we had not used such magic since our ancestors came and created this land we call home. We poured over reams of ancient texts, and learned that only a child, descended directly from our first King, could capture the Egg. When we were ready, we sent a large contingent of Elven Riders to accompany and protect the boy chosen for the perilous task. And, although only two in the entire company returned, one was the boy, carrying the prize that cost so many precious lives. We defeated the Demon and drove her and her evil servants into their prison and used the Egg to seal it.

"But, in our arrogance, we believed that we had rid ourselves of the Demon for all time. At first, we took precautions—examining the seal vigilantly—but, as the centuries slipped by, we looked at it only occasionally. Finally, we did the unthinkable. We forgot about Hate and evil, and in our forgetfulness, we allowed her to escape."

The old King paused and looked at Miranda, his eyes troubled. "We failed," he said, shaking his head sadly. "And because of our failure, the Demon now once more marches toward Gregor's Kingdom."

Gregor, King of the Dwarves, stamped his boots on the wooden floor and shuffled to his feet. "Can't hold for long. A day. Two days," he growled. "Can't sit and talk. Must act."

Ruthar nodded. "My friend's words are true. Even as we speak, more creatures are pouring through the breach and speeding toward their Mistress." He turned back to Miranda.

"The Serpent's Egg is one of the magics the Demon fears. She can neither capture it nor use it. But she *can* destroy it. Hate remembers only too well the last time we used the Egg. She knows that a young boy left here and returned with something that took away her power and all that belonged to her. That is why she has to destroy you, Miranda. You are the only one who can capture the Serpent's Egg."

"Why me? I didn't know anything about the Serpent's Egg," protested Miranda, "or about Hate . . . or Elves . . . or Dwarves . . . until—"

"It does not matter," said the Druid, speaking for the first time. "*She* knows about *you*."

"How can she know about me?" cried Miranda. "I don't understand how I come into any of this."

The old King took Miranda's hand. "But you *do* know," he said gently. "And you have known for some time, now."

"No!" cried Miranda, pulling her hand away. "It's not true."

"She *knows*?" The Druid addressed the King.

"Tell him, Miranda," Ruthar said gently.

Miranda looked at him, her eyes begging him to spare her—to lie to her if necessary. "Please, say it's not true."

The old man shook his head sadly, and looked slowly about the room. "Miranda is an Elven girl, directly descended from King Elester. She is the only one who can capture the Serpent's Egg. She is the only one who can help us now."

Suddenly, from the other end of the room, a head of unruly, chocolate-coloured hair poked up from under the table.

"Wow! Mir," said Nicholas, beside himself with excitement. "You, an Elf! This is so cool!"

Miranda burst into tears and ran from the Council.

CHAPTER SEVENTEEN
THE BLOODSTONES

"Is it such a terrible thing to be one of us?" asked the Elf, dropping lightly onto the grass at Miranda's feet.

Elester and King Gregor had found the girl, a small, dark form, huddled on the wooden bench in a small grove of oleander near the still pool in the park outside the Council Hall. The old Dwarf paced in a circle, mumbling to himself.

"Never could talk to young folk. Noisy and rude. Least thing makes them cry. Nothing wrong with Elves. Should apologize."

Miranda bowed her head. "I'm sorry," she whispered, filled with shame.

"Not you," barked the Dwarf. "Me! I apologize. Don't think sometimes. Blurt what I'm feeling."

Despite herself, Miranda couldn't help smiling at the Dwarf's discomfort. "You don't have to apologize. Everything you said back there is true. I'm just a useless kid."

"Humph!" muttered the Dwarf, resuming his pacing.

Miranda looked from his short square-bodied shadow to the younger man sitting on the grass. She could see him clearly in the moonlight. He was so still that, without thinking, Miranda reached out and lightly touched his shoulder. "I never knew my father, or my grandparents. Mom never talked about them. I didn't know who they were."

"She never told you they were Elves?" Elester asked, astonished. Miranda shook her head.

"Wrong. Shouldn't hide things. Come back to haunt you," muttered the Dwarf.

"I know you are afraid," continued Elester gently. "Please tell me what you fear."

When the girl finally spoke, both Elf and Dwarf had to strain to catch the words. "I'm afraid of dying."

"Girl, fear is good," snorted Gregor. "Fools fear nothing." He stopped pacing and faced her, sturdy legs apart, hammy fists on hips. "You up to this?" he asked.

"That's the problem. I don't know what I'm supposed to do. I'm sorry I ran away from the Hall, but everything's so confusing." Miranda twisted her hands in frustration. "I don't even know what the Serpent's Egg is." She caught the flash of white as Elester grinned.

"Then I will share with you what little I know," said the Elf. "The Egg is real. The Serpents only appear to hatch a new egg, and that does not happen more than once or twice every hundred years." He fell silent for a moment, then added wistfully. "I would give anything to finally see what I have only read about."

"I'm still confused," cried Miranda. "Just because we need the Egg now doesn't mean the Serpents are going to have one ready for us."

"True," said Elester. "We had to resort to a bit of our own magic to trick them into hurrying the process."

"Naim said you never interfered with Nature," said Miranda, frowning at the Elf.

"By simply taking the Egg, we are meddling with Nature. But it does not hurt the Serpents, and its magic is good for all living things, including snakes, if it gets rid of the Demon." The Elven Prince shrugged. "There is a difference between hurting Nature and giving her a little help from time to time."

"I guess," said Miranda, turning red and glad that no one could see her face clearly in the moonlight. "But, how did you trick the Serpents?"

"I do not know because I was not present. But I would guess that we used a Fire Stone that our ancestors brought when they first came to this world. It is a wonderful thing—cool on the outside, but liquid fire inside. This stone creates an atmosphere that draws the Serpents to the surface, thinking that it is time to hatch the Egg."

Miranda's eyes widened. "How big is this Egg?"

"From what I have read, it is about the size of a dew fruit?"

"What's a dew fruit?"

"Melon. Grows in the dew," explained Gregor.

"But how big is it?" persisted Miranda.

"As big as an ostrich egg," said Elester.

"And the Serpents?" asked Miranda, shuddering.

"They are big. But how big I do not know."

"Just my luck," said Miranda. "More Demons."

"No Demons," said Gregor. "Fire Serpents. Not evil."

"That is true," agreed Elester. "They do not belong to Hate. But they are dangerous, because they are poisonous."

"How do they expect me to get this egg away from poisonous snakes?" asked the girl, knowing that she was going to fail or maybe even die.

Gregor stomped up to the girl and sat on the bench next to her. "Won't be alone, girl. Don't worry. Be there with you."

Miranda looked at the Dwarf gratefully. "Are you saying that you'll come with me? I don't have to do this by myself?"

"Is that what you thought?" asked Elester, amazed that the girl had even contemplated undertaking such a task alone. No wonder she was petrified. "I, too, will accompany you on your quest."

Miranda felt relief wash over her like sleep. "I know in my heart that I have to do this thing," she said, suddenly feeling that, with

Elven magic and the fierce Dwarf beside her, she might stand a chance.

"Good girl. Nothing else to do. Destroy evil ones."

"We know that the magic of the Egg was used a thousand years ago," said the Elf. "But we have no knowledge of what the Serpents do when they appear or even where they come from. I have heard many stories, but I do not wish to repeat them for fear of misleading you. I have read that, for a few seconds during the hatching ritual, the Serpents let the Egg out of their grasp. That's the window of opportunity—when you must snatch the prize before it hatches."

"Then run like the Devil," added the Dwarf.

Miranda laughed easily. "That's the one thing I know how to do."

Gregor nodded. "Time to fight, time to run."

Sometime later, Miranda yawned, and the Dwarf lumbered to his feet, mumbled, "Hit the sack. Leave early. Long ride," and ambled off toward the Hall.

Miranda grinned. "I was terrified of him at first, but he's really nice."

"'Nice' is not the word I would have used to describe the King of the Dwarves," said Elester, rising from the grass and stretching. "But he is right. We leave at dawn. The quest has begun, Miranda."

They walked in silence through the park, lost in their own private thoughts. Despite yawning, Miranda felt wide awake. She was eager to see her friends and tell them about the Council and the Serpent's Egg. When she reached the villa, she turned to bid Elester goodnight and to say that she was proud to be of his race, but the young Elf was gone.

Her companions were waiting in the living room. So was the Druid. From their expressions, she realized that they had been worried about her.

"Are you really an Elf?" asked Penelope, eying Miranda suspiciously. "Aren't you worried that your ears are going to grow long and pointy?"

"You're so stupid, Penelope," said Nicholas. "Why don't you just shut up?"

"It's OK," said Miranda. "I don't think my ears are going to change and if they do, well, don't worry, it's not contagious." She walked up to the Druid and looked him squarely in the face. "I don't feel that I'm going to be very helpful, but I will come with you to find the Egg."

The Druid took her hands. "I never doubted it," he said. "Now to business. We have much to do. I have already briefed your companions so they know about the Serpent's Egg and what is required of you. They also know that we leave at dawn for Gregor's Kingdom."

Miranda looked at her friends. She saw Arabella, grim faced, staring at her as if she were seeing a ghost.

"You don't know what you're doing, Mir. You don't have to go with them. Tell them to find someone else."

"There is no one else," said the Druid. "Miranda is the only child in Ellesmere who can trace her roots all the way back to the first Elven king."

Miranda went to her friend. "That's what they told me, Bell, and I believe them. I am the only one who can do this." She laughed bitterly. "And I have thought about it. In fact, I've thought about nothing else since we left Ottawa."

Arabella scowled at the Druid. "It's all your fault," she cried. "You got a bunch of kids to do your dirty work and you're going to get us killed." She grabbed Miranda's arm. "Don't you see? It's got nothing to do with us. Let's just go home."

"You're wrong, Bell. If we don't stop the Demon now, we won't have any homes to go back to." She shook her friend gently. "You know those creatures were in Ottawa. You woke me up. You saw them."

"It was dark," protested her friend. "I don't know what I saw."

"I'm going with you, Mir," said Nicholas. "Bell can go home if she wants, and she can take Penelope and that little Muffrat with her. And good riddance!"

"And good riddance to you, too!" yelled Penelope, snatching up her poodle and flying out of the room.

Arabella pulled away from Miranda and glowered at Nicholas. "You know what. I used to think you were my friend. But now, I'd rather be friends with that lake monster. At least it's got more charm." Before Nicholas could think of an equally rude reply, Arabella turned on her heels and stormed up the stairs. The slamming of her bedroom door shook the little house.

Miranda and the Druid crossed their arms and glared at the boy, until he wriggled uncomfortably.

"What? I'm sick of her whining all the time. OK?"

"Go to them and mend your friendship," said the Druid. "Before it is too late. Arabella is afraid and surely, you, who are also afraid, can understand that."

Nicholas sighed. "Yes, sir!" he said, saluting the Druid and stalking angrily to the door. With his hand on the doorknob, he turned back. "But I'm going with Miranda, no matter what. So you better find me a magic sword or some awesome enchantments." Then he was gone.

"Magic sword, indeed!" said the Druid, easing his tall frame into one of the wingback chairs near the fireplace. Then he searched inside his cloak and produced a small metallic pouch that was attached to a fine silver chain. He passed the pouch to Miranda. "I have brought you something from Ruthar."

Miranda knelt on the floor in front of the fire. "What is it?" she asked, amazed at the softness of the metallic cloth.

"Open it and find out," said the Druid.

Eagerly, the girl opened the pouch and poured the contents into her hand. There were six smooth oval stones, deep green streaked with fine red lines. She looked at Naim, questioningly.

"They are Bloodstones," he said. "They belonged to your father. Now they are yours."

"They're beautiful," breathed Miranda, picking one of the stones out of her palm and holding it up to the firelight. "Did you know I was an Elf?"

"Yes."

"Why didn't you tell me?"

"Would you have believed me?" he asked.

The girl hesitated before shaking her head. "Probably not. In Canada I wouldn't have believed it, but here . . . I don't know . . . it's different." She stared into the fire. When she spoke again, the Druid could barely make out the words. "Naim, did you know my father?"

The old man thought for a minute. "Yes," he said, "I knew Garrett. He was a friend."

"He's dead," said the girl quietly.

"Yes, he is dead," answered the Druid, his face lined with pain.

"How did he die?"

"Miranda, I know you wish to learn about your family. And I will tell you, but not now. Now you must sleep. It will be dawn in a few hours." The Druid stood up and patted the girl's shoulder. "But I will say this. Your father was the most courageous man I have ever known and he died bravely. I miss him more than I can say."

Miranda hopped to her feet and stared into the Druid's navy blue eyes. "I never knew my father, but I want to know all about him," she said. "Do you promise that you will tell me?"

The Druid returned her look, solemnly. "You have my promise."

"When?"

"Soon."

"When is 'soon'?"

"I will tell you before you return to your own land."

Satisfied for the moment, Miranda rubbed the cool oval stones between her fingers. They felt like butter in her hands. But she also felt something else. A pulling sensation as if she were melting into them. "Are they magic?" she asked, already knowing the answer.

"The power of the Bloodstones is very great," answered the Druid. "Perhaps the most potent magic that the Elves possess."

"How do they work? Can they make me disappear?"

Naim laughed. "My dear girl. I do not know what they can do. For that, you would do well to consult Elester. But I know that there is one stone for each of the senses."

"But there are only five senses. What's the sixth stone for?"

"That, too, I do not know. I think even the Elves have lost the meaning of the sixth stone." He walked to the door. "Like King Ruthar, I, too, feel the magic in you, Miranda. You may be the one to rediscover the power of the sixth Bloodstone. I have a strong feeling that it will mean the difference between life and death in the dark days ahead."

After the Druid left, Miranda found the kitchen and, weak with hunger, made herself a giant sandwich, which she washed down with a glass of milk. Then she mounted the stairs to her room. But before she finally crawled into bed, she placed a chair in front of the full-length mirror fastened to the closet door and sat there, staring at her image, holding the Bloodstones tightly in her hand. She focused her thoughts on the Stones, willing herself to disappear. The pull of the Stones was stronger than before, but nothing happened. The girl finally admitted defeat.

CHAPTER EIGHTEEN

DUNDURUM

It seemed that she had just fallen asleep when Miranda heard the pounding on her door and Nicholas yelling, "Time to get up!" Hopping out of bed, she was surprised to feel so refreshed. She showered quickly and dressed in the same clothes she had worn only hours ago. Before leaving her room, she slipped the silver chain over her head, tucking the pouch with the Bloodstones inside her sweater. She opened the door to find Arabella waiting in the hall, backpack slung over her shoulder.

"I'm not a very good best friend, am I?" said Arabella. "I want to come with you, if you're still speaking to me."

"Of course you're coming," said Miranda, wrapping her arms about the other girl. "Did you really think I'd let you off the hook that easily?" She paused for a second and then added: "Is everything OK with you and Nick?"

"Yeah, he actually apologized. Then I apologized. I think we both realized that we've been acting like a couple of dorks. He even apologized to Penelope." Arabella looked at her friend. "I'm really sorry about everything. It's just that I've never been afraid of anything except heights and vampire movies before. Sometimes I think I'm trapped in a bad dream and can't get out."

"I know the feeling," said Miranda. "But we will do this thing, Bell, and then we'll go home. If we stick together, I don't think even the Demon can hurt us." She grabbed her backpack and put her arm around Arabella's shoulder. "Now, lead me to the kitchen. Nick said breakfast was ready and I'm so hungry I could eat a horse."

"Don't say that, I love horses," said Arabella. "And anyway, we're not eating here, in a mere kitchen. Pl-ease! We're breakfasting in the Dining Hall. Nick said he'd meet us there."

Miranda laughed. "Kitchen, Dining Hall, who cares. Just give me food." Then she looked at her friend. "Where's Penelope and you know. . . . ?"

"Muffy and Penelope have been up for hours, dying to get started."

"You're joking," said Miranda.

"No, seriously, they're coming with us." She grinned. "I wonder if it has something to do with Elester?"

Miranda pulled Arabella to a stop. "Has anybody told her what we're doing? About the Serpent's Egg and everything?"

"We tried," answered Arabella. "But who knows what she absorbs."

"I've got a bad feeling about this," mused Miranda, who, at the time, had no way of knowing how prophetic that feeling would turn out to be.

The large Dining Hall was packed. Nicholas was there, seated next to the Druid. Miranda saw Elester, listening patiently to Penelope, who couldn't seem to tear her eyes away from the handsome young Elf. Gregor, the Dwarf, sat apart from the others, wolfing down a mountain of scrambled eggs and baked beans as if it were the last meal he would ever have.

Miranda smiled, a feeling of unbelievable happiness welling up inside her. These people were her friends. They were here, together in this room, because of her and what she must do. And they believed in her enough to risk their lives to help her capture the

Serpent's Egg. For the first time in her life, she felt that she had a real family.

"Hey, Mir! Bell! Over here." Nicholas grinned, waving the girls to his table.

Breakfast was perfect. To start, the companions had a fruit drink made from oranges, dew fruit, and persimmons, blended into a frothy nectar worthy of the Gods. Next came a tray of roasted miniature potatoes and a bowl of hot, melted cheese seasoned with nutmeg and peppers. Miranda and her friends slathered the cheese on the potatoes and ate until they were stuffed, and then they ate more. Since nobody seemed to be paying attention to them, the young companions ordered bowls of strong Elven coffee, which they topped with thick, sweetened cream. Miranda said it tasted like coffee ice cream, hot ice cream. When they got silly, Naim gave them a fierce look, barking at them to wipe the white cream mustaches off their upper lips.

"It is time to go," announced the Druid, abruptly getting up from the table.

The silence that fell over the room was absolute. All eyes were on the tall man as he turned to face the others. "It is time to go," he repeated, peering about the Dining Hall. "All of you know the purpose of our journey. We are the Trust that will accompany the girl, Miranda, to the Serpents' Cave. It is a terrible thing we ask of her, and now I ask something of you. Send your thoughts out to the Demon. Hinder her. Confuse her. Draw her mind away from the Trust and the girl. Buy us time with your thoughts."

"Well said," shouted the Elves, tapping their coffee bowls with their spoons.

"Did you understand a word of that?" groaned Nicholas to no one in particular.

"Don't need thoughts. Need sharp Dwarf steel," muttered Gregor, pushing himself away from the table, his heavy boots scraping on the smooth wood floor.

The doors into the Dining Hall swung open and King Ruther made his way to the Druid. He embraced each of the travellers, and then turned to Miranda. "When you come back to us, I will speak with you about your family," he said. "There is much to tell, because they have a long and noble history."

Miranda flushed, smiling proudly. "I'd like that," she said.

The King of the Elves held the girl in his arms. "My thoughts travel with you," he whispered, before turning and leaving the Dining Hall.

The first faint glimmer of dawn was already visible in the eastern sky when the sleek boat slipped out of Bethany harbour, veering toward the eastern shore of Lake Leanora. It was a fast craft, powered by cold fusion, which the Elves had perfected thousands of years earlier.

Miranda ventured out onto the narrow deck, her hands gripping the guardrail as she turned her face into the wind. Now that they were actually on their way, she was overwhelmed by doubt. "What have I done?" she asked the wind. "Everybody believes that I can do something that I know I can't do. When are they going to discover that I'm not what they think?"

She slumped onto the deck, near the stern, out of the wind, bracing her legs against the railing. Stretching the neck of her sweater, she reached for the Bloodstones. She poured them into her open palm, and closed her hand over them. *How did my father use them?* she wondered. Once again she felt the pull of the stones, a magnetic force, drawing her into them. She fought the sensation and the stones released her immediately. *What are they trying to tell me?* There were five senses. This time, she chose hearing, concentrating on the sounds about her. Nicholas and the others were somewhere on the boat. Could she hear what they were saying? She listened intently.

A sudden noise startled her. She shivered, surprised to find that she was soaked to the skin, rain streaming down her neck. How long had she been sitting here? Quickly, she dumped the stones into the pouch and hid it under her sweater.

"SO THIS IS WHERE YOU DISAPPEARED TO," a gruff voice bellowed.

Miranda relaxed when she saw the Druid. He joined her on the deck, pulling his old cloak tightly about him to ward off the strong wind.

"WE ARE DOCKING NOW," he shouted, the wind snatching at the words.

Miranda grabbed the railing and pulled herself up. Her eyes followed the Druid's arm as he pointed ahead to a cluster of dark clouds. "DUNDURUM!"

As they disembarked, Miranda questioned Elester about Dundurum.

"It's the Dwarves' country," he said, jumping lightly onto the dock. "Look there!" He waved his arm before him.

At first, Miranda and the others did not know what they were looking at. All they saw were a few arched doorways barely recognizable in the cloud of black smog that covered the entire area. And then, the sun broke through the overcast sky and the black smog became solid—the land of the Dwarves rose up and up, disappearing into the clouds.

"It's a mountain!" cried Miranda, gazing in awe.

"Look Muffers. See the funny country?" said Penelope, holding the poodle in her outstretched arms.

"The Dwarves live in the mountain," explained the Elf. "All of their towns are inside."

"How many towns?" asked Nicholas, his eyes as round as silver coins.

"I do not know for certain, but more than ten."

"It looks dark and gloomy," said Penelope, clipping a bright pink leash onto Muffy's rhinestone collar and dropping the animal to the ground. "That's probably why Dwarves are so short."

The mountain home of the Dwarves began life millions of years ago as molten magma spewed from the belly of a volcano. For many more millions of years, the magma flowed, pushing the cooled crust higher and higher from the core, until it solidified into a black igneous rock the Dwarves called "Agni." The mountain within the volcano continued to grow upward and outward, pushing through the cone and eroding the outer shell of the parent mountain that gave it life and form, until only it remained. Its base was spread out over six hundred square miles. It rose fifteen thousand feet into the sky.

Miranda felt overwhelmed by the terrible beauty of Dundurum. It was a magnet that drew and held her eyes. At the base of the peak, she saw a magnificent, carved pylon—the main gateway into the heart of the Dwarves' country. Looking up, she saw hundreds of similar archways carved into the face of the mountain. *Windows*, she thought. They were similar to the one over the main entrance of the Centre Block back in Ottawa.

"The Dwarves really were on Parliament Hill!" she cried.

The Elf looked at her, puzzled.

"Naim said the Dwarves were in my country," she explained. "He said they built our government buildings."

"I do not mean to contradict the Druid," said Elester, dryly. "But I think you'll find he was mistaken. Gregor's people do not leave their mountain, nor do they work for others."

At that moment, the King of the Dwarves called to them. "The lodge. DunNaith. Quick bite. Short rest. Start journey."

They followed the Dwarf King along a wide boulevard inside the mountain. As impressive as Dundurum appeared from the outside, Miranda had expected the interior to be bleak and dark. She was astonished at the soft brightness. It was like sunlight without the harsh glare. The girl wondered what made it bright, and then she saw the gemstones—huge, finely cut and polished chunks of topaz and tourmaline, set in the walls, and she realized, with a start, that the stones were reflecting the sunlight through miniature openings in the stonework.

The walls on both sides of the street were intricately carved into a complex history of the Dwarf nation, from the reign of Gregor the First to the present King. Miranda grinned as she recognized Gregor's familiar stocky figure poised in triumph over the body of a strange, hideous beast.

"This is so amazing," breathed Nicholas. "Dad's not going to believe this."

"You're right," said Miranda. "He won't believe you and neither will anybody else."

The boy looked at her sheepishly. "I forgot. I guess we can't talk about any of this, can we?"

Miranda shook her head. "Only among ourselves, and maybe Mom."

"I'm going to write about it," said Penelope. "Fantasy books are big business, you know."

"I hate it when she gets a good idea," whispered Arabella.

"Yeah," agreed Nicholas. "It'll probably be a best-seller."

As they entered the city of DunNaith, the sound of children's laughter echoed from the walls. It was such a happy, unexpected sound that Miranda felt a smile spread across her face in response. The streets were alive with Dwarf men and women going about their daily activities. Miranda glanced up and saw the windows cut into the rock. There were hundreds of them, as far up as she could see. A young, dark-haired girl waved to her, shyly, from one of the windows. Miranda grinned and waved back. The Land of the Dwarves was as different from Ellesmere as night from day and, although Miranda's heart was bound to the land of the Elves, she almost wept for the majesty of Dundurum.

The lodge was a massive structure carved out of the living rock. Here, arched windows, set high in the sloped ceiling, allowed light from outside to enter the room. Gregor's "quick bite" turned into another feast, with a distinctly Dwarfish flair—platters of sweet sauerkraut with lingon and juniper berries, topped with sausages stuffed with honey, herbs and garlic. The Dwarves washed it down with a strong local black beer, called Boot.

"Its name derives from the teaspoon of black boot polish in each bottle," said the Druid, slapping the companions' hands when they tried to sneak a sip of the potent brew.

Since Dwarves eat quickly, the feast was over in ten minutes and King Gregor announced that they had lingered long enough. It was time for the Trust to press on. They exited on the opposite side of the mountain, where a group of younger Dwarves had led the Druid's stallion and the Elven horses from the ship. The second leg of the journey had begun.

CHAPTER NINETEEN

AMBUSH NEAR THE DEVIL'S FORK

iranda rode behind the Druid on a magnificent red roan stallion. Avatar was the only non-Elven horse in the company. On his far travels to the Isles of Sand, a cluster of seven floating islands in the Last Ocean, the Druid had found the wild animal drowning in one of the quagmires that appeared at random throughout the Isles. He saved the horse and, to his amazement, instead of running away, the loyal creature stayed with him.

Penelope, grinning like a Cheshire cat, insisted on riding with Elester who, amiably, tucked Muffy into a pouch that hung from the saddle of his gray Elven horse, Noble. Even the stern Druid smiled at the sight of the little dog's head poking out of the pouch, the wind whipping its long ears straight back like fluffy pink socks.

Since Arabella and Nicholas had riding experience, they were given their own mounts. Arabella's horse was a dappled gray mare, called Marigold. Nicholas rode Fetch, whom the Elves nicknamed "Sprite," because of the young stallion's swiftness.

With the company rode a half-dozen Elven Riders, members of King Ruthar's special Guard, the finest protectors on Ellesmere

Island. Miranda thought they looked fierce in their black pants and shirts, with black scarves around their necks. Sara, a tall, slim Rider, nodded at Miranda who grinned and waved back. Just ahead of Sara, Nicholas, clad in black and wearing the short sword he had been given for his training, beamed from ear to ear as he rode proudly beside his new friend, Laury, Captain of the Riders. The only member of the Trust who looked completely out of place on a horse was King Gregor. Miranda giggled at the sight of the short, stocky Dwarf, his face a mask of terror as he tried to control his frisky mount.

For once, the Druid was in high spirits, talking readily, answering Miranda's questions without his usual grumbling. She took advantage of his expansiveness to ask him again where they were going, and almost fell off the horse when he told her.

"Elester already told you that our final destination is a cave in the eastern foothills of the Mountains of the Moon or, as the Dwarves call them, the White Mountains."

"How far away are they?"

"I will tell you, because if anything happens to me and the others, you must go on alone. Besides Gregor, Elester and me, you are the only one who shares this knowledge."

"Can I tell my friends?" asked Miranda.

"I cannot stop you from telling the entire world if you want," answered the Druid. "But I would strongly advise against it, for the simple reason that a person cannot tell what he or she does not know." He waited a minute to see if the girl were going to argue. When she remained silent, he continued. "The Mountains of the Moon are about a two-day ride from The Devil's Fork, which is where we will make camp tonight. From the Fork, we take the Northwest Road, skirting the village of Diputs Seno, and turn North, following a little-used pass through the Spikes, a ring of jagged mountains, surrounding Indolent's land."

"What's Indolent?" asked Miranda.

"Indolent is a wizard, who was once a Pledge in my Order," Naim replied curtly.

"What does that mean?"

"It means he wanted to become a Druid."

"Did he ever get to be a Druid?"

"No."

Miranda gave up. Again, getting information from Naim was like trying to pry open an oyster shell. They rode in silence for a few minutes and then the Druid gave Miranda more precise directions and made her memorize them. Just as she thought she had worked hard enough for one day, he made her memorize the route she must take inside the Serpents' Cave. "Going in is easy," he said. "Now repeat the directions for finding your way *out* of the cave."

When Miranda could recite the directions to his satisfaction, the Druid brought up the Bloodstones.

"You say you felt them reaching out to you?"

"No, I felt them trying to pull me into them."

"And you resisted?"

"Yes—it's a horrible feeling. It scares me," said Miranda. "Naim, I haven't got a clue how to use the Stones. I've tried and tried, but I'll never figure it out. King Ruthar should have given them to someone who knows how to use them."

"Patience, girl," said the Druid. "You will discover their use, perhaps when you least expect it."

They rode until dusk, making only brief stops along the way to feed and rest the animals, and work the stiffness out of their own tired limbs. Worried about the Bloodstones, Miranda went in search of Elester. She found him rubbing down Noble, talking soothingly to the animal as he worked. Sensing the girl's approach, the gray horse lifted his head and whickered softly.

"I came to ask you about the Bloodstones," Miranda said, stopping to run her hand over the huge animal's velvet face. Noble nudged her and nibbled her clothing.

"He wants a treat," laughed Elester. "Here." He tossed a carrot to Miranda. "You can feed him." Then the Elf sat on a tree stump and looked at the girl. "What do you wish to know about the Stones?"

"Everything," she cried. "Why I can't use them, for one thing?"

"How do you know you cannot use them? Have you tried?"

"I've been trying ever since your father gave them to me," said the girl.

The young Elf thought for a minute. "Bloodstones are like people. Each one has a different purpose and personality. My father has a Wisdom Stone. But it does not make him wise."

"What good is it then?"

"My father's wisdom allows him to use the Stone."

"I don't get it," said Miranda.

"You have to trust yourself, Miranda. The Stones are always working, but they have to be directed by the one who possesses them."

"Can anybody use them?"

"No. The Stones are part of a family's bloodline. The ones you have belong to your family, just like a sister or brother. They are useless to anyone else."

"You mean, because I'm an only child, if I suddenly died, nobody else could ever use them?"

"That is true. But someday you may wish to pass them on to your children."

"I might," agreed Miranda. "But for now, I just wish I could make them work."

While the others slept and the Elven Riders rotated the watch around the perimeter of the camp, Miranda huddled by the dying embers of the fire, thinking about the Bloodstones and Elester's advice to trust herself. Finally, she curled up on the hard ground and fell asleep.

Hate, the Demon, came for her then, no longer a nameless formless terror breathing down her neck, but a huge hissing creature bearing in one clawed hand the hideous black stake with the human head stuck on the end. It came for her with such loathing, such evil purpose that no mere Elven power could stand against it. So Miranda did what she had always done in the dream. She threw down the Bloodstones, and ran. She ran and ran, knowing that she could never, never escape this evil thing. But still she ran.

She sat bolt upright, gasping for air and fighting something heavy that was pinning her to the ground, smothering her. It was the Druid's cloak. He had placed it over her while she slept. She breathed rapidly, her heart pumping loudly.

And then someone, it sounded like Nicholas, shouted.

"AMBUSH! RUN!"

Suddenly the dark shape of the Druid bent over her and his strong hand gripped her shoulder. "Get up, girl! The Demon's creatures are all about us." The Druid paused only long enough to pick up his old cloak and slip it over his shoulders.

"No!" Miranda cried, jumping to her feet, unsure whether this was still part of the nightmare. The sound of howls drove the dream out of her mind. She saw Naim ahead, little more than a black shadow, moving swiftly toward the horses. The girl grabbed her backpack and raced after him.

"The forest is crawling with the filth," said the Druid, whistling for the red roan stallion. "You and Penelope must take Avatar."

The great horse appeared out of the trees, stamping the ground, his eyes white with loathing for the evil creatures, whose scent filled his nostrils.

"But—" cried Miranda, tense with fear.

"Do not argue," snapped the Druid, stroking the animal's face as he quickly slipped the bit into its mouth and slid the reins over its sleek neck. Then he turned to the girl. "Trust the horse. He knows what to do." He caught the girl's shoulders. "Listen to me. When you ride out of here, do not look back, do not turn back, no matter what. Even if you see them drag me, or another down, do not turn back. If you do, you will die. Ride until you reach The Devil's Fork and then take the road to the left. If I am not there by then, continue along that road until you reach the village of Diputs Seno. But do not, under any circumstances set foot within the village borders. Hide yourself off the road and wait for me on the outskirts." He gave the girl's shoulders a quick, but gentle, shake. "Have you been listening?"

When Miranda nodded, he said. "Now, get the others and bring them back here, quickly, while I attend to Marigold."

"Where are you—?"

"Do as you are told," he snapped. "Now go!"

Miranda turned to obey, uncertain whether the tears in her eyes were the result of fear or the Druid's harsh words. She followed Muffy's sharp yelps, and found Arabella and Penelope crouched in a clump of bushes, frantic with fear. Penelope was crying, trying to hold onto the squirming, snarling poodle.

"The horses! Come on!" shouted Miranda. Then she noticed that Nicholas was nowhere in sight. "Where's Nick?" she yelled, peering through the darkness, trying to spot the boy among the dark running forms of the Elves. Off to her left, she recognized Sara advancing on a pale, ghostly shape, her sword poised to strike.

"We couldn't find him," cried Arabella, her eyes wide with terror. "He was with Laury earlier."

Miranda pointed to the black form of the Druid. "Over there! Go!" Both girls took off as if they had been kicked from behind. Miranda risked another quick look for Nicholas before dashing after the others.

"MOVE!" thundered the Druid, as the howls grew louder.

"We can't leave without Nick," cried Miranda.

"USE YOUR HEAD, GIRL. WHAT CAN YOU DO FOR THE BOY?"

The Druid lifted Miranda and flung her onto Avatar's back as if she were a sack of feathers. Then he swung Penelope up behind her. "You will need both hands to hold on," he said to Penelope. "Give me the dog!"

"NO!" screamed Penelope, stuffing Muffy into her jacket and zipping it up quickly.

For an instant, Miranda could have sworn she saw smoke coming out of the Druid's ears, but then he shrugged and spoke softly to the horse. "Ride like the wind, Avatar. Keep them from harm."

The powerful stallion dug his hoofs into the hard ground and took off for the road, like a bullet, plowing through the brush and leaping over barriers with the ease of a champion. Marigold whinnied and followed with Arabella bent low over the mare's neck, hands gripping the reins. The fierce shouts of the Riders mingled with the howls and screams of the attacking creatures and filled the air about them. Miranda clutched the reins and held on for dear life. Behind her, Penelope squeezed her so tightly that the Elven girl could scarcely breathe.

Nicholas was keeping watch with Laury when he saw the shadow dart across the moonlit ground between two evergreen trees. At first he thought his eyes were playing tricks on him. He blinked and peered into the darkness, his senses keen and alert. Then, the shadowy form paused, and Nicholas caught a glimpse of a pair of glowing red eyes. For a second, the boy froze, fear stabbing at his heart. With a start, he realized that, until this moment, he hadn't really believed in Miranda's Monsters. Oh yes, he knew something was after her. Too many people said so, for him to doubt. But he hadn't seen anything scary, except maybe those bubble things that had carried them to Ellesmere Island.

But, the sight of the creature slinking through the shadows changed all that. Before he knew it, he had drawn his sword and was shouting at the top of his lungs. "AMBUSH! RUN!"

As Avatar cleared the camp, a huge, pale form leaped out of the trees ahead. At first Miranda thought it was one of the THUGs, but then she realized it wasn't large enough. No, this was one of the creatures she had seen on Parliament Hill. It was one of the Hellhags! The horse saw the creature too, but instead of turning away, galloped straight at it. Panicked, Miranda pulled on the reins with all of her strength, but the big horse followed its own instincts. The girl dropped the reins and wound her fingers in Avatar's mane. She had to hold on and trust the horse.

The Hellhag, expecting the stallion to veer away in terror, saw the twister coming at her and froze, confused, like a deer stunned by a bright light. And then, Miranda's heart stopped as Nicholas flew out of the bushes directly between Avatar and the Hellhag, his sword swinging wildly at the snarling beast. It happened so suddenly, Miranda didn't have to time to shout a warning to the boy. Two thoughts raced through her mind at the same time: *He doesn't see us. We're going to trample him.* But Avatar was swift and agile. In seconds, the stallion had leaped over Nicholas and smashed into the creature, knocking it under its powerful hooves, leaving behind its twisted, broken carcass.

For an instant after, Miranda slumped forward in the saddle. She closed her eyes tightly, praying that when she opened them, she'd be far away from the shouting and screaming. She simply clung to Avatar's mane, as they fled for their lives. When she finally lifted her head and risked a quick look behind her, she was relieved to see Marigold galloping on the stallion's heels, Arabella's face flat against the mare's neck. There was no sign of the Hellhags. There was no sign of the Druid, or Nicholas, or the others. They were alone.

Muffy chose that moment to wriggle out of Penelope's jacket and leap to the ground. The tiny dog raced around in a circle and then, picking up the scent of the Hellhags, took off in pursuit—a swift pink blur, its staccato barks dying away in the night.

CHAPTER TWENTY
DIPUTS SENO

"GO BACK!" screamed Penelope.

Miranda hesitated for a minute. She remembered the Druid's orders not to turn back no matter what. But they couldn't leave the little dog out here alone. Muffy might have the heart of a lioness, but in the end, she was no match for the Hellhags. Miranda shivered, thinking about what the monsters would do if they caught the miniature creature. *Stupid poodle*, she thought. *Stupid Penelope for bringing her stupid dog.*

She felt for the Bloodstones, pouring them into her hand. Then she held them tightly and sent her thoughts into the Stones and out to the tiny fierce hunter. She thought she could hear the sound of faint barking in the distance and, suddenly, an image of a snarling pink terror surrounded by four of the grisly beasts filled her mind. Slowly, she opened her hand and replaced the Stones in the pouch. Did she really see the dog, or was it just her imagination? She did not know.

"I'm sorry," she said, urging Avatar into a gallop. "We can't go back."

"Miranda, please. I can't leave Muffy," wailed Penelope. "If you won't go back, then let me down. I'll find her."

Miranda felt terrible. She looked to Arabella for help, and saw tears shining on her friend's cheeks as she scanned the road ahead.

"I don't want to leave Muffy behind. But we can't go back. We just can't."

They rode for a long time in silence. Miranda could see that Avatar was tiring and, because she sensed that the proud animal would run until his heart stopped, she pulled on the reins and the horse came to a stop. Stiff and sore, the three girls dismounted and led the horses along the dirt road, keeping to the middle and peering fearfully at the dark shadows along the sides. They tried to comfort Penelope but the unhappy girl did not respond, except to sniffle loudly every few minutes.

Miranda felt so depressed, she wanted to cry too. Her decision to abandon Muffy gnawed at her conscience. She worried that she had made the decision to leave the dog, because she was too terrified of the Hellhags to turn back, and not because of the Trust. Was destroying Hate more important than saving one rotten little poodle? She didn't know. But, deep within, she felt that if she said yes, it would be the wrong answer, and if she said no, it would also be wrong. Maybe there was no right answer.

She kept looking over her shoulder, hoping the others—the Druid, Nicholas, Elester, Gregor—would appear like magic on the road behind them. Or Muffy. Were they safe? If they escaped, they should have been here by now. What if they were dead?

"We're coming to a fork in the road," said Arabella, pointing ahead. "Which way do we go?"

"Left," answered Miranda. "We have to go off the road before we get to a place called Diputs Seno."

"We'll ride the rest of the way," said Arabella, slipping one foot in the stirrup and swinging her body into the saddle as though it were as natural as sitting on a chair.

Miranda looked at Penelope and, for the first time since Muffy had run off in pursuit of the Hellhags, the other girl giggled.

"Yes?" asked Arabella, innocently.

"Uh, we've got a small problem," said Miranda. "Getting off the horse was easy, but how do we get back on?"

Avatar stood several hands taller than the mare, but after a lot of combined lifting and shoving, Miranda and Arabella managed to get Penelope on Avatar's back. Miranda ended up walking.

They reached the outskirts of a village at daybreak.

"'Welcome to Diputs Seno, population 232. No comparisons or long meals allowed. No trespassing.'" Miranda grinned as she read the sign. "Does that mean you're welcome to go into the village, but if you do, you're trespassing, so you really can't go in?"

"Who cares about some stupid sign," said Penelope, yawning and stumbling from tiredness. She sank into the tall grass by the side of the road and, within minutes, was fast asleep.

"I like the part about no comparisons or long meals," added Arabella. "Remind me not to say that long meals are way more fun than short ones."

"ARREST THEM!" shouted a loud voice.

The girls almost jumped out of their skin as they heard horrific crashing sounds coming from the bushes on both sides of the road. Then, the foliage disappeared, trampled flat, as a dozen fat, almost completely round creatures wobbled onto the highway and surrounded the two startled girls. Miranda stifled a giggle at the sight of the puffed up, gnomish bodies. She also noticed the hefty wooden clubs clutched tightly in their chubby hands.

She guessed that they were all roughly the same size, about four feet. *Vertically and horizontally*, she thought, fighting to keep a straight face. The odd-looking creatures were clad in black hide overalls that fitted like a second skin and on their feet were grimy, gray socks under black leather sandals. In the pale, early morning light, their wart-encrusted bodies were the bleached green colour of lima beans. They had no necks.

"Arrest the four-legged DEARS, too," commanded one of the round people, obviously the leader. But as more of the strange creatures wobbled toward the horses, Avatar whinnied loudly, rearing up on his powerful hind legs, hooves slashing the air in front of him. The Wobbles, as Miranda now thought of them, tumbled onto the road in panic, and several rolled into the ditch where they covered their eyes with their hands and stayed there until it was safe to come out. With Avatar in the lead, the two horses wheeled about and galloped into the trees.

"What are you arresting us for?" asked Miranda, amused by the seriousness of the silly creatures.

"The charges are trespassing on Simurgh land, Edict 175, and making comparisons, Edict 412(a)," recited the leader, as if he said this many times every day. He motioned to one of his underlings. "Cousin Slugs, read them their rights and bring them to the Pen." He turned his back and started wobbling along the road toward the village.

"Just a minute," said Arabella. "We haven't broken any of your laws. We're not even on your land."

The Simurghs erupted in laughter, their funny round bodies bouncing off one another, but their open mouths showing deadly sharp pointed teeth.

"That's what they all say," said one of the creatures, eyeing the girls slyly, and running its long, goat-like tongue over its lips. Miranda turned away in disgust.

The leader stopped, his back to the girls. Suddenly, his head rotated one hundred and eighty degrees and he eyed the prisoners. His mean spiteful face turned black with loathing. "Our land starts ten feet behind you, DEAR," he spat, lips drawn back, exposing the wicked teeth. "What are the DEARS going to say next, Cousins?"

"IT'S NOT FAIR!" chanted the Simurghs in unison.

"You're right. It's not fair," said Miranda, green eyes blazing.

For a second, the leader's small, pink eyes met the Elven girl's clear gaze, and then he looked away abruptly, shaken by the resolve he saw there. "To the Pen," he ordered, his head spinning grotesquely. "Sut will know how to deal with them."

As the wall of round Simurghs shepherded the girls along the road, one of the strange beasts read the prisoners their rights: "YOU HAVE THE RIGHT TO ADMIT GUILT. YOU HAVE THE RIGHT TO DIE FOR THE GLORIOUS KINGDOM OF SUT."

"Isn't this where we're supposed to be getting scared?" asked Arabella, feeling the urge to laugh and cry simultaneously.

Too late, Miranda shot her friend a warning glance. One of the Simurghs punched the girl in the back, knocking her to her knees on the road. Arabella gritted her teeth to keep from crying out in pain. She stretched out both hands to cushion her fall, and felt the dirt scraping away the skin on her palms.

"Bell!" screamed Miranda, lashing out at the Simurghs with arms and legs. She kicked the nearest one in the stomach, and jammed her elbow into the nose of another, before the creatures overpowered her, bouncing her from one round body to the next, until she was black and blue and utterly defeated. The Simurghs clamped heavy iron manacles about the girls' ankles. The rough edges cut into their soft Elven boots and chafed against their skin. By the time they reached the village, the bottom half of their boots was the colour of blood.

"PRISONERS HALT!" ordered Kroak, the leader, who was waiting for them outside a large round outdoor pen, enclosed by a high log wall, the tops tapered to sharp points. He opened a strong iron gate, grabbed the girls by the hair, and flung them through the opening into the Pen.

CHAPTER TWENTY-ONE

SUT

rouching in the tall grass by the side of the road, Penelope watched the queer roly-poly creatures shackle her two companions and march them in the direction of the village. Long after they disappeared, the girl remained in her hiding spot, sobbing and growing more frightened by the minute.

"What am I going to do?" she cried, thinking that it would be dark soon. Finally, after an hour of pulling her hair and biting her perfectly manicured nails down to the cuticles, it dawned on the girl that she had better think of something fast. "But what?" she muttered. "I can wait here and hope that nasty Druid person shows up which might be never, or I can go back and look for Muffy and the others. But what if I can't find them? What if they're all dead and those horrible beasts are still around?" The only other course open to her was to rescue Miranda and Arabella. The big question was how?

Then she remembered how Stubby, her homeroom teacher, had bought the Muffy story without blinking. If anyone had told her that the expensive gifts her parents showered upon the teacher made it easier for him to believe the wild story, she would have laughed. No! It was her cleverness alone that earned her extra time to complete the assignment.

Penelope wracked her brain, discarding one idea after another. She thought about the Simurghs. Who or what is Sut? The Simurghs had said that Sut would deal with the prisoners, so whatever sort of creature it was, it must be important. For a minute, the girl stared off into the distance. Suddenly, a light flickered on in her head. "Yes! It just might work!" she cried, leaping to her feet and stomping purposefully toward the village.

Miranda sat on the dirt floor of the Pen, her back against the log stakes near the gate. She tore the pockets out of her pants and ripped the cloth into narrow strips which she stuffed between the shackles and her torn boots to ease the pressure on her raw, bleeding ankles. Through tears of pain, she looked at Arabella. The other girl was staring in shock at her inflamed hands.

"Oh, Bell! Here. Let me wrap them." Gently, she took one of her friend's hands in her own and wound the cloth around the deep cuts, talking soothingly while she worked. "It's OK. I promise you we'll be OK. We're going to get out of here." Her lips tightened in anger. "And then we're going to burn this place to the ground."

Arabella's face relaxed into a grin. "I like the part about torching this place." She looked at Miranda and made a face. "You should see yourself. You're a mess."

"You should talk," said Miranda.

"What do you think they're going to do to us?" asked Arabella. "They're awfully fat. I wonder what they eat?"

"Stop!" cried Miranda, her flesh crawling. "I don't want to hear this." She picked up a small stick from the ground, absent-mindedly scratching her initials in the dirt. Suddenly, she stared at the stick as if she were seeing it for the first time. Then she wriggled around and pushed the stick between the tightly joined logs, scraping the dried bark until she had carved out a tiny peephole in the wall.

At that moment, the heavy gate swung inward, and Kroak wobbled into the Pen, followed by another of the ugly creatures dragging a big wooden crate.

"Get up, DEARS," Kroak ordered. The girls hobbled quickly to their feet, ignoring the shooting pain in their ankles.

"No more playing. It's time for the DEARS to earn their keep," snarled the creature.

Miranda wanted to drive her fist into his horrible, grinning face. But she merely clenched them tightly and bowed her head, to hide the anger written there in capital letters.

"Come on, Cousin Slugs, you lazy slime, get that crate over here," yelled Kroak.

Slugs glared knives at his superior. But Kroak noticed the look and swung his club at his companion, catching him on the side of the head, cracking the creature's skull. Puling like a cat, Slugs dropped the heavy crate and grabbed his head with both hands, jumping up and down and spinning like a top. Miranda's stomach lurched as globules of green pus laced with bright red blood poured out of the gaping wound in the Wobble's head and flew in all directions. Suddenly the creature's eyes opened wide and it toppled over and then lay still.

Kroak kicked the fallen carcass and then turned his mean pig eyes on the horrified girls. The Simurgh pointed at the crate. "Now get to work, DEARS." Then he grabbed one of the dead creature's legs, spun around and wobbled out of the Pen, dragging Slugs behind him.

Miranda crawled over to the crate, lifted the lid and peered inside. The stench made her gag. She dropped the lid as if it were burning hot and moved back quickly.

"What's in there?" asked Arabella, anxiously, imagining the crate crammed full of dead Simurghs.

"A basin, a can of water, some soap," answered Miranda, her face green. "And a crateful of dirty Wobble socks."

"Forget it," said Arabella. "I'd rather die."

"Me too," said Miranda, pressing her eye to the peephole in the wall and then falling back in shock.

"What?" cried Arabella.

"Penelope!" gasped Miranda.

"What about her?"

"She's out there. In the middle of the road, coming toward the village."

"What? Is she out of her mind?"

"Who knows?" answered Miranda, reaching instinctively for the Bloodstones and pulling the pouch out of her sweater. "She's stupid enough to march up to the Simurghs and tell them to let us go or she'll call 9-1-1."

"What's that?" asked Arabella, eyeing the tiny metallic sack in her friend's hand.

"What?" said Miranda, astonished. She didn't know what she was doing with the magic stones or how they got into her hand. But, since they were there, she wanted to try out an idea. Ignoring Arabella, she gripped the Bloodstones tightly and peered through the crack in the wall, feeling the irresistible pull of the stones, stronger than before. She thought of sight and sound, reality and illusion, the lone girl marching resolutely into the village and the malevolent Wobbles, cute comic creatures with wicked pointed teeth. Then she released her thoughts, sending them out in a wide circle that encompassed both the Pen and Penelope, one unblinking eye glued to the small opening between the logs.

"Sut sent me for the prisoners," said Penelope, in a deep, gruff voice that sounded exactly like Penelope trying to disguise her voice. "Hand over the two prisoners immediately!" The girl shook her head in frustration. "Too wimpy. OK. Try it again. The prisoners. Bring them to me."

She was so intent on practicing what she was going to say when she faced the Simurghs, she almost died of heart failure when she suddenly realized that she had entered the village and was already facing them. Directly ahead, two dozen of the creatures were spread out in a straight line before a tall wooden enclosure. They were waiting for her, their beady eyes glinting cold and cruel.

The Simurghs trembled with glee, chittering like monkeys, as they watched the trespasser draw nearer. They were all thinking the same thing. *Three in one day. Sut will be pleased. Maybe he'll let us keep one.* And then the ground shook and a hush fell over the village as Sut, the dragon, lumbered toward the flabbergasted Wobbles, orange flames erupting from the beast's open mouth, singeing the stiff bristles growing out of the warts on the Simurghs' bodies, and scattering their thoughts like clouds in a high wind.

"BRING THE HUMANS TO ME!" Penelope commanded, folding her arms and trying to look as fierce as a lion. She couldn't believe her eyes when the Wobbles cringed in fear, arms raised to protect their heads. The one they called Kroak threw himself at the dragon's feet, groveling in the dirt, and licking the creature's huge clawed feet.

"Does the DEAR Master want both of the humans?" he wheedled. The dragon opened its mouth, and Kroak shrieked in terror. Then he sidled to the iron gate, unlocked it, and disappeared inside.

Miranda couldn't believe her eyes when she saw Penelope change into a huge, fire-breathing dragon. But she dared not halt the flow of her thoughts through the stones in order to tell Bell what was happening. She knew, without knowing how, that if her thoughts wavered, the illusion would revert to reality. If that happened, they were finished. The gate flew inward and Kroak hurried over to the girls.

"Sut wants you," he grunted as the heavy manacles fell away from the girls' ankles. He caught a handful of hair and yanked them to their feet. "Get a move on! Chop-chop!"

"What's going on out there?" asked Arabella, limping through the gate behind her friend. Then she saw the dragon. "Ahhh!" she screamed, turning back toward the Pen, only to find her way blocked by Kroak's solid round form. The Simurgh sneered at the girl's fear, grabbed her by the arm, and dragged her to the dragon.

Before they escaped, Miranda had one last thing to take care of. She thought her brain would explode as she bent her thoughts on the Dragon. As if it were yawning, Sut opened its mouth and blew a sheet of flame along the ground toward the Pen. Sparks danced in the air and clung to the stakes, igniting the dry wood. As the Pen burned, the dragon grasped the girls by their arms and, with a mighty lash of its tail, turned and lumbered down the road. Suddenly the great beast wheeled back toward the Simurghs. The movement was so unexpected that Miranda's concentration wavered and the illusion faded.

"KNEEL!" shouted Penelope at the stunned Wobbles.

"Now you've done it!" said Miranda crossly, looking over her shoulder as dozens of the furious creatures charged at the three girls, nasty wooden clubs poised to strike hard.

CHAPTER TWENTY-TWO

ESCAPE

"UN!" shouted Miranda, knowing that, with their injuries, neither she nor Arabella could outrun the irate Wobbles if they stuck to the open road.

"Head for the trees," she said, breathing heavily. "We'll try to lose them in the woods."

The three companions veered off the road, crossed the ditch, and entered the forest, a few feet from the spot where they had been arrested only a few hours earlier. Close behind, the chittering of the Simurghs was suddenly drowned out by the snap of wood splintering, as they, too, left the road and crashed through the trees, tracking the girls.

On a hill, a short distance away, crouched in a thicket of tangled bushes and vines, the THUG watched. Its red eyes glowed dimly as they followed the Elven girl. For long seconds, the creature remained motionless, gloating with the knowledge that the girl would not escape this time. A shudder racked the THUG's body as it remembered the pain Hate had inflicted on it and its three brothers when she had learned that the girl had fled from Ottawa with the Druid. The enraged Demon had driven her sharp iron stake deep into the THUG's body, again and again, puncturing its vital organs and bursting its black heart. Then she had made the creature whole again, cauterizing the fatal wounds with red liquid fire, but leaving the pain. "As a reminder," she had hissed.

In its long service to the Demon, the creature had never thought. It was a thing of action, kept alive for only one purpose. To kill. To kill for Hate. But the unbearable pain it carried as a constant reminder of its only failure had changed all that. The emotionless killing machine was now a thinking, cunning assassin, a hundred times deadlier than before. And all of its dark thoughts were bent on Miranda.

The THUG moved cautiously out from the cover of the thicket. Then it paused, stilling its harsh breathing, and listened intently. For an instant, it had sensed another presence nearby. It remained motionless for a long minute before hunching its huge shoulders and melting into the trees.

A short distance downwind, Avatar watched the THUG. When the black creature finally stirred, the stallion lifted his head, snorted softly, and trotted after the humans.

"Listen!" said Miranda, coming to a sudden stop. "I think we've lost them."

"Good, because I need a rest," gasped Arabella, sinking to the ground, and lifting the bandages to examine the angry cuts on her hands and the raw weeping flesh around her ankles. "We can't keep running blindly," she cried, holding up her swollen hands, palms outward.

Miranda lowered herself onto the trunk of a fallen tree, knowing that her friend was right. They had to stop and rest. "Let's go until we find a place to hide for the night. Then we'll decide what to do next," she said, trying to hide the awful hopeless feeling creeping over her.

"Lead on, Penelope," groaned Arabella, getting up slowly.

But the other girl didn't respond. She sat on the ground staring at a clump of plants with beautiful pale turquoise leaves and strange white pods. When she looked at her companions, her eyes were bright as if she had a fever.

"What's wrong?" asked Miranda, jumping to her feet and rushing to the girl.

"I've read about this plant," said Penelope. "But I thought it had died out a long time ago. It's called 'Pearl's Tears.' The leaves are poisonous, but inside the pod is a small sac, called the tear of the pearl. If we can find some water and soak the teardrop, it'll help your hands and ankles."

"Are you serious?" asked Arabella suspiciously, thinking of the girl's habit of lying. "Are you sure it's the pods we're supposed to use?"

"Not the pods," snapped Penelope, breaking off a handful and stuffing them in her jacket pocket. "What's *in* them. If you'd listen for a change, instead of criticizing all the time, you'd have heard me say in Bethany that I knew a lot about herbal remedies." She turned to Miranda. "We can go now. Just remember, we need water, so keep an eye out for a spring."

Penelope's small, but important, discovery worked wonders on the dispirited trio. Their weariness and hopelessness dropped away and they set out eagerly, each secretly hoping that she would find the spring before the others.

"Over here!" shouted Penelope. "Water!"

They had been walking for over an hour when Penelope let out her triumphant cry. And, sure enough, when Miranda and Arabella joined their companion, they saw the narrow, clear stream bubbling swiftly over the smooth rocks, on its way to a great lake or river far beyond these lands. Beside the stream was a flat, grassy space, almost totally enclosed by a circle of thorny bushes. They had found both water and a place to hide for the night.

"Yes!" cried Miranda, happily, grabbing her friends by their arms and leading them in a wild dance, around and around, in a parody of some ancient tribal rite of passage. Falling onto their stomachs in the soft grass by the stream, the girls dunked their heads into the swiftly flowing water, shrieking as the cold hit them and turned their skin to gooseflesh. Then they drank deeply, scooping up water in their hands. When they had satisfied their thirst, the girls huddled close together on the grassy bank, chatting happily. Their voices, high and excited, echoed from the tall trees.

"I need something to soak these in," said Penelope, breaking the pods and collecting the delicate tears on a leaf.

"There's nothing," said Miranda, frustrated that they had the pods and the water, but no container. "I've looked everywhere."

"Wait," cried Penelope, reaching for her backpack and digging through her possessions until she produced a small plastic container. "Muffy's water bottle," she cried, excitedly, holding it up. Throwing the backpack on the ground, she unscrewed the cap and poured the Tears of the Pearl plant into the container. "Here," she ordered, passing the bottle to Miranda. "Fill it. It's better with hot water, but this way'll work. It'll just take longer."

While the Pearl tears dissolved in the cold spring water, the three friends sat or lay prone on the grass, listening as Penelope told her companions how she had come up with the idea for their rescue. "I knew it would work, but I have to say I was a bit nervous."

"Admit it, you were scared out of your mind," snorted Arabella.

"Well, maybe I was more than a bit nervous, but you have to admit, I was brilliant." She frowned. "The only thing I don't understand is why the Simurghs started chasing us. Especially after they let me take you in the first place?"

"You know, don't you Mir?" said Arabella, looking at her friend strangely. "It's got something to do with that little silver bag around your neck, right?"

Miranda nodded, reaching for the metallic pouch and pouring the stones into her hand. Gazing into deep green, the colour of her own Elven eyes, Miranda told her friends how she had used the Bloodstones. For a second, after she had finished, the others stared at her in silence.

Penelope was the first to protest. "Are you saying you turned me into a dragon?" she spluttered, glowering at Miranda. "Without my permission?" Then she looked away and tossed her head. "I didn't need your help, you know."

"Oh, shut up!" said Arabella. "There's something seriously wrong with you if you think for one minute the Simurghs would have handed us over to you."

"But they did, didn't they?" quipped Penelope. "So there!"

Miranda broke in before she had a major tiff on her hands. "Listen!" She looked at Penelope. "First of all, you were never a dragon. The stones made the Simurghs and us think that's what they were seeing. Remember when you said, 'Bring me the humans'?"

"I don't remember what I said, but yeah, it was something like that."

"The Wobbles didn't hear your voice at all. They heard the dragon. And, believe me because I was watching through the wall. It was the most horrible voice I've ever heard."

Penelope looked as if she'd seen a ghost. "Y-you m-mean. . . ."

Arabella smirked, as the other girl's eyes widened in horror. "If Mir hadn't made you look and sound like a Dragon, you'd have been Wobble food."

Miranda felt sorry for Penelope, even though it served her right for always thinking herself cleverer than anyone else. "It's over now," she said. "But what you tried to do was really brave."

"Or stupid," muttered Arabella, under her breath.

Penelope ignored her and spoke to Miranda. "Why was I the only one who didn't see myself as a Dragon?"

"I honestly don't know."

"I almost lost it when that ugly little creature started licking my boots."

Miranda giggled. "Me too. You should have seen the look on your face." She crawled along the ground and wrapped her arms about Penelope's boots. "Does the DEAR Master want both of the humans?"

Arabella and Penelope shrieked and shrieked. Penelope jumped to her feet, backing away as Miranda advanced toward her. "You sound exactly like that Kroak thing. Get away!"

When things quieted down, Penelope, keeping a wary eye on Miranda, edged closer to the other girls and slipped to the ground. "What happened when we were leaving? Why did those nasty things suddenly start chasing us?" she asked.

"Because I lost focus and the stones stopped working. The Simurghs saw us as we really are—just three harmless kids."

"What I don't understand is how you knew that Sut was a dragon?" asked Arabella, baffled.

"I didn't," answered Miranda, looking as puzzled as her friend. She also wondered how an illusory dragon had burned the wart hairs off the Wobbles and torched the Pen.

Penelope was fascinated by the magic stones. She could not take her eyes off them. When Miranda finally dumped them back into the small pouch and slipped the silver chain under her sweater, she felt the girl's eyes following her every movement.

Before turning in for the night, Miranda and Penelope ripped more fabric from the legs of their pants and made new bandages for Arabella's hands and ankles. They soaked the cloth in the herbal water and wrapped it around the cuts. When Miranda finally applied the wet cloth to her own ankles, she was surprised at how quickly the Pearl tears acted on the raw, angry wounds. The pain disappeared even as the liquid touched the chaffed skin.

"I've been thinking about what we should do next," she said softly. Up until a few minutes ago, the girls had been talking and arguing in normal voices, and Miranda had not been the least bit concerned about anybody eavesdropping on their conversation. But, talk of the Serpent's Egg changed everything. Nobody must know where she was going. She looked at Arabella. *Not even my best friend*, she thought, sadly.

"I don't have much choice about what I have to do," said Miranda. "We don't know where Nick and the others are. We could spend months wandering about searching for them." She took a deep breath, as if to give herself courage. "Since I'm the only one who can capture the Serpent's Egg, it makes sense for me to go where Naim and Ruthar said I would find the Serpents' Cave."

"Where's that?" asked Arabella.

"I can't tell you," answered Miranda, reaching out quickly and touching her friend's arm. "Bell, I don't know what the Demon can do. Naim said her magic is evil, but it's still magic and it's very powerful. I don't know if she could read your mind. I only know she can't read mine."

"How do you know that?"

Miranda shook her head, puzzled. "Honestly, Bell. I didn't know until I said it." She looked at Arabella. "You're not going to believe this, but I think the stones told me."

"That's so weird!" whispered Arabella. "Anyway, we have to stick together, so I'm coming with you." She held her hand out and Miranda covered it with her own.

"I'm coming too," said Penelope, adding her hand to the top of the pile before curling up on the soft grass. "I want to see this Serpent's Egg. Do you think it's valuable?" she asked, and was asleep before Miranda could answer.

Talking about the Serpent's Egg had made Miranda edgy. She lay on the grass, tossing and turning, until finally, she gave up trying to sleep. Finally, she rolled onto her back and stared at the stars, thinking about all that had happened since she had left Ottawa in the middle of the night. When would she see her mother again? She thought about Nick and the Druid, saying a silent prayer for their safety. She missed them, even Gregor, the gruff Dwarf, and especially Elester. She wondered if Muffy had escaped the Hellhags. Sleep must have come then, because the next thing she remembered was Arabella's hand on her shoulder and the girl's voice saying it was time to go.

As they came out from the shrubs that protected their hiding place, Miranda felt a stirring within the Bloodstones, almost as if they were trying to communicate with her. She shrugged and stepped into the forest. Suddenly, she knew, even before she heard the ghastly chittering, that the Wobbles were all about them. But that wasn't what made her blood run cold. Off to the right, outside the circle of Simurghs, in the darker shadows, she saw a pair of glowing red eyes. The companions were trapped.

CHAPTER TWENTY-THREE
THE WINGED STORM

here was no escape. At least a hundred Simurghs surrounded the three girls. In the pale predawn light, they appeared translucent, like fat green ghosts. They pressed forward, chittering excitedly, sharp teeth bared.

"Not feeling very clever now, are you, DEARS?" spat Kroak, elbowing his way through the press of round Simurghs. He stuck his thumbs in his ears, wobbled his pig eyes, and lunged at the girls. "BOO!" he squealed.

Penelope and Arabella reacted as if they had touched a live wire, screaming and leaping a foot off the ground. But, Miranda didn't budge. She was determined that this puky little creep would not have the satisfaction of knowing how much she feared him.

He leered at her now and pointed. "What shall we do with that one?" he asked. "Yes. You, DEAR!" His head swivelled to face the Simurghs. "SHALL I PULL OUT HER HAIR?"

"NO!"

"SHALL I CUT OFF HER FEET?"

"NO!" screeched the Wobbles. "SKIN HER!"

From the dark shadows beneath the tall trees, the hulking black monster watched the negligible Simurghs toying with the humans.

At first the THUG had found it amusing, but now it irritated him. It was time to end this. Driven by Hate's incessant need for blood, the hooded creature moved swiftly out of the shadows, ignoring the Wobbles except for those that happened to be in its direct path to the Elven girl. Before the unsuspecting creatures spotted the Demon's servant, nine Wobbles lay on the ground, skin hanging in tatters from bodies that resembled burst balloons.

The sight of their dead companions drove the Wobbles berserk. They forgot about the humans as they closed in on the THUG. They attacked in a swarm, like a school of piranhas, tearing at the THUG's thick hide with razor sharp teeth, and pounding him with their heavy clubs. But a hundred Simurghs were a mere nuisance to the THUG. They could slow him, rip his flesh, and bruise his body, but they could not kill him. He could not die.

"FOLLOW ME!" shouted Miranda, turning away from the skirmish and bounding through the trees like a frightened deer. Her companions needed no urging. They were on her heels in a flash. The Elven girl didn't think about where she was leading her friends. She didn't care. For her, right now, the running was the goal. She ran as she ran in her dream, full out, blindly, heart pumping wildly, lungs bursting, hope dying.

And ahead of her, like the answer to a desperate prayer, like a tiny flame at the end of a black tunnel, the great stallion, Avatar, waited, still as night. Miranda's heart sang with gladness when she saw the Druid's horse. Calling its name over and over, she raced toward the animal and leaped onto its back, landing on her stomach and clutching the saddle to keep from sliding off the other side. When she finally maneuvered herself into an upright position, Miranda grabbed Penelope's outstretched hand and, with Arabella pushing the girl from below, pulled her up onto the horse's back.

"Where's Marigold?" cried Arabella, looking about wildly for the gray mare.

"Just get on," shouted Miranda. "She can't be far away."

Arabella finally made it onto the horse's back with help from the other two. Clucking softly, she flicked the reins and Avatar stomped his front hooves and lashed his long tail. Carrying his Master's young charges, the noble red roan stallion fled that place, flying through the trees like the wind.

The THUG swatted the Simurghs, squashing them like flies. At his feet, at least two dozen of the disgusting creatures lay dead, their bodies and severed body parts already putrefying in the warm, early morning air. But still, they came at him and died horribly, like their companions.

When he saw the humans dash into the forest, the THUG roared with fury, grabbing the nearest Wobble, which just happened to be Kroak, and ripping its head off in one swift movement. Then he flung the remnants of the creature aside and waded through the pile of bodies, forging a bloody trail as he hastened in pursuit of the Elven girl. Hate's enemy! His enemy! The Druid's evil horse might be fast, but it could not run forever. Soon it would grow weary, like all living things. When it did, the THUG would be there, ready to pounce.

As Avatar carried the girls deeper and deeper into the forest, Miranda felt that time had stopped. Past, present and future fused into a never-ending race to nowhere. She might have dozed off, but she couldn't have said for sure. Then, with a jolt that almost catapulted the companions into the trees, Avatar faltered and came to a complete stop. His once shiny coat was slathered with sweat and his breathing sounded heavy and laboured. It was clear that the horse could go no further.

The THUG saw the big animal stumble. Tasting the sweet blood of victory, he sprang forward, narrowing the distance between them by half. But, Avatar, who had caught the creature's scent earlier as the horse watched the THUG watching the humans, sought and found within his constant heart a well of reserve strength. The chase was on again.

Miranda knew it would be a short race. No matter how determined the big horse was, he could not keep running. His strength would fail any moment now. Instinctively, she clutched the Bloodstones, but she did not feel the familiar heavy tugging sensation. They were useless, just like their owner. Wasn't that what Gregor had called her at the Council of Bethany? Useless! Tears filled her eyes and she cried softly. She cried for Avatar, who was about to lose his life because of her. She cried for the Druid and all the others, her best friends, who had risked everything to follow her. Finally, she cried for herself—because, for a brief moment, she really believed that she had stood a chance of saving the world. But now she knew better. Nobody could win a fight against Hate and the THUGS, especially a ten-year-old "useless" nobody.

"There is one last thing I can do," she whispered, as the great stallion slowed to a walk. Avatar halted at last, utterly spent. He turned to face the creature who had come to kill one or all of the humans. Before her companions could stop her, Miranda slipped to the ground.

"ARE YOU OUT OF YOUR MIND?" screamed Arabella, hysterically. "WHAT ARE YOU DOING?"

Miranda ignored her. She stroked the horse's neck, soothing the trembling animal and whispering urgently in his ear. "Take my friends and run away now, Avatar. It's me they're after." Then she kissed the downy face, shook her fist at the approaching THUG, and dashed into the trees.

The storm came out of nowhere. It struck with the ferocity of a twister, blotting out the sun, roaring and crashing like thunder. The howling wind tore into the tall trees, uprooting them and hurling them about as if they were matchsticks. Giant boulders rolled helter-skelter, shattering everything in their paths.

Avatar reared up and neighed fiercely, seeking the source of the chaos that had erupted all about them. His instincts screamed at him. *Protect the humans!* The horse leaped over a huge boulder, his hooves pounding on the hard forest floor as he tried to escape. He surged forward, dodging hurtling trees and swerving around broken hanging branches. The big-hearted stallion gave it all he had, but he could not outrun the tempest. It caught the animal and the two riders, and swept them up and away.

"It's the end of the world," thought Miranda, laughing at the storm, almost daring the flying trees and rocks to smash the life out of her. If they didn't, the THUG would. The evil creature was close behind her now. She didn't have to look over her shoulder to know that. She could feel its closeness like a breeze stirring the hairs on the back of her neck.

Miranda ducked under a low-hanging branch, plowing through the sharp needles that pricked her hands like a swarm of black flies. Coming out the other side, she suddenly skidded to a stop. A high rock wall loomed ahead. She looked about frantically, but there was no way around or over the barrier. There was no escape. For a second, she stared at the obstruction, shaking her head, not in disbelief, but in resignation. She took a deep breath and exhaled slowly, letting her shoulders go limp. With every fibre of her being screaming out in horror, Miranda clasped the Bloodstones, turned around, and waited for the THUG.

The creature's red eyes burned into the Elven girl. This time there was no wicked Druid to help her. No galling Simurghs in the way. Just the two of them, alone in the forest.

The half-dead thing laughed soundlessly. There was one thing left to do before he dispatched the girl. He would throw off the loose black hood and let her look upon his face. After that, she would beg him to kill her. One enormous clawed hand reached for the hood while the other shot toward Miranda. Before she squeezed her eyes shut, she caught a glimpse of a hideous gold skull embedded under the skin on the creature's left forearm. It seemed to be leering at her.

The storm reached the paralyzed girl first, snatching her out of the Monster's clutches even as its giant hand closed about her. The THUG exploded in rage, kicking and clawing at the stone wall, as if it were to blame for the loss of the girl. It turned its red gaze skyward and fell back, shaken and confused. The black storm was moving swiftly to the east, *against the wind*. For long minutes, the THUG stared at the sky. Then, it hunched its massive shoulders and began moving toward the east.

CHAPTER TWENTY-FOUR
TYPHON'S HAUNT

"DON'T EVEN THINK ABOUT IT!"

Miranda froze. She had been struggling to free herself from the iron grasp of whatever had captured her when she heard the booming warning. But she also heard something else, a small voice calling her name.

"Mir! Is that you?" came the thin whisper.

It sounded like Bell. *But that's impossible*, thought Miranda, looking about. When she spotted her best friend, she didn't know whether to shout with relief or wail in despair. They were all there, Avatar, Penelope and Arabella. They, too, had escaped the THUG only to find themselves miles above the clouds in the clutches of this unknown terror.

"AND NO WHISPERING!" roared the big voice. "OR I'LL EAT ALL OF YOU THIS MINUTE!"

Miranda tried to unscramble her thoughts. She touched the scaly, webbed limb that was clamped about her like a vise. One thing was crystal clear. The sudden violent storm was really a gargantuan flying creature of some sort, whose powerful wings had created the maelstrom that had shaken the ground and torn up the trees. She couldn't see enough of the monster to confirm her worst fears, but she knew her captor. The Bloodstones had already revealed its name. Only this time, it was not an illusion. They had been captured by Sut, the dragon!

"Are you going to eat us?" she asked, her voice reflecting the trembling of her body.

"THAT'S FOR ME TO KNOW," roared the Dragon, suddenly snapping its monstrous wings against its body and plummeting toward the distant earth.

Miranda and her companions went numb with fear. They plunged straight down, faster than sound, scattering clouds and a large flock of Canada geese. The enraged birds honked furiously after the hurtling missile, before regrouping and continuing their migration.

Miranda's eyes were glued on the mountain range below rocketing toward them. The dragon would never be able to pull out in time.

"HELP!" she screamed, squeezing her eyes shut and willing herself to faint before they smashed into one of the jagged peaks.

The Dragon sensed the humans' terror and grinned wickedly. It was a trifling pleasure but, in its vast experience, fear was the perfect tenderizer. Seconds before they surely must crash, the colossal black dragon spread its wings and leveled out. Sparks as big as cars flew from its scaly belly as it skimmed the rocky ground. In a flash, the Dragon changed direction, soaring up the face of a gigantic mountain and landing on a ledge before the mouth of a cave.

The creature folded its wings, opened its giant claws and, as if it were throwing dice, rolled the captives into the cave where they landed in a tangle of arms, legs and hooves. The dragon bent its massive body and wriggled through the small opening. Inside, it rose to its full height and glared at the prisoners.

"ALWAYS NEED A LITTLE PICK-ME-UP AFTER A LONG FLIGHT," boomed the Dragon, looking furtively about the cave before picking up Avatar by the saddle, tilting back its enormous head, and dangling the bucking, kicking animal over its open mouth.

"No!" screamed Miranda, kicking the Dragon's monstrous foot with the same result as if she had kicked the wall of the cave.

"I will take the animal and the humans," came a cold, forbidding voice from the cave opening.

The three companions wheeled about in astonishment. Framed in the entrance to the cave stood the tall, cloaked form of the Druid.

"Naim!" shouted Miranda, feeling a surge of hope wash over her. She took a step toward him, but the Druid, eyes fixed on the Dragon, raised his hand in warning and the girl froze.

At the sound of the voice, the huge Dragon tensed, as if its mother had just caught it doing something naughty, but the creature did not look toward the mouth of the cave. A faint stream of smoke drifted from its wide nostrils, as it slowly set the horse down onto the floor of the cave. "What do you want, Druid?" it demanded. "You have no business with me."

The Druid snorted and crossed the cave to where the red roan stallion stomped nervously. He placed his hands on both sides of the animal's face and looked into its dark eyes for long seconds. He stroked the horse until it was calm and then turned to the Dragon.

"You have made it my business by bringing the humans to your Haunt, Typhon," said the Druid. "I would know how you came upon them before I take them from this place."

"Typhon?" Miranda looked at Arabella, mouthing the name and raising her eyebrows questioningly.

Arabella shrugged. "What happened to Sut?"

"Where's Penelope?" whispered Miranda, suddenly noticing that the other girl was nowhere in sight.

Arabella looked about in surprise. "She was here a minute ago."

The Dragon glared at the Druid. "There is nothing to tell. Another had cornered the girl. I happened to be flying over the area and I thought it would be amusing to take the prize away from it. I was mistaken. That is all." The creature turned away. "Now take what you came for and leave."

"The day you just happen to be flying—"

"BE VERY CAREFUL, DRUID," warned the Dragon, the smoke from its nostrils turning to a thin flame.

But the Druid did not back down. "What was this creature that had the girl cornered?"

When the Dragon didn't reply at once, Miranda turned to the Druid. "It was one of the THUGS."

"THUG! SHMUG!" roared Typhon. "It has nothing to do with me."

"Yet, you rescued the girl," said the Druid, studying the Dragon curiously.

"I DID NOT RESCUE ANYONE," said Typhon. "IN FACT I WAS JUST ABOUT TO EAT THEM WHEN YOU SO RUDELY INTERRUPTED."

"Have you been flying so high above the clouds that you do not see what is happening on earth?" asked the Druid quietly.

"I AM RUNNING OUT OF PATIENCE," snapped the Dragon. "WHAT HAPPENS IN YOUR WORLD DOES NOT CONCERN ME." It fixed the Druid with a glassy stare. "IT NEVER HAS."

The Druid's eyes blazed and he gripped the staff angrily. "You will remember those words with great bitterness, Typhon, when the Elves are gone from Ellesmere and the wind blows through the vast empty halls of Dundurum. When all life has been extinguished, where will you look for the livestock you have stolen for centuries? Where will you hunt when the forests have been turned to ashes, the land bled dry? What will you do when you are hungry and there are only your Dragon kin left?"

The Dragon laughed, a deep rumble that shook the walls of the cave, dislodging several large rocks and sending them tumbling to the floor.

"DON'T YOU EVER TIRE OF LISTENING TO YOURSELF, DRUID?" The creature raised one gigantic limb and pointed to the mouth of the cave. "AND DON'T FORGET THE ANIMAL AND THE HUMAN BRATS."

"We're not brats," protested Miranda before she could stop herself. "But I'd rather be the Demon than be like you."

The Dragon whipped its head toward the girl, bending its neck until they were nose to nose. Miranda heard Arabella gasp and sensed the Druid staring at her in surprise. She gulped, raising her hands protectively and backing up until she bumped into the hard wall of the cave. "At least Hate knows which side she's on." She continued in a rush. "Maybe someday she'll even be sorry for what she's done. But if you do nothing, you've already chosen evil. And the worse thing is, you can never be sorry because you'll never realize that you've done anything wrong." She flushed and looked down at her boots. "I know this because, at first, I didn't want to do anything either."

For a minute, there was absolute silence throughout the cave. Then the Dragon raised its head, lashed its titanic tail and roared. "GET OUT! NOW!"

CHAPTER TWENTY-FIVE

THE THIEF

"It took courage to face the Dragon back there," said the Druid softly, as the companions and the stallion, Avatar, picked their way cautiously down the steep mountain track. He put his hand on Miranda's shoulder and chuckled softly. "The old tyrant did not know whether to roast you alive or throttle you."

"It didn't do much good," answered the girl.

"Perhaps not," agreed the Druid. "But knowing Typhon as I do, I am certain that he will fret over what you said and, in the end, who can say. He may prove to be a formidable ally."

"The Simurghs called him Sut," said the girl.

"Those despicable creatures call him Sut because he terrorizes them. It is the way of a Dragon to use another name when it practices deceit. As you know from first-hand experience, the Simurghs are not very intelligent."

Miranda nodded. "I think that's what makes them so horrible. You never know what they're going to do next."

"Yes," said the Druid. "What they lack in brains, they make up for in cunning. I am responsible for what happened to you at their hands, because I underestimated them. The Simurghs never hunt outside their own lands, but once they lose a captive, they will track it to the ends of the earth to get it back. When I told you not to enter Diputs Seno—to wait for me near the village sign—I thought you would be safe enough. It did not occur to me that they would move the sign well within their own borders."

"But how does Typhon deceive them?"

"Typhon agreed not to eat them as long as they provide living things for the Dragon's hunger." The Druid laughed softly. "The deceit is that Typhon does not eat Simurghs."

"That's not very funny," cried Miranda, remembering with a shiver how close she and her companions had come to being eaten by the Dragon.

The Druid laughed louder. "If it is any comfort, I do not believe Typhon would have eaten you."

Miranda shot him a dark look. "But you don't really know for sure, do you?"

At that moment Penelope shrieked. "THAT'S MINE! GIVE IT BACK!"

"Be quiet!" hissed the Druid, turning quickly. "You have just announced our whereabouts to any of Hate's minions who are surely in this area." He glowered at Arabella. "Did you take something that belongs to Penelope?"

"No," said Arabella. "It's not hers."

"Liar!" said Penelope.

"You're the liar," snapped Arabella, and then she threw something at the other girl. The large stone landed with a dull "thud" on the ground at Penelope's feet, where it sparkled like a burning coal.

"What is that?" asked the Druid, frowning as he reached to pick up the blood red gemstone.

"It's mine," insisted Penelope.

"Answer me, girl. Where did you get this ruby?"

"I found it, all right? Finders keepers."

"You stole it from the Dragon," accused Arabella. "That's what you were doing when you disappeared in the cave."

"So what?" snapped Penelope. "You're just jealous you didn't think of it. Anyway, everybody knows that Dragons have a treasure hoard. For your information, they don't go out and buy it. They steal it. All I did was take something that wasn't his in the first place. I don't call that stealing."

"I call it stealing," said the Druid coldly. "Dragons may eat foolish, meddlesome girls, but hear me. They do not steal."

"B-but, I thought—"

"That is the problem. You did not think," snapped the Druid. "Listen to me. Dragons do not covet riches for their value. Their hoard, as you call it, is a measure of their Clique's honour and courage. And it is earned, every gem and gold piece. Typhon is the guardian of the treasure. If he loses it, he loses face and the entire Clique loses honour." He stopped and stared at Penelope, who was squirming like an eel on a fishing line. "Now do you understand what you have done?"

"H-How was I to know? I-I—"

"What else did you take from the Dragon?"

"Nothing. Honest. You've got to believe me. I didn't know—"

"Enough!" said the Druid. "You will go back and return what you have taken."

"I can't! I won't go back there!" cried the girl. "You can't make me."

"No, I would not make you," answered the Druid. "But Typhon will discover the theft soon enough and I would not want to be in your shoes when he leaves his cave to hunt for the one who stole honour from his Clique."

Penelope turned her back on the others and burst into tears. "I-I d-didn't know," she sobbed.

Miranda felt sorry for her friend even though she had brought this latest fiasco on herself. Then she realized, with a shock, that she thought of Penelope as a friend when only a few days ago she couldn't stand the sight of her. But now, after having come so far and shared so much, things were different. She couldn't imagine what would have happened to her and Arabella if Penelope hadn't rescued them from the Wobbles. *She's still a pain in the butt, though*, she thought, sighing deeply.

"Come on Penelope. I'll go back with you," she said, taking the other girl's arm and starting the steep climb back up the mountainside.

"Wait for me," cried Arabella, not wanting to be left alone with the Druid.

When they reached the Dragon's cave, Penelope drew back and started crying again. "I can't go in there. I know it's going to eat me." She grabbed Miranda's sleeve. "Let's just leave the jewel here where the Dragon'll be sure to see it when he comes out," she whispered desperately.

Miranda gave her a long look. "Penelope, remember it took guts to walk into Diputs Seno to rescue us. You can do this." She exchanged looks with Arabella.

Before Penelope could protest further, the other two gave the terrified girl a hard shove in the middle of her back and propelled her into the Dragon's Haunt.

Penelope skidded to a stop, inches away from Typhon, spinning her feet in a desperate attempt to run backwards out of the cave. She risked a glance at the mammoth creature, who appeared to be sleeping. Quickly, trying not to make a sound, the girl took the huge ruby and set it on the floor of the cave near the Dragon's head. She looked furtively about and then opened her backpack and produced a sock filled with smaller gems. She poured the gems into a pile on the floor next to the ruby.

For a second, she looked from the gemstones to the Dragon who was snoring loudly. Then she slowly reached toward the pile of small stones, and snatched a deep blue sapphire that was cut in an oval shape. Quickly, she dropped it into the sock and, turning away, stuffed it into her backpack. When she looked back at the Dragon, her heart leaped into her throat. The creature's huge eyes were wide open and they were boring into her. Without saying a word, she slowly pulled the sock from her backpack, shook the gemstone into her hand and put it back on the pile.

"So, you are the thief," said the Dragon, exhaling a spurt of flame toward the trembling girl.

Penelope jumped back as if she were on fire. "I gave them back to you. All of them," she cried. Then she turned and ran toward the mouth of the cave.

Typhon whipped its giant tail to block the entrance. The girl was trapped inside the Haunt with an irate Dragon.

"YOU, ELVEN GIRL, GO AND TELL THE DRUID THAT I WILL RETURN THE THIEF WHEN SHE HAS BEEN PUNISHED."

"What are you going to do to her?" asked Miranda weakly, suddenly overcome with guilt for having pushed the girl into the cave.

"THAT IS NOT YOUR BUSINESS," roared Typhon. "NOW BE GONE!"

Miranda didn't need to be told twice. Before the Dragon had finished roaring, she and Arabella were halfway down the mountain track.

CHAPTER TWENTY-SIX

THE CIRCLE OF FIVE

he girls slipped and skidded down the steep trail, as if the Dragon were breathing fire down their necks. When they reached the spot where the Druid waited, their lungs were screaming for air.

"HELP! HELP!" they cried in unison.

The Druid moved swiftly to meet them.

Miranda clutched his sleeve. "Naim, you've got to do something!" she gasped, between deep breaths.

"What is it?" asked the Druid, removing her hand and squeezing it tightly.

"Typhon's got Penelope," cried Arabella.

"And he won't let her go until he's punished her," Miranda said, freeing her hand from the Druid's grasp and tugging on his cloak. "Come on! Hurry! We've got to get her out of there."

To the girl's surprise, the Druid threw back his head and laughed. "I do not know what you expect me to do, but I have no intention of climbing that hill again tonight. Nor will I interfere in the Dragon's business."

"How can you laugh?" cried Miranda angrily.

"I can laugh because I know what the Dragon will do to the girl and you do not," said the Druid.

"What will he do to her?" asked Arabella, her eyes misty. "It's all my fault. I should've let her keep the stupid ruby."

"No," said Miranda. "It's my fault, I pushed her into the cave."

"I helped," said Arabella.

The Druid wagged a long finger at them. "It is the girl's own fault for taking something that did not belong to her. She, alone, is responsible for her actions."

"What's he going to do to her?" repeated Miranda, seeing the image of Avatar dangling over the Dragon's open mouth.

"Very well, I will tell you, but first you must give me your word that you will not tease your friend about her punishment?"

"I promise," said both girls simultaneously, crossing their hearts (and their fingers).

The Druid sat on the boulder and tried hard to keep a straight face. "Typhon will make her polish the treasure," he said. "With a cloth and a large bowl of Dragon spittle." Then his face broke and he laughed until tears streamed down his face.

Miranda burst out laughing. "Dragon spit! Ohhh! That's so gross!"

As the three companions continued their trek down the rugged path, the only sounds echoing off the mountain were the occasional sudden hoots of laughter at the thought of Penelope up to her elbows in Dragon spit.

When they reached the base camp, Naim led Avatar to a shelter the Riders had built for their horses. Arabella raced ahead, searching anxiously for Marigold and letting out a whoop of joy when she spotted the gray mare. Miranda ran toward the campfire where Elester sat on the ground, hands about his knees, eyes focused on the flames. When Miranda called his name, he looked up and smiled grimly. Beside him stood Gregor, King of the Dwarves. From the way the Dwarf stomped his heavy boots on the hard ground,

Miranda could tell that he was deeply agitated. Quickly, she scanned the campsite and then her eyes came back to rest, questioningly, on the Elven Prince.

"Where's Nick?" she asked, alarm signals going off in her brain.

Elester glanced at the Dwarf, who ignored him and looked into the air, whistling softly.

"He's not here," said the Elf quietly.

"I don't understand," said Miranda, turning cold. "Where is he?"

"Went off an hour ago. Riders searched. Boy vanished. Bad business," muttered Gregor.

Miranda sank onto the hard ground near the fire, thankful for the warmth. "Why would he go off on his own? That's not like Nick. Something must've happened to him."

Elester took the girl's hands and covered them with his own. "Believe me, we have searched everywhere. There were no signs of a struggle. Whatever happened, it looks as though Nicholas left willingly."

"What's this about the boy?" asked the Druid, suddenly appearing through the trees.

"He's gone—disappeared!" cried Miranda.

The Druid and Elester exchanged meaningful looks. "Indolent!" said the Druid.

"That is my thought," agreed the Elf. "If it had been the Demon, we would have found the boy by now. She does not take hostages."

"Are you talking about that wizard? The one you said wanted to be a Druid?" asked Miranda.

Naim lowered his tall frame onto the ground beside the girl. "Yes, the wizard Indolent. I knew him, once, a long time ago. He studied with the Druids, as a Pledge, but he was never a member of the Circle of Five." He threw a stick onto the fire. "He was a clever fellow, too clever for his own good. He quickly mastered our arts and looked for ways to expand his own power. It was not long before he began to use the things we taught him for purposes that went against the Druid Code."

"What sort of purposes?" asked Miranda.

"He experimented with a forbidden magic—to control people's minds. Of course he couched his vile purpose in the sort of timeworn phrases that oppressors have always used. 'For the benefit of the people,' he said. 'No more wars,' he said. We ordered him to cease his experiments on innocent animals. He would not listen. At a conclave with the other members of the Circle, we unanimously cast him out. Since my voice was the loudest raised against him, he blames me for his fall."

"But what does he have to do with Nick?" asked Miranda, not liking what she was hearing about the wizard Indolent.

"I do not know the answer to that," said the Druid. "But if Indolent has learned of our Trust, he will try to make trouble, you can be sure of that."

"You mean he'd use Nick as a hostage to get the Serpent's Egg?" asked Miranda, her mind racing with possibilities.

"That is what I fear," answered the Druid, his face troubled. "What I do not know is what he intends to do with the Egg. He cannot use the magic."

"Unless the wizard is in thrall to the Demon," said Elester quietly. "In that case he intends to destroy the Egg before we can use it."

"What are you talking about?" cried Arabella, suddenly joining the group. "Some wizard's got Nick?" She sat on the ground beside Miranda, picked up a stick and whacked the flames angrily, sending a shower of sparks fluttering through the air like fireflies. "Wait 'till I get my hands on that wizard. He'll rue the day he was born."

Miranda put her arm around Arabella and pulled her close. "*Rue* the day?"

"Yeah! When I get finished with him, he'll be sorry he ever messed with the kids from Ottawa."

King Gregor stomped his feet on the ground and held his sides, rocking back and forth with laughter. "He's yours. When I'm done."

Arabella sighed. "When is it going to end?"

"When Egg's found and Hate's gone," answered the Dwarf, in his typical curt manner.

"But, we'll find Nicholas before that?" Miranda said, looking to Naim for confirmation. But the old man did not reply. He was lost in his own thoughts, his unblinking gaze fixed on the flames.

Later, while her friend slept, Miranda sat beside the Druid on a log by the fire. She touched the gold ring on his right hand. "Please tell me about the Druids and the Circle of Five."

At first she thought he hadn't heard her. But then he sighed and stretched his long legs toward the fire. "Very well. But I will make it brief if we are to ride to Indolent's Castle in the morning." He picked up his staff and rubbed one hand along the smooth pale wood. "Now then, what do you wish to know?"

"Everything."

"Humph!" Naim snorted. "There are always five Druids, no more, no less. But there are many Pledges. These are men, women and children, not to mention Indolent, who suddenly feel the call and answer it. I had never heard of Druids until one day I felt something calling me. I was only a lad. But it was such a compelling summons that I left my parents' house without so much as a 'farewell' and followed the bidding for many months, not knowing where I was going, or even why. I only knew that I could not resist."

He stopped and poked the burning logs with the end of the long staff, his eyes looking far away at something only he could see. "One evening, just before sunset, I stood on a hill and saw in the valley below, a circle of tall white marble stone tablets shining like a beacon. I even knew the name of that place — Druid's Close. I knew that I had come home, and I knelt in the green grass and cried like an infant."

Miranda felt tears flood her eyes. "That's sad," she said, sniffling loudly. "Did you ever go back to your mother and father?"

The tall man shook his head. "No. I never saw my parents again. They have been dead for a long time now."

"But what did they think happened to you?"

"I do not know," answered the Druid quietly. He cleared his throat and when he spoke again, his voice was husky with emotion. "I spent many long years studying and learning the use of Druid power and, one day, after the death of one of the Elder Druids, I was admitted into the Circle of Five." He polished the yellow stone on his finger with his left thumb. "I was given the Druid's stone and my staff." He removed the ring and held it out to the girl.

Miranda was surprised that the ring was so heavy. She gazed into the yellow oval stone. A small black line shaped like the letter "S" was visible in the centre of the gem. A minute red line ran from one end of the black "S" to the other and over the head of the letter was a tiny amber-coloured crown inset with dots of rubies. Miranda was fascinated. She had noticed the ring the very first time she had met the Druid in her home, but she had not looked at it closely. And then, to her horror, the small black "S" suddenly moved, wriggling like a worm.

"Ahhh!" she cried, dropping the ring as if it had bit her.

"Yes," said the Druid, leaning over to retrieve the ring. "It is a live serpent within the stone. We call it the Druid's Egg, and it is the symbol of my Circle and of that other Egg which we seek."

CHAPTER TWENTY-SEVEN
STONE STEW

hey set out early in the morning, the horses' hooves leaving dark trails in the wet grass. Miranda's heart was heavy with sadness when she saw Fetch trotting behind the Riders. She half expected to see Nicholas grinning from the saddle. Why had he left camp without telling anyone? she wondered. That and other questions haunted her. What sort of mind magic could Indolent have used to ensnare the boy? It must have been awfully powerful to trick her friend who, next to Arabella, was the most suspicious person she knew.

It turned out to be one of those rare perfect days. The pine-scented air was crisp and clear. Fluffy white clouds frolicked across the brilliant blue sky like frisky lambs, and the sun smiled on the travellers, warming their hearts and lifting their spirits. It was early afternoon when Miranda heard the shout from one of the Riders who had been scouting the land ahead. "Over there! The Castle!"

The Elven girl peered around the Druid, shading her eyes with her hands. In the distance, perched precariously on the edge of a steep cliff, the Castle of Indolence jutted into the sky like an insult. On three sides, the Spikes rose like a jagged wall. At that moment the sun vanished behind the black cloud that hovered like a living thing over the Castle. A cold wind cut into the travellers like knives, chilling them to the bone and filling them with melancholy. Miranda cried out in despair. The black abomination was a gaping wound, a festering sore on the earth, cut off from the living world by blackness and gloom. Miranda felt something menacing reach out from the desolation and settle on her like a blanket.

"It is not pretty," muttered the Druid.

Miranda nodded silently. She could find no words to describe the sinister, crumbling structure and the black aura that hung over it like death. She reached for the Bloodstones, wanting to feel their smoothness in her hand. Closing her fist about the stones, she almost fell off Avatar's back when she saw Nicholas, brown hair falling in his eyes, blood oozing from a cut on his left temple and trickling down his cheek.

"Nick!" she cried, reaching out to the boy only to grasp at nothing.

"What is it?" said the Druid, pulling Avatar to a stop.

"I saw him!" she cried. "Nicholas! He's in the Castle, and he's hurt."

"You used the Bloodstones? Is this the first time?"

"I don't know if I'm using them or not," said Miranda and she told him how the Stones had made Penelope appear as a Dragon to the Simurghs.

"If you are able to create a Dragon and see into Indolent's Castle without trying to use the Stones, imagine what you might do if you tried," said the Druid.

Miranda thought about what the man said. One stone for each of the five senses. Creating the illusory Dragon, took both the sight and sound stones and, yes, the touch stone too. What was the sixth stone for? How could she control them? She had tried to make herself disappear but had been unsuccessful. What was she doing wrong? If they only worked when *they* wanted to, what good were they?

When the company stopped to rest the horses and grab a quick bite, Miranda found Elester among the Riders, unsaddling and rubbing down Noble. Sensing that the girl wished to speak with him privately, the Elf motioned her away from the others.

"What is it?" he asked, searching her eyes.

Miranda told him how the Stones had created the illusory Dragon and revealed that Nicholas was a prisoner in the Castle of Indolence. "I'm afraid that we're going to get to the Serpents' Cave and I won't know how to use them when I need them. How can I find the Serpents if I can't see?"

Elester nodded and waited patiently for the girl to continue.

"Can you help me?" she asked, kicking the ground in frustration. "I've been given a gift that I don't understand."

"Tell me what you did when you saw Penelope walking into the Simurgh's village," said Elester. "What were your thoughts?"

Miranda sighed. "That's easy. I thought she was stupid."

The Elf frowned. "Miranda, think."

"I thought I had to do something to protect her. I didn't even realize the Stones were in my hand at first. Then I thought about the Simurghs waiting for her and I let my thoughts go into the Stones. I could feel them taking my thoughts and shooting them out all around. That's all I did."

"Miranda, the Bloodstones have their own knowledge. They have been here a long, long time. In a way, you were controlling them. You told them by your thoughts to protect the girl. And they did."

"But I didn't know what they were going to do. Before I go into that cave with the Serpents, I have to know."

"Show me the Stones," said the Elf.

Miranda pulled the thin silver chain out of the neck of her sweater, opened the metallic pouch and poured the Bloodstones into her hand.

Elester looked at her mischievously. "Shall we use them to play a trick on the others?"

Miranda grinned. "We can try, but I'm telling you they won't work."

"Wait here," said the Elf, fetching a pot from one of the saddlebags. He filled it with water from a water skin and carried the pot to Miranda. "Now, find me some big stones."

Miranda looked at him questioningly, but she gathered a handful of stones.

"Put them in the pot," said Elester.

The girl did as she was told, wondering what sort of trick they were going to play on the others with water and stones.

The Elf grinned and Miranda found herself smiling along with him. Elester strolled toward the Riders and placed the pot on the campfire, before returning to Miranda's side.

"Now, trust the Bloodstones. We are going to make a stew with water and stones. Think of the pot and imagine the stew simmering on the fire. You want the others to smell the mouth-watering aroma until they cannot resist getting up and looking into the pot. Then you want them to fill their bowls and eat the stew."

Miranda was giggling now. "It won't work," she said but she was keen to try. She closed her hand over the Stones and stared at the pot, forming a picture of her mother back home in their cozy kitchen, and trying to remember all the things she put into her stew. She imagined the ingredients, starting with plump, seared chicken breasts, then adding carrots, potatoes, snow peas, sweet potatoes, pearl onions and mushrooms on top of the chicken. Next, she filled the pot with rich, foamy stock seasoned with herbs, spices, and a teaspoon of red currant jelly and thickened with rich cream. Finally she set light, fluffy dumplings to steam on the top. By the time she had built the illusion, she was so hungry, she almost believed that a real stew bubbled in the pot over the hot embers.

Miranda concentrated on holding the image together. Nothing happened. The Riders moved about, checking the horses or cleaning their sharp swords. Arabella crouched by the fire, poking it with a stick. Naim sat apart, staring off into the distance, lost in some dark place. Just as she was about to give up, to the girl's astonishment and dismay, the Druid stirred, sniffing the air as he looked toward the pot. Then he got up and, taking a small metal bowl, filled it with the stone stew. The others, including Arabella, suddenly roused, drifting toward the pot, their mouths watering. They filled their bowls to the brim and settled contentedly around the fire.

Elester was doubled over with silent laughter. Then the Druid locked eyes with Miranda and leisurely set his bowl on the ground, a slow grin spreading over his face. When Arabella stuffed a dumpling into her mouth, Miranda couldn't hold the image any longer. She burst out laughing, arms wrapped about her sides. Arabella bit into the dumpling, or tried to, her face wrinkling in disgust as she spat the stone onto the ground. The Riders looked into their bowls and saw water and stones and shook their heads in disbelief.

"All right!" shouted Miranda joyfully. Then she looked at the stern faces of her victims and grinned sheepishly. "Sorry," she said, bursting into laughter again. "But isn't it great? I did it! I actually used the Bloodstones."

"Next time you feel the urge to practice with magic, try something that will not break our teeth," said the Druid irritably, but Miranda caught the twinkle in his eye.

Just before the company broke camp, a shout came from the surrounding trees. The Riders drew their swords and spreading out, converged on the sound. They emerged from the trees leading a Dwarf, who appeared close to collapse.

"Dury!" shouted King Gregor, stomping toward the exhausted man, the companions on his heels.

Miranda felt a hard lump form in her throat at the Dwarf's words.

"The Demon . . . army . . . reached the Gates of Dundurum."

For a second, everybody went quiet, staring at Gregor in shock. Then the King of the Dwarves suddenly looked at Miranda. "Sorry.

Know I promised. But must go home."

Miranda nodded. "I know," she said, fighting to control her anger. She desperately wanted to tell Gregor not to worry. She would get the Egg and destroy Hate. But she knew, in a small detached part of her mind, that the chances of capturing the Egg were one in a million.

"We have run out of time," said the Druid. "I underestimated the Demon. I thought that we would have the Egg before she reached Dundurum. But I was wrong. She has pushed her armies hard and now they stand at Gregor's front door." He clasped the Dwarf's shoulder. "Go, my friend. Your people need you now. The Trust will go on. How long can you hold against the Demon?"

"Two days. Maybe three," snapped Gregor, stomping toward the horses. "We'll make her pay."

Elester caught Gregor's arm. "Send word to my father. We will stand with our friends in Dundurum."

The companions watched silently until Gregor, with the messenger riding behind, were a dark speck on the horizon. Then, with heavy hearts, they mounted their horses and rode toward the trees. Miranda looked back at the campsite where, a moment ago, she had laughed as though there were no such Monster as Hate, the Demon. She wondered if any of the Trust would ever laugh again. Suddenly, she saw a figure flying out of the woods into the clearing, waving its arms frantically.

"Stop!" she shouted, tugging on the Druid's cloak.

"Wait for me!" screamed Penelope, looking desperately over her shoulder as she ran after the horses. The company turned and stared at the bedraggled girl in surprise, except for Miranda and Arabella, who exchanged knowing grins.

"What happened?" asked Arabella innocently, as Elester caught Penelope by the arm and swung her easily onto Noble's back.

"Just shut up," barked Penelope, lapsing into a silence that lasted all the way to Indolent's Castle.

CHAPTER TWENTY-EIGHT

THE CASTLE OF INDOLENCE

icholas felt the deep cut on his temple and winced with pain. His head throbbed and the rest of his body felt as though he had been dragged behind a train for a week. He opened one eye and tried to focus on the blurry lines streaking across his vision. The floor was moving, making him dizzy. Then he sat up with a start. The floor wasn't moving. It was the wall-to-wall carpet of giant cockroaches covering the floor that was moving. Jumping to his feet, he brushed at his clothing frantically, dislodging several of the large insects and stepping on them—the loud "Splop!" turning his stomach. He pounded on the floor with his boots, and the bugs scrabbled toward the walls and under the rotting baseboard. In a second, they had vanished.

Nicholas looked about, turning his throbbing head cautiously. He was surprised to find himself in a large gloomy room and not locked in a dungeon somewhere. What happened? *How did I get here?* he wondered, wrinkling his nose in disgust at the squalor of the place. Dirt and grime covered everything. Garbage was strewn about the floor and dark patches of something slimy covered the walls. No wonder the place was infested. Out of the corner of his eye, he saw the bugs inching from the holes in the walls. He stomped hard on the floor and the filthy insects pivoted and scuttled back into the cracks.

Suddenly, he remembered what had happened. It was the dog—Penelope's rotten little poodle. Nicholas gritted his teeth in anger. He had survived the Hellhags' attack at The Devil's Fork only to be led into a trap by the treacherous Muffy. He shuddered as images of the Hellhags flashed through his brain. The evil beasts had struck the camp with such swiftness and ferocity that, even now, Nicholas broke out in a cold sweat at the thought. At first, the Riders had stood fast, drawing their swords and slaying several of the four-legged fiends before they heard the howls of a great swarm of the creatures advancing to reinforce their half-dead sisters.

As they ran toward the horses, Laury gripped Nicholas's arm. "Keep your sword unsheathed and be ready for anything. It is an Elven blade and these devils will think twice before coming at you." The Captain of the Riders had grinned and clapped Nicholas on the back. "Good job back there," he said. "If you had not raised the alarm, we would not be standing here now."

Nicholas had felt his neck burn at the unexpected praise. Then they had fled from the Hellhags, only discovering when the King's Riders regrouped that the Druid and the three girls were gone.

Elester had led the company hard in pursuit of the missing companions. Last evening they had come upon the Druid, horseless, sitting on a big rock in a small clearing at the base of Mount Oranono, one of the highest peaks in the Mountains of the Moon. The Druid had disappeared up the mountain, saying that he hoped to return before long with the girls.

Shortly after Naim left the camp, Nicholas had been sitting around the fire with Elester and Gregor, listening to the Riders' tales of their adventures among the Red Giants of Vark, when he thought he saw something move at the edge of his sight. Turning toward the trees, he was surprised to see Penelope's little dog standing stiffly within the shadows, the red from the campfire reflected in its microscopic eyes.

Curiously, Nicholas moved away from the fire toward the miniature poodle. "Hey! Muffrat," he called. "What're you doing here? Where're Mir and the others?"

As the boy drew nearer, Muffy backed away, turning and dashing a dozen feet into the trees before stopping and facing the boy. Each time Nicholas got within touching distance, the poodle shot off like a bullet, leading the boy deeper and deeper into the forest. She wants me to follow her, thought Nicholas, alarmed that something might have happened to Miranda and the other girls. He looked back the way he had come, but he could see nothing. There was no moon that night and the forest was a black place of blacker shadows. For a moment he worried about getting lost, but the dog seemed to know where it was going.

"Wait a minute," he said, coming to a sudden halt. Ahead, the poodle had turned and was waiting silently, its tiny red eyes burning in the darkness. "That's no reflection," he whispered, a feeling of dread creeping over him. "Something's seriously wrong." The last thing he remembered was turning to run, a shout forming on his lips. But he was too late. Before he could struggle, a heavy blunt object caught him hard on the left temple and he toppled over into blackness as deep as the shadows.

Nicholas heard the sound of a key turning and the door suddenly burst open. A tall, lean man glided gracefully into the room. In the dim light, Nicholas could see that he was as tall as the Druid and would have been much taller if it were not for the grotesque hump on his shoulders and upper back. He wore a long blue robe with loose wide sleeves and, tucked under one arm, was a short thin rod. The long thick hair on the man's head was a dirty yellow, with black streaks. Nicholas noticed several large bald patches where scabs had formed on the creature's scalp. He shuddered, wondering if the man had pulled his own hair out by the roots in a fit of rage. The boy looked at the stains on the man's robe and the tattered hem and frayed seams, and curled his lips in disgust.

The humped-back creature closed the door, locked it, and threw the key into the air where it simply vanished. Then he turned to the boy. "Well, well! What have we here, little one?" he said, petting the pink poodle nestled in his arms. "And what can our guest do for us today, hmm?"

"Who are you?" demanded Nicholas, reaching for his Elven sword.

"Is this what you're looking for?" asked the man, a cruel smile spreading across his face. He raised his arm and the sword suddenly appeared in his hand. He waved it in the air.

Nicholas stared at the strange man boldly, feeling chagrined at the loss of the fine blade. "My friends will be looking for me by now, and when they get here, you're going to regret the day—"

"SILENCE!" snapped the man, dropping the sword and pointing the thin rod at the boy.

"Grrrrr!" snarled the poodle, baring its teeth.

Nicholas felt as if his tongue were glued to the roof of his mouth. He could move his lips but the sounds that came out were garbled and meaningless. Could the Druid stand against magic so powerful that it could control your tongue? he wondered. Was this man one of the Demon's slaves?

"I am Indolent the wizard and you are an insolent boy," said the misshapen creature, moving into the room and waving the rod at a pile of logs in the huge fireplace against the far wall. Instantly, the logs burst into flames. More giant cockroaches erupted from the cracks in the logs, their bodies igniting and popping apart.

The wizard Indolent opened his arms and the poodle leaped to the floor, yapping furiously as it sped after one of the insects skittering across the stones. Nicholas noticed that Muffy's rhinestone collar had been replaced with a thick, black leather one, studded

191

with sharp steel spikes. The dog caught the large bug and crunched on it, chewing and chewing until Nicholas thought the grisly sound would drive him crazy. Finally, Muffy's body convulsed as it swallowed the roach and the dog looked toward its new master for approval, its short fluffy tail wagging like a gossip's tongue.

"That's a clever, good doggie," cooed the wizard, reaching down to stroke Muffy, but his eyes never left the boy. "I will loosen your tongue to answer my questions."

Nicholas didn't react. He wriggled his tongue, and waited.

"Where is the Druid taking the girl?"

"Druid? Girl? I don't know what you're talking about," said Nicholas, hoping that he sounded convincing. Neither the Druid nor Miranda had been at the campsite when the dog had lured him into Indolent's clutches, so there was a slim chance that the wizard would believe him.

Indolent waved the rod again. The next instant, a pair of invisible hands gripped the boy's shoulders and hurled him through the air and across the room. Nicholas cried out in pain as he felt his body connect with the wall. He collapsed in a heap on the floor, the breath knocked out of him.

"The bad boy lies. Bad lies," sang the wizard, scooping up Muffy and kissing the creature's lips. "Does he not, my sweets?" The dog agreed with one sharp bark, then it wriggled out of the wizard's arms and darted toward Nicholas, barking and snarling.

Nicholas looked away in disgust. "What have you done to Muffy?" he breathed, pressing his arms tightly against his tender ribs.

The wizard's answer was another painful demonstration in flying. Nicholas felt himself being hoisted high into the air and then dashed against the floor. This time he knew he couldn't get up on his own. Groaning softly, the boy lay on his back in the dirt, one outstretched arm bent at an impossible angle.

"I will have the Serpent's Egg," said the wizard. "I will learn its power, but I need the girl."

"I'd die before I told you anything," whispered Nicholas.

"Moron!" spat the wizard. "I am not some common murderer. Indolent does not have to kill." He smiled at Nicholas as if they were best friends, but when he spoke his voice was like ice. "I will repeat my first question. Where is the Druid taking the girl?"

"Eat worms!" muttered Nicholas through clenched teeth. Then the boy shook his head as if he had suddenly awakened from a long sleep. He yawned and looked at the wizard lazily. "Please don't be mad at me. I'll tell you what you want to know."

CHAPTER TWENTY-NINE

DRUID V. WIZARD

he black cloud that hung like a shroud over the Castle of Indolence suddenly burst and rain poured down upon the travellers in torrents, soaking them to the bone. Lightning ripped across the sky, jagged daggers stabbing into the ground about them, scorching the earth and splitting huge trees as if they were twigs. Thunder cracked like the sound of a thousand cannons, battering the companions' eardrums and driving the horses mad.

Eyes white with terror, Marigold reared and bucked, throwing Arabella into a river of mud. The Riders, undaunted by the sudden deluge, managed to control their mounts, but not even the stout-hearted Elven horses would go any farther.

"HURRY!" shouted Miranda, "BEFORE WE'RE TOO LATE!"

"WHAT DO YOU SEE?" roared the Druid, at the same time urging Avatar into a gallop. The mighty stallion surged forward, streaking like a missile past the screaming horses and quickly leaving them behind.

"IT'S A FEELING," answered the girl. "I JUST KNOW NICK'S IN TERRIBLE DANGER."

The Druid gripped the staff tightly, knuckles white with anger.

"HARM ONE HAIR ON THE BOY'S HEAD AND YOU WILL ANSWER TO ME," he bellowed, his fury matching that of the storm.

Amidst the clamour, Elester spoke softly to the frightened animal as he caressed Noble's long neck. He used the Elven language and the horse's ears twitched as if it understood his every word. The gray stallion was descended from Kings of Horses and, as it listened to the Prince of Elves, the blood of its proud ancestors coursed through its veins. Without exception, Noble's progenitors—a long line of proud fighters, had been tested in courage and loyalty and not been found wanting. For a moment, the intrepid animal went as still as stone, then it lunged after Avatar, following on the red roan's heels like a shadow.

Indolent knelt on the dirty floor beside Nicholas, cradling the boy's head gently in his arms. "I've got a surprise for you," he said.

"What?" asked Nicholas, smiling at the wizard, his heart aching with love for this kind, gentle man.

"Then it wouldn't be a surprise, would it?" answered the wizard. "But first, tell me, where is this cave you mentioned earlier?"

"The Serpents' Cave?" asked the boy, his eyes glazed and his voice a monotone.

"Yes, yes! The Serpents' Cave," snapped Indolent impatiently, suddenly releasing the boy and jumping to his feet.

"Ouch!" Nicholas felt his head hit the hard floor. He didn't understand what had upset his dear friend. But, despite the throbbing in his temples, he smiled at the wizard, hoping to please him. "If you really want to know, I'll tell you," he said.

At that moment, the huge door burst from its hinges, crashing into the room and cracking down the middle as it hit the floor. Indolent spun toward the sound, the magic rod extended threateningly. He recoiled when he recognized the dark figure looming in the doorway.

"Druid!" He spat the word as if it were a cockroach in his mouth.

"To what do I owe this dubious pleasure?"

Naim ignored the wizard and strode across the room to Nicholas, motioning to his companions to remain outside the room. He stood over the boy, taking in the broken, twisted arm and the cuts and bruises on his head and face. When he finally acknowledged the wizard's presence, the Druid's face was dark with fury.

"I have come to take away your power," he said in a terrible voice.

The wizard cringed as if he had been punched, but he recovered quickly, and sneered at the Druid. "You wormed your way into the Circle of Five by spreading filthy lies about me. But you cannot deceive me. Spiteful, lying, slanderous, spawn of a hag. You have no idea of the power I wield."

"I did not lie," said the Druid. "You overreached, Indolent. All you ever wanted was power and more power. Greed was your undoing. Even now, you would have the Serpent's Egg at any cost. Tell me, what black promise has the Demon made to you in exchange for this prize?"

"You know NOTHING," screamed the wizard. "I am INDOLENT—not one of your spineless followers. I do not trade with the Demon." He waved his arms, cackling like a demented woman. "But you—SHE has plans for you, Druid. Better you die here, now." Even as he ranted and raved, a blue flame erupted from the tip of his wand. He flicked his wrist, shooting a stream of fire at the Druid.

From the doorway, Miranda and the other companions watched in horror as the flame streaked toward Naim. But, the Druid did not move. He raised his right arm, almost casually, and the staff drew the blue fire into itself, as effortlessly as snuffing out a candle. Before the companions could blink, the Druid pointed the staff toward Indolent, releasing the wizard's own magic, now transformed into a white-hot liquid inferno.

The wizard saw the firestorm exploding toward him. He shrieked in terror, leaping high into the air and clinging to one of the heavy wooden ceiling beams. He spluttered with rage as the Druid's fire ripped through the place where, less than a second earlier, he had been standing. The white blaze incinerated everything in its path.

"I have taken your fire," said the Druid, laughing ruthlessly.

Peering around the shattered doorframe, Miranda scarcely breathed as she witnessed the Druid's terrible power. It fascinated her and terrified her at the same time. He terrified her. She did not know this cold, emotionless stranger, whose harsh laughter turned her blood to ice.

Suddenly, Penelope screamed, grabbing Miranda's arm and startling her companions. "Look! It's Muffers!"

Miranda looked over her shoulder into the long hall and saw the fuchsia poodle immediately. She also saw its red eyes, glowing angrily at the intruders. Penelope held her hand out toward the dog. "Muffsey! Come here, darling," she called, and instantly snatched her hand back as the tiny creature growled and snapped at her. "Her eyes! What have they done to her? And what's that around her neck?"

The poodle inched closer, limbs stiff with anger, her once curly fur sticking straight out, the sharp spikes on her collar glinting like crystal. Elester removed his cloak and, holding it in front of him, advanced slowly toward the vicious animal. Like a bolt of lightning, Muffy sprang at the Elf, but Elester was faster still. He caught the charging animal in his cloak and swiftly brought the edges together, forming a sack. Holding the sack at arms' length with one hand, he pulled a thin cord out of a small pouch at his waist and passed it to Miranda. The girl didn't have to be told what to do. Quickly, she tied the cord tightly about the top of the sack and slumped back against the door in time to see Indolent release his hold on the beam and drop lightly to the floor, arms raised above his head.

In the instant it took for the wizard to fall from the ceiling, Miranda saw something that triggered a terrifying memory. The wide sleeves of the creature's robe dropped, exposing a pair of pale,

197

withered limbs. On the creature's left forearm was a mark she would never forget. She had seen it once before, embedded under the skin on the THUG'S left arm as it reached for her, just before Typhon snatched her out of its grasp. It was the sign of the Demon, a human skull! This was no coincidence. Only one explanation made sense. Indolent was lying. He was one of the Demon's creatures.

Shaking uncontrollably, the girl grabbed Elester's arm. "Hate knows I'm here. I have to get away now." She looked across the floor where Nicholas had raised himself onto his good arm and was shouting at the Druid to leave his friend alone. "But we can't leave Nick."

Elester nodded. "You and Penelope go to the horses. I'll get the boy and meet you there." He handed the wriggling, snarling sack to Penelope. "Take this."

Penelope gently set it on the floor. "Unless you're planning to take the Druid's horse, how are we all going to ride out of here?" she said, not looking at her companions. "You go. I'll wait for him." She nodded toward Naim. Miranda couldn't believe her ears. Penelope had never thought of anything or anyone but herself and Muffy in her entire life. Miranda was sure that the girl had only rescued her and Arabella from the Wobbles because she thought it was the least dangerous thing to do. Now, here she was suddenly offering to stay behind and let the others go on without her.

"Thank you," said Miranda, her voice breaking as she hugged Penelope. "You'll be safe with Naim." Blinking back tears, the Elven girl turned and disappeared down the dark hallway.

She reached the horses only seconds before Elester appeared through the wind and rain, carrying a protesting Nicholas in his arms. The gray stallion whinnied softly at the sight of the Elven Prince. Elester gently laid the boy on the wet ground. "I must tend to him before he can ride with us."

"I don't want your help," growled Nicholas. "He promised me a surprise. I want my surprise."

"I do not think you would have liked Indolent's surprise," said Elester.

Miranda saw the Elf take a bottle from the small pouch at his belt. "What is that?" she asked as he forced some of the contents of the bottle into the boy's mouth. It was a vivid red liquid.

"It's poison. He's going to poison me," yelled Nicholas, trying unsuccessfully to spit out the substance that swarmed over his tongue as if it were alive, and then slid down his throat.

"It is a healing phage," replied the Elf, screwing the cap on the bottle and replacing it in the pouch. Then he set Nicholas's broken arm and bound it snugly against the boy's body.

"A 'phage'?" asked Miranda.

"I do not think this is the proper time to tell our friend that he has just eaten a mouthful of spiders," grinned the Elf.

Miranda gagged loudly. "Live spiders! You're not serious?" But she could tell by the look he gave her that it was true.

Elester helped Nicholas to his feet and propped him against the courtyard wall. The Elf leaped onto Noble's back. With Miranda pushing from below, he lifted the boy and held him in his arms as if he weighed no more than a feather. Miranda stood on top of the wall and slid onto the horse behind the Elven Prince.

"Our path leads to the Serpents' Cave," said Elester quietly, urging the big stallion into a gallop. "We dare not stop until we get there."

Miranda did not reply. She squinted through the driving rain into the darkness ahead, as Noble carried her swiftly toward her destiny.

CHAPTER THIRTY
THE BROKEN WAND

ndolent waved his wand frantically, conjuring up the air, compacting it and forming it into a behemoth with the power to dash the Druid to pieces. Under the wizard's control, the shadowy form of the hulk towered menacingly over the room. Hands as big as houses reached toward the Druid, seizing him by the shoulders and tossing him from one giant paw to the other as if he were a rag doll.

Naim slid out of the creature's grasp, landing nimbly on his feet. Working quickly, the Druid planted the staff firmly on the floor in front of him, gripping it with both hands. The staff shook violently and then a thin black spiral of smoke or fog drifted out from its base growing and writhing like a cyclone, inhaling dirt and small insects. The black hole gyrated faster and faster, consuming chairs and tables. Flaming logs flew out of the fireplace and disappeared into the void. The looming creature recoiled as the suction caught the monstrous foot that was descending like a meteor to crush the life out of the Druid. But it didn't stand a chance. A high, thin wail echoed through the Castle of Indolence as the creature stretched into a long dark string and was subsumed into the vortex.

The Druid thumped the ground with the staff and silence settled over the room, all signs of the terrible disturbance gone as if had been a thing of the mind. He looked about for the wizard, finally spotting the trembling creature clinging to a pillar at the far end of the room.

"I have taken your control," said the Druid, advancing upon the wizard. "Now, give me your wand."

"You think you're so clever," screamed Indolent, backing away. "But SHE is coming and I will have power that will show up your Druid magic for what it is—childish tricks."

Naim laughed. "You never understood, did you, Indolent? A Druid has no magic."

"N-no magic? Then how—? What—?"

"My power comes from within. It is me, and it can never be taken away," continued the Druid. "Even now, you are overreaching. Do you think Hate will reward you when you do not produce the Egg? Listen to me, Indolent. Leave this place now and take yourself far away before the Demon discovers that you are of no use to her."

Indolent rubbed the skull on his left forearm as though it burned his skin, then he raised the wand toward the Druid but, before he could evoke its magic, Naim swung the staff, flicking the wand into the air and catching it in one swift movement. He raised his knee and snapped the thin rod in two.

Indolent choked on his rage. "I may not be able to give HER the Egg," he snarled. "But I will give HER you."

Naim shook his head sadly. "Look around you. See what you have become. Look at the filth of this place. Look at yourself. You have become what you have tried to turn others into—an indolent creature." He turned his back and walked toward the doorway. "Do you still think that you are indispensable to the Demon?" He paused beside the huge fireplace and tossed the broken wand into the dying embers. It ignited like hot oil, bursting into a roaring flame before

abruptly sizzling out. The Druid watched until only ashes remained. Then he strode from the room.

"You should kill me, Druid," screamed Indolent, who was once a wizard. "Because when I rise like Phoenix, I will come looking for you."

The Druid's shoulders shook with silent laughter. "Seriously delusional!" he muttered, thinking that Miranda would approve of his choice of words. He looked about for the girl now, but she was nowhere to be seen. Then he spotted Penelope peering fearfully into the room.

"Where is Miranda?" he asked anxiously.

"She's gone. With Elester," said the girl, avoiding the Druid's stern gaze. "She said the Demon knew she was here."

"How did she know that?" muttered the Druid, more to himself than to the girl.

"I don't know," cried Penelope. "Stop asking me things I can't answer."

"Forgive me," said the Druid. "I am not thinking clearly. Of course you cannot answer my questions. If she is with the Elf, they are on their way to the Serpents' Cave. We must hurry. The girl may need me." He noticed the sack by the girl's feet. "What is that?"

"It's Muffy!" cried Penelope, using her sleeve to wipe the tears from her eyes. "That nasty wizard did something to her. She tried to bite me."

Naim smiled and patted the girl's shoulder. "The spell has been broken. You will find that your dog is as good as new." He snorted. "Or, perhaps I should say, as bad as ever. But let us not take any chances. Leave the dog in the sack until we are far from this place. Now, let us make haste."

At the moment the Druid snapped Indolent's wand, Nicholas stirred as if he had just awakened from a long sleep. For a second, he thought he was still in the clutches of the insane wizard and he fought to free his arms.

"I will not harm you, Nicholas," said Elester, one strong arm clamped on the boy's chest holding him still.

"Elester? Is that really you?"

"Yes," said the Elf. "Miranda is here too. Now, I will release you if you promise not to fight."

"Fight?" said Nicholas, puzzled. "Fight what?"

"Not what," said Elester. "Me."

"Don't you remember, you thought Elester was trying to poison you?" asked Miranda.

The boy shook his head, utterly bewildered. "The last thing I remember is that wicked warlock thing using some kind of magic to throw me around the room." He felt his bandaged arm. "He broke my arm, too."

"The wizard's power is gone," said Elester. "Otherwise you would still be calling him 'friend.'"

"You're joking," spluttered the boy. "That scumbag . . . my friend. . . ." He turned his face away to hide his shame.

"You were powerless against Indolent's bonding spell. It changed your perception of the man," explained the Elf kindly.

"He took my sword," groaned Nicholas.

As Noble carried the three companions farther and farther from the Castle of Indolence and closer to the Serpents' Cave, Miranda's apprehension grew. She shut herself off from the sound of Nicholas droning on about all that had happened to him, starting with Muffy luring him into the woods. Doubts clouded her mind and she felt numb with exhaustion.

Elester brought Nicholas up to date on Miranda's capture by the Simurghs. The boy's eyes opened wide in wonder when he got to the part where Typhon, the Dragon, rescued her from the THUG.

"A real Dragon!" said Nicholas, softly. "I wish I'd been there."

Suddenly, Noble slowed and came to a stop. "We are near," said Elester.

Miranda shivered from the icycles forming on her back. The Elven

prince helped the others down and then dismounted. "We must walk the rest of the way."

"I don't know what you did to my arm, Elester," said Nicholas, rubbing the injured limb. "It doesn't hurt a bit."

Elester grinned, thinking about the microscopic red spiders that were, even now, busily knitting the torn ligaments in the boys arm. He looked at Miranda, but the girl had moved away and was staring at the dark opening of the cave.

"Is that it?" asked Nicholas, pointing in the direction of Miranda's gaze.

The Elf nodded. "You should wait for us here."

The boy shook his head vehemently. "No! I can't let Mir do this alone. I know you'll be there too, but it's different for me. I've known her all my life." Then he added bitterly. "So far I haven't done much to help her."

"It's going to be very dangerous, and we may have to fly from this place faster than you can run with that arm."

"I'm going," said Nicholas, stubbornly.

Elester nodded grimly. "Then know that my first duty is to the girl. To get her and the Egg to Ellesmere at any cost. If you delay us, I will leave you behind."

Nicholas paled. He knew that the Elf was speaking the truth. "Don't worry about me," he said. "If I thought for one minute that I'd put Mir in danger, I wouldn't go."

Elester did not reply. He reached into a saddlebag and took out a coiled length of thin cord which he slung over his shoulder. Then he walked quickly to the girl, and took her hand. "We must go."

Miranda bowed her head, allowing the young Elven Prince to lead her through the tangled underbrush and over rough boulders toward the dark yawning hole in the mountain that, at this moment, looked a thousand times more frightening than Dilemma's gaping jaws.

A short distance behind the companions, four abysmal black

shapes came together and slipped through the scrub. When they reached the spot where the three humans had dismounted, they paused briefly and fixed their red-eyed gaze on the mouth of the cave. Noble, ears pinned back in anger, swished his tail and cantered into the brush.

CHAPTER THIRTY-ONE
CATASTROPHE

rabella saw the black cloud over the Castle of Indolence break up and drift away.

"The wizard's magic has failed," said Laury of the Riders, coming to stand beside her. "Come. We ride to the Castle. That is where we will find your friends."

The other Riders were already mounted, impatient to be on their way, as Arabella ran toward Marigold, her sodden, muddy clothes squishing with each step. Within minutes, the company was riding swiftly toward the ugly crumbling Castle.

Naim sprinted across the courtyard toward a pair of iron gates that hung askew on bent hinges. He whistled to Avatar, at the same time looking over his shoulder for Penelope. The girl was not there.

"THUNDER AND LIGHTNING!" roared the Druid, turning to retrace his steps. What was the matter with the foolish child? Did she not grasp the fact that every second they tarried here brought Hate closer? He had taken only a few steps when Penelope appeared in the doorway. "Hurry girl, or I will leave you for the Demon," he shouted impatiently.

Penelope heard the Druid urging her to run, but she didn't care anymore. It would be better if he did leave her behind. Nobody would miss her. In fact, they probably wouldn't care if they ever saw her again. She had never seen this Demon, but she would rather face her than be around when the others found out what she had done. Ignoring Naim's frantic gestures, she hesitated in the doorway, slumping against the frame, clutching the Muffy sack against her chest and wishing with every fiber of her being that she were dead.

The sound that suddenly shattered the night jolted the girl out of her depression. It came from above—a long strident hissing that pierced Penelope's heart. She looked up at the sky and saw the massive black shadow hovering overhead, its great cloak spread out like a plague. The stench of evil raining down from the creature made her gag. She had been afraid of the Simurghs and the Dragon. She had known terror when she had gazed into the red eyes of the THUG, but those fears were nothing compared with the mind-snapping horror that paralyzed her now, as Hate, the Demon, dropped from the sky.

The Druid did not look up at the Demon. He kept his eyes on the girl frozen in the doorway. He leaped onto Avatar's back and urged the animal into a run. The big stallion reared once and took off like a shot. The Druid, bent low over the horse's neck, reached down and caught Penelope by the collar and swung her onto the horse in front of him. Avatar wheeled about and thundered across the courtyard, through the iron gates and into the cover of the stunted, misshapen trees that surrounded Indolent's castle.

"I'm sorry. I'm sorry," sobbed Penelope. "I called the Demon and she came."

"Nonsense!" snapped the Druid. "Hate has no interest in you. Indolent brought her here."

"You don't understand," cried the girl. "For my punishment, I said I'd rather face the Demon than all of you."

Naim shook his head. "My dear child. I do not know what you

are talking about. What have you done that is so terrible?"

Penelope buried her face against Avatar's neck and cried like a baby. When she finally spoke, the Druid had to strain to catch the words. "I took the stones."

Naim sighed. Would the girl never learn?

"We do not have time to deal with the Dragon now," he said. "I will go with you to return the stones if we are still alive when this day ends."

"Not the Dragon's stones," cried Penelope.

The Druid felt his blood run cold. "You have the Bloodstones?" he asked, his voice deadly quiet.

"I thought I could use them to change Muffy back. I didn't think about Miranda. I've made a mess of everything. I wanted to die," she wailed. "And the Demon came. Oh, it's too horrible!" She wound her fingers in Avatar's mane and held on tightly, expecting the Druid to throw her off the horse at any second.

"Listen to me," said the Druid. "It is easy to talk about wanting to die until you come face to face with death. Nothing you did is worth your life." He patted the girl's shoulder and his voice turned gruff. "Now give the Stones to me and stop that noise. I must think."

From a distance, Arabella and the Riders saw the monstrous black form descend from the sky and hang over the Castle of Indolence for a minute before drifting down to land in the courtyard. Although Arabella had never seen her, she knew that this terrifying blackness was Hate, the Demon. She was petrified, but she also burned with anger. This was her friend's nightmare come true—the creature who was going to destroy Miranda if somebody didn't stop her first.

Thinking that Miranda, Nicholas, and the others were inside the Castle unaware of the evil that was stalking purposely across the courtyard, she pressed her heels into Marigold's sides and the gray mare broke into a gallop. She didn't have a plan, she only knew that her friend was in trouble. "Hold on Mir. I'm coming," she said, ignoring the shouts from the Riders.

No one spoke as the trio stood at the mouth of the Serpents' Cave. Elester listened for the sound of the THUGS, or the Hellhags, or even the Demon herself. He knew Hate's creatures were near. He could smell them. But they made no sound. Nicholas peered into the cave and quickly drew his head back. "It's black as crows in there," he said. "We'll need a torch or something."

"A light will alarm the Serpents," said Elester. "Miranda has the Stones."

"What stones?" asked Nicholas, puzzled.

"He doesn't know about them," said Miranda, reaching under the neck of her sweater for the thin silver chain. Abruptly, she turned away from the others, the air escaping from her lungs as though the Demon were squeezing her to death. The Bloodstones, the only hope she had of capturing the Serpent's Egg, were gone. Holding her stomach, she reeled away from the mouth of the cave like a drunk. It was all over. She had lost the stones.

"Mir! What?" asked Nicholas, hurrying after her.

"Go away," she pleaded, sinking onto the hard ground and burying her face in her hands. "I'll be OK." She had to be alone— to think. What happened to the Stones? How could she have been so careless when they were so important? She could never find her way in the dark cave without them and the Serpents would kill her for sure if they saw her grab the Egg.

Hate's going to win, and it's my fault, she thought, tears filling her eyes. What am I going to say to the others? She saw the Druid in her mind. Tall and lean, his narrow face creased with deep lines, he reached out and took her hand. "I never doubted you," he said, the remembered words hurting worse than a kick.

She let her mind travel across this land that the people in her

world could no longer see. Her heart ached as she pictured the beauty of Ellesmere Island, home of the Elves. Her people! She saw King Ruthar gazing at her through eyes filled with shame because his ancestors had ignored the evil that Hate had done to others. She thought of Typhon, the proud Dragon, who believed he was immune to evil. And what about Dundurum? She could not bear the thought of Hate smashing the Dwarves' magnificent mountain home to dust. She heard King Gregor's voice again. "I'll be right there beside you." Well he wasn't here, but Miranda felt that his thoughts were never far from the Trust. She wondered if the Druid were also thinking of her.

Sick at heart, Miranda climbed slowly to her feet and looked to where the daylight ended at the mouth of the dark cave. "Demon," she whispered. "I came all this way to destroy you. If you think I'm giving up now, think again." Then she walked toward her companions. "I'm ready," she said.

Elester nodded. He picked up the coiled rope and placed it over the girl's left shoulder, holding one end in his hand. "I know that the Bloodstones will show you the way in the dark, but we must know where you are whatever happens," he said. "Let it out as you go. I will be holding one end." Then he knelt on the ground and placed his hands gently on Miranda's shoulders. "Trust the Stones, Miranda. Trust yourself."

Miranda nodded, hoping, without hope, that Elester would suddenly say that it was all a mistake and she didn't have to go into the darkness. She waited for a second, but when he didn't speak, she turned and stumbled blindly into the black mouth of the Cave.

The Druid kept glancing over his shoulder as he clutched Avatar's reins and urged the fine horse to a faster pace. The stallion's coat glistened with sweat but Naim could not let the animal slow down. Hate may not have noticed them in the Courtyard, but she would soon know that they had been at the Castle and had left shortly before she arrived. He thought about Indolent and sighed deeply, wondering what horrible punishment Hate would exact for his failure. He felt sad because, although he had never been close to the man, he had studied and trained with him for many years.

A picture of Miranda formed in his mind. Surely by now, she had discovered her loss. He saw her clearly, striding undaunted into danger without the Bloodstones to guide her. He sent his thoughts out to the girl, telling her to wait because he was coming to her.

Ahead, he saw Noble, chomping grass in a small clearing. The Elven horse raised its head and whickered contentedly as the Druid reined in Avatar and swung Penelope to the ground. When he had dismounted, he faced the girl.

"If you wish to do something for the Trust, you will remain here with the horses and keep them safe and quiet until they are needed. When Hate comes, they will be frightened. You must not let them run away. Can you do that?"

Penelope chewed her lip nervously. "Will the Demon come after me?" she asked.

"Right now, Hate's thoughts are bent on one thing," answered the Druid. "You need not fear her."

"OK, I'll watch them," she said, thinking that maybe she didn't want to die after all.

"Good," said the Druid, giving her shoulder a gentle squeeze. Then he turned away and ran toward the Serpents' Cave, following the rough path through the underbrush that Miranda and the others had taken earlier. He strained to identify the figures crouched near the mouth of the cave peering into the darkness. The boy, Nicholas, was there. And Elester. But not Miranda. Naim clenched his fists in anger. He was too late. The girl was in the Cave, alone in the dark. Without the Bloodstones, she had less than one chance in a billion of capturing the Egg.

CHAPTER THIRTY-TWO
THE SERPENTS' CAVE

iranda waited just inside the cave for her eyes to adjust to the sudden darkness, wrinkling her nose at the smell of mildew that permeated the stale air all around her. It took all of her strength not to turn around and take that one step out into the sunlight. She fumbled for the wall of the cave, sliding her hand along the cold, rough surface as she took her first cautious steps forward. Without the Bloodstones, she had to rely on her own limited senses to find her way deep into the cavern where the Serpents performed their ancient ritual with the Egg.

Folded up in her pocket was the crude, but accurate, map the Druid had made for her. It showed a confusing maze of tunnels branching off in all directions. Naim had marked her route in red ink and had made her memorize the way into the cave. Then, to her surprise, he made her memorize the way out, something she never would have thought of. She remembered how she had complained at the time, but now she was glad that she knew the way by heart because, without a light, the map was useless. She repeated the going in directions to herself. "Right hand on wall. Fourth tunnel on right, turn right. First tunnel on right, turn right. Left hand on wall.

First tunnel on left, turn left. Right hand on wall. Third tunnel on right, turn right."

Miranda felt that she had been walking forever, but she was moving slowly and had lost all sense of time. What if she missed one of the branching tunnels and had to go back and start over? No! She mustn't let that happen, for if it did, she would never reach the Serpents in time. Each time she paused to let out more rope, she gave it a gentle tug. The small gesture gave her comfort and made her feel less alone. As she made her way deeper into the tunnel, she tugged on the cord more frequently, seeking courage and strength in the thought that the cord was her lifeline back to the world of the living.

Except for the hollow "drip-drip" of water echoing from a source somewhere ahead, the cave was as silent as a tomb. Then her ears picked up another sound—a faint scraping noise. She stiffened, holding her breath, straining to pinpoint the sound that seemed to be coming from all directions at the same time. There it was again. She listened intently. It was coming from behind. Someone or something was moving toward her in the darkness.

She slid her right hand along the wall, shuddering whenever she felt a thick cobweb cling to her skin. A small hairy insect ran up her fingers toward her arm. She pulled her hand away as if she had been burned, brushing frantically at her clothing. She took a few small sliding steps forward, loathe to touch the wall again. But she had to use it to guide her if she hoped to get anywhere. Just as she had begun to think that she would never find the Serpents, she reached out to touch the wall only to discover that she had arrived at the first tunnel. She almost called out with relief. Instead, she gave the cord a sharp tug to share the moment with her companions.

After that, whenever she reached a new tunnel, she pulled the cord. Turning right at the fourth tunnel, she found another passage almost immediately. She paused and listened. The dripping sound was louder but so was the dull scraping noise in one of the tunnels

behind her. "It's coming for me," she whispered. Was it following the cord? Did it have the cord in its hands? Shaking uncontrollably, she slipped the coil off her shoulder and let it drop to the floor of the cave.

She counted the tunnels as she moved slowly but surely along the passage. Finally, she reached the third passage. This was it! Thoughts of the Serpents drove everything else out of her mind. They were coming here to hatch the Egg. A lot of snakes. A lot of *big* snakes. How was she going to get the Egg when she couldn't see an inch in front of her face? "What am I going to do," she whispered. "They're going to bite me. Or swallow me alive." She hugged herself tightly and rocked back and forth, moaning silently.

The light came from the ground about twenty feet ahead. It was a pale shimmer, like daylight showing through a tiny scratch on a black window. But it was enough for Miranda to make her way into the large underground chamber and feel along the walls for a hiding place. Her fingers found a narrow crevice where the rock wall had split as if it had been struck by a giant axe and, despite her fears about what else might be lurking in there, she squeezed her body into the crevice and waited, eyes fastened on the pale light coming out of the ground.

Miranda gripped the rough edge of the wall so tightly her fingers ached. She stared, mesmerized, as the light spread along the crack in the floor of the cavern. A burst of vapor issued from the rent with a sound like a dying breath. The ground split wider and wider, the pale light turning to yellow and then to hot flickering red. Heat escaped out of the hole, turning the cavern into an oven.

Suddenly, without a sound, a nightmare-sized head rose from the crack, followed by a massive body that writhed and flexed as it surged out of the fire. The huge head swayed back and forth as the creature's yellow eyes travelled about the cavern. Then, it slithered onto the floor of the cave—a fabulous creature, all black, with a thin red line running along its back from its broad head to the tip of its tail. The flat part of its head bore a mark in the shape of a crown, the orange-red colour of molten lava. The giant Serpent opened its great mouth and Miranda stifled a scream at the sight of the two sharp fangs protruding from the reptile's upper jaw, each longer than a pencil.

Within minutes eight huge Serpents had risen out of the molten fire. They slithered along the floor of the cave, contorting and winding about each other in a tangled knot. Miranda stared, fascinated and repulsed by the spectacle of the squirming, twisting reptiles. Suddenly, mysteriously, a golden Egg floated up from amidst the entangled vipers. With a start, Miranda realized that the Serpents were hissing at the Egg. It was their combined hissing that kept it suspended. As the hissing increased in volume the Egg rose high into the air before dropping rapidly toward the floor. Miranda stopped breathing as the pale gold Egg fell. Surely it must hit the ground and smash open. But, before the astonished girl's eyes, the Egg stopped abruptly and hung, floating in the air just above the Serpents.

When the snakes hissed the Egg into the air again, Miranda was ready. She wiped the sweat out of her eyes and then, quick as a flash, she wriggled out of the crevice. Eyes on the golden Egg, she jumped over the gaping crack in the floor, feeling the heat melt the soles of her boots and scorch the legs of her pants. She saw the Egg begin to fall as she charged into the midst of the Serpents, dodging or vaulting over twisting black bodies the size of large tree trunks. Then she leaped high into the air and her hands closed so tightly on the Egg that she was afraid it would burst. The shell was warm and she felt the Egg pulse in her hands.

The snakes were aware of her now and they reacted instantly. Yellow eyes glared at her with hatred. The hissing changed to a horrible screeching. The vipers' huge jaws snapped wide as they recoiled sharply for an instant before striking at the girl.

Miranda didn't look back but she could hear the Serpents side-winding across the cavern floor in pursuit. She hugged the Egg to her chest and ran toward the exit tunnel as fast as her legs would carry her. She reached the tunnel, relieved that only one Serpent at a time could fit into the small opening. Another twenty feet and she'd be in the long passage. "Turn left," she said, knowing that she had to use all of her strength to get as far away as fast as she could while there was light. Miranda flew into the long passage, skidding as she tried to make the left turn without losing momentum.

Regaining her balance, she plowed ahead. Then, she staggered as she felt something sharp stab into her shoulder. "Keep going," she said, knowing that the coldness already circulating through her body was a deadly toxin ejected from the Serpent's fang as it bit deep into her flesh.

"Don't stop." The words were softer than a whisper and thin with despair. What was wrong with her legs? She couldn't feel them anymore. "Please, please! Don't let me die now. Not now." Her legs buckled and she fell to her knees, holding the Egg protectively against her chest. When her knees collapsed, she fell onto her side. The Egg slipped out of her arms and rolled toward the rock wall, stopping and rocking back and forth less than an inch from a jagged chunk of rock that had fallen from the roof of the cave.

Miranda lay on her side on the hard, rock floor. The Egg! She must guard the Egg. She reached for it, but her arms wouldn't move. She wondered why she couldn't move her limbs but could still see and hear. She heard the Serpents screaming behind her, slithering through the small tunnel, coming for her. "So tired," she whispered, but no sound came from her lips. The Elven girl tried to close her eyes, but they wouldn't obey her, either. She felt herself rising out of her heavy, paralyzed body. Up and up she rose, repeating Naim's directions. "First tunnel, turn left. . . ." Then she felt nothing at all.

CHAPTER THIRTY-THREE
ATTACK

ate dropped to the ground, furious that the weasel of a wizard had not contacted her with news of the girl. The Demon snarled savagely and bared her fangs. She had left her armies at the base of Dundurum and raced through the skies to answer the sudden surge of fear emanating from the tattoo on the wizard's arm. What had frightened the vain little man? The answer came to her immediately. The Druid!

"COME TO ME, INDOLENT!" she hissed, the sound shaking the crumbling Castle walls. The Demon swept through the front entrance and stopped dead. The place was deserted. The wizard had fled. She did not need to search the Castle, she knew, instinctively, that nothing human remained within these walls. Her long tongue whipped about her face as she caught the metallic scent of blood. On a dark marble table against the wall, she spotted the thin gold wafers that she had pocketed under the wizard's skin to shape the skull tattoo. Indolent had torn the skull out of his arm, and only a short while ago because the pieces of skin mixed with the sticky blood on the gold slivers had not yet begun to curl.

The Demon shrieked with rage, lashing out with her black stake and smashing and smashing the marble table until it was reduced to gravel. Suddenly, she stiffened. The THUGS! They were near—very near. Their presence could mean only one thing. The girl was also near. Hate's rage became a hiss of pleasure as she turned and stormed out of the Castle. She had taken only a few steps when Arabella rode through the gates into the courtyard.

The gray mare skidded to a stop and reared up on her hind legs, screaming in terror at the sight of the huge black creature. Heart in her throat, Arabella quickly slipped to the ground. "Go, Marigold!" she breathed, slapping the animal gently on the rump before racing toward the crumbling courtyard wall. "Oh, Mir! What have we got ourselves into?" she whispered, looking over her shoulder in time to see Hate raise her stake and point it at Marigold. The Elven horse wheeled about and made a beeline for the gates, her hooves pounding the cobblestones echoed like applause.

Arabella held her breath, hypnotized, as the Demon-fire erupted from Hate's iron stake and streaked toward the fleeing horse. "Oh no, you don't! Run! Oh please run!" she prayed. And, as if she had heard the girl's plea, the mare shot through the gates and plunged down a steep embankment less than a second before the red lightning blew away the gates and the wall for fifty feet on either side.

Arabella's knees folded and she collapsed on the ground, weak with relief, but too frightened to peer over the wall. She felt that she would do anything as long as she never had to look upon that creature ever again. But mingled with her fear was a deep anger. This Monster was after her friend—had invaded Ottawa and driven them from their homes. Arabella gritted her teeth. She'd like to see the Demon scared for a change. She'd like to see the creature's head fall off. She'd like to see the creature die.

Poking her head over the wall, Arabella saw that the Demon's attention was still focused on the fleeing horse. She crouched and followed the low wall toward the Castle.

Hate didn't bother to search the courtyard for the human. Since it was not the Elven girl, she had no interest in killing one stupid, piddling child when her great army was poised to kill an entire nation. She had wasted enough precious time here already. Now she must join the THUGS. But, before she flew to the place where her servants waited, the Demon stood in the courtyard and hissed until the Castle of Indolence collapsed upon itself and settled into dust.

"MIR?" Arabella felt the marble floor buckle beneath her feet as she dashed along the dimly lit hallway, keeping clear of the walls which threatened to come down and crush the life out of her. Just ahead, a great slab of stone crashed to the floor, dissolving in a cloud of dirt that made the girl choke. Without pausing, she pulled the neck of her sweater up and over her mouth and nose to filter out the thick dust.

"MIRANDA?" She yelled, but the sound that came from her throat was a mere whisper.

As the castle crumbled, and more chunks of marble and other stone broke away from the walls and ceiling and tumbled to the floor, Arabella suddenly went blind. She couldn't see an inch in front of her. Gulping and coughing, she froze in the middle of the passage, only jumping like a puppet on a string when a chunk of the ceiling fell near her.

"We have trouble," said the Druid, coming up behind Nicholas and Elester, and startling them. Both the boy and the Elf turned quickly.

"What sort of trouble?" asked Elester.

The Druid took the silver pouch out of his cloak and poured the Bloodstones into his open palm. "This sort of trouble."

"She knew," said Elester, shaking his head in wonder. "And still she went to find the Serpents."

"What's going on?" demanded Nicholas. He pointed to the Stones in the Druid's hand. "And what does a bunch of stones have to do with Mir?"

The Druid ignored him. "One of us must go after her, Elester. Without the stones, she will fail. And she will die."

"I will go," said the Elf.

"Hey! Listen!" said Nicholas. "What's this about dying? If Mir's in trouble, I'm the one who's going after her."

The Druid flashed the boy an angry look. "Young man, I do not have time to explain things to you nor do I wish to argue. You are not going anywhere. You will remain here and you will be quiet, or—"

"Or what? You'll turn me into a toad?" The boy shook his head in disgust. "Give it a rest."

"Not a toad," said the Druid, looking about. "A tree stump."

"Yeah, right," said Nicholas.

"You have been warned," said the Druid.

Elester scooped the Bloodstones from the Druid's hand and poured them into the silver pouch, dropping the chain over his head. As both men moved toward the mouth of the cave, he touched the Druid's sleeve. "There are others here besides us," he said, keeping his voice low so Nicholas couldn't hear. "Be careful, Druid friend. They will attack if they see the girl."

"Yes," answered the Druid, clasping the Elf's shoulder. "Just find her."

Elester nodded and passed the end of the rope to the Druid. Then he disappeared into the Cave.

The Riders thundered through a gap in the wall at the back of Indolent's Castle. The roar of the imploding structure was deafening, drowning out the screams of the horses and the shouts of the men and women. Leaping from his horse, their Captain, Laury, pointed toward a jagged opening in the building's exterior wall where, a moment before, a door had stood closed and bolted. He covered his nose and mouth with his black neck scarf, winding the ends about his head. Motioning for two of the company, Jarol and Sara, to follow him, he moved cautiously into the castle. The rest of the

Riders didn't have to be told what to do. They found some sturdy beams among the ruins and used them to prop up the opening.

"Over here, Sir!"

Laury's heart leaped into his throat when he saw the pair of boots sticking out from beneath the heavy slab of marble. Quickly, he cleared away the loose gravel and smaller chunks of stone, while his two companions examined the marble block.

"Arabella, can you hear me?"

No answer.

"If you can hear me, move either foot!"

Fearing that he might miss a slight movement in the murky darkness, he placed his hands on the girl's ankles and waited. Nothing. He wasn't surprised. Nobody could survive after being hit by a piece of marble that must weigh close to 500 pounds. He only hoped that death had come swiftly. He did not want to be the one to tell her friends that she had suffered horribly.

Suddenly he felt both feet wriggle. "Good. Now, I want you to move your right foot if you can speak." No movement.

"OK. Move your right foot if you are hurt." No movement. Laury was amazed. "Is the stone touching you? Use your right foot for 'yes' and the left for 'no'." Left foot.

"Will it hurt you if I pull your ankles?" Arabella wriggled her right foot, then the left foot.

"You moved both feet. Does that mean you do not know if it will hurt?" Right foot. "I will pull you very slowly. If it hurts, move either foot and I will stop."

"Sir!" Jarol's voice was harsh. "We dare not move the stone. The only thing that is keeping it from the girl is a small piece of wood. And that could snap at any second. Hurry and get her out, Sir."

Laury grabbed Arabella's ankles and pulled. Feeling no resistance from the girl, he continued pulling until at last she was free. Arabella managed a weak grin as she stared into the faces of her rescuers.

Jarol and Sara each took a firm grip on one of her arms and moved quickly back through the castle the way they had come. Laury peered under the marble block just as the wooden support cracked and the mass of stone smashed to the floor.

Hate wrapped her cloak about the THUGS, holding them close to her as she observed the humans. The hooded creatures basked in the Demon's stench, in her depravity, their demented minds seething with malice toward the human enemies. The mass of poisonous snakes about the Demon's middle hissed at the intrusive THUGS, thrashing and wriggling in protest. Hate ignored them. When the tall Elf disappeared into the Cave, she gently pushed two of the THUGS away, holding them with her probing red gaze and sending her orders without speaking.

When the girl appears, smash the Egg and slay her and the others. Do not fail me, my THUGS. They are not to leave here. Do you understand?

The THUGS bowed their heads. They understood. *When it is done, follow me. By sunset tomorrow, Dundurum will be mine.* She watched as the two creatures moved to carry out her orders. Then she wrapped her arms about the others, spread her huge cloak and rose like thick smoke into the air.

Elester picked up the coil of rope from the cave floor where Miranda had dropped it. He scowled, angry at himself for having alarmed the girl. She must have been frightened half out of her wits when she heard the sounds of someone following her in the blackness. Did she drop the rope in a panic and try to flee? Or did she place it here, to mislead her pursuer? Was she hiding nearby at this moment, waiting, listening?

"Miranda!" he whispered softly. But, except for the sound of water trickling into an underground stream or pool, he heard nothing.

How was he going to find the girl? He had been so intent on following the rope to get to her quickly, he had not counted the openings into the branching passages. He wondered how Miranda had made it this far, totally blind. Even with his keen Elven sight, he had difficulty picking his way along in the dark.

Turning to retrace his steps, Elester hesitated. A light flickered from a side tunnel farther along the passage. He walked cautiously forward, until he came to a junction. Following the light, he turned left and instantly staggered backwards as the heat hit him. Sweat formed on his face and head and streamed down his neck. The tunnel ahead glowed with a bright reddish orange light reflected from some tremendous heat source. Elester's pulse raced. He knew that he had found the place where the earth had split open to release the Serpents.

He had learned about the Serpent's Egg when he was a child on his father's knee. Ever since then, he had longed to be there when the earth opened and the giant vipers erupted from the fire to perform their strange ritual. But, as he raced along the passage, it was the last thing on the young Elf's mind. All of his thoughts were directed toward the girl. He had to find her, protect her, get her away before it was too late.

Suddenly, like one of the Serpents rising from the molten magma, Miranda flew out of the fire, her arms wrapped about the golden Egg. Elester froze in his tracks, stunned. She had done the impossible. But how? He opened his mouth to call out to her and shut it immediately. No! After what she had just been through, the girl had to be in a state of shock. He must not startle her. The best thing to do was to wait for her here.

The huge Serpent's head flashed around the corner and struck at the girl before the Elf knew what was happening. He saw her stagger, and his heart went out to her.

"NO!" he shouted, streaking toward Miranda, slipping the silver chain over his head as he ran. He saw her fall to her knees and struggle to get up before collapsing in a heap on the stone floor.

He reached Miranda seconds before the Serpent slid its full length around the corner. She lay on her side, eyes open, one arm extended toward the Egg. Quickly, Elester wrapped one powerful arm about her limp body and slung the girl over his shoulder. Then he scooped up the Egg and ran, not back the way Miranda had come, but straight down the nearest tunnel where his sharp Elven hearing had picked up the steady sound of water trickling into a pool.

The THUGS waited patiently, watching the Druid. The old fool sat on a tree stump, his back facing the mouth of the cave, the long wooden staff cradled in the crook of his arm. He appeared to be asleep with his eyes closed, chin resting on his chest. Well, soon he would sleep forever. When the Druid stirred and looked over his shoulder into the cave, the THUGS edged closer. They didn't care if he saw them now. Their eyes glowed with only one purpose. Smash the Egg and kill the humans.

The Druid leaped to his feet, reaching into the mouth of the cave even as Elester burst into the open with Miranda slung over his shoulder. Naim took the girl from the Elf and gently laid her on the ground beside the tree stump. Rising to his feet, he turned and brought up the staff. Elester placed the Egg on the stump next to the girl and slipped the silver chain holding the Bloodstones about Miranda's neck. Then, he moved to stand with the Druid, his Elven sword unsheathed.

The two black creatures moved as a single entity toward the humans. They crashed swiftly through the brush, clawed feet plowing deep furrows in the ground. They stopped about ten feet from their victims and glared at the feeble creatures, their eyes burning with hatred. The sound of their breathing dragged through the air like knives cutting into sandpaper.

"GO BACK TO YOUR CRONE WHILE YOU STILL CAN!" commanded the Druid, suddenly rising into the air to tower over the startled

THUGS. The creatures fell back, momentarily confused by this enemy's power.

Then, one of the THUGS screamed and lunged at the Druid, slamming into him and knocking him to the ground. In a flash, the creature slashed at the Druid's throat with razor sharp claws. But Naim moved faster. He brought one arm up in time to fend off the deadly strike, smashing his elbow into the blackness beneath the creature's hood and then throwing the Monster away from him. Before the THUG regained its balance, Naim was already on his feet, the staff raised. White fire exploded out of the wood and streaked toward his attacker, striking the THUG in the chest and burning through flesh and bone to expose the creature's black heart. The creature looked at the open wound and shrugged. The old fool could not kill it. Its body convulsed with silent laughter as it charged at the Druid.

Elester felt his strength begin to fail as he pulled his sword out of his attacker's gut. No matter how many times he stabbed the creature, it kept coming at him. He winced in pain at the wounds the creature had inflicted on him. The front of his clothing was one large bloodstain. Until now, the young Elven Prince had never considered that he might die far from his beloved Island and the thought broke his heart, filling his eyes with tears of sadness.

And then, suddenly, the storm that was Typhon, the Dragon, swept down from the sky. One giant limb scooped up the girl and the Elf, and scraped through the dirt toward the Druid, who barely managed to grab the Egg and the tree stump before being lifted into the air. With its other forelimb, the Dragon picked up the THUG that had battled the Druid and, in one smooth motion, opened its huge jaws and dropped the creature into its mouth.

Before the Dragon's teeth came together, the THUG learned the terrible lie on which it had been nourished by its Mistress. It could die.

CHAPTER THIRTY-FOUR
THE HEALING

n the peaceful blackness of Miranda's mind, a tiny spark would not be doused. It grated on her nerves, making her edgy. "Go away! I need to sleep." But the light tugged at her, drawing her into its buttery softness. She recognized the feeling. But, no, this time there was a difference. It was she who was absorbing the Bloodstones into herself. "Go away!"

The light spoke to her then, not in words, but she heard it. "No! No! You are dying! The Serpent's venom is flowing to your heart. Use us! Use us!"

"Then will you leave me alone?"

"Yes! Yes! But hurry."

Annoyed, Miranda forced herself to follow the light of the Stones deep within herself. She entered her heart and slowed its workings until the blood and the toxin in her veins scarcely flowed. She swam through blood then, thick and metallic, and found the black poison. The stench and the filth of it made her cry out in anguish. She fought the black death, sluggishly at first and then with all of her remaining strength. And, as she fought, the light grew brighter and brighter. She forced the poison from her blood, pushing it through her skin, out of her body. The blackness left her and soaked into the white sheets on the bed in her Healing room on Ellesmere Island.

The Elven Ministers had done all they could for the girl. They exchanged glances with Laurel, the First Minister, and shook their heads sadly. Laurel turned to the old Druid slumped forward in the chair by Miranda's bed, and went to him and gently placed her hand on his shoulder.

"It is the end, Druid friend," she said. "Her heart is failing."

The Druid nodded slowly. He took Miranda's hand and felt the slick wetness even as he saw the black poison oozing from the girl's pores, and from her eyes, and ears, and mouth. He pressed his thumb against her wrist, feeling for a pulse. At first there was nothing, and then he felt it—a weak flutter. She was still alive and as he held his thumb gently in place, the flutter became a faint throb that swelled into a strong, steady rhythm. The Druid turned away from the bed and used his sleeves to wipe the tears from his eyes. He went away then, and the news of the girl's healing spread through Bethany like a ray of sunshine.

After Miranda had bathed and put on fresh clothing, and the black sheets had been burned, the Druid returned. He sat in the deep armchair and listened, without interrupting, while she told him all that had happened in the Serpents' Cave. When she finally fell silent, he stared at her as if he were seeing her for the first time. She seemed healthy enough, on the outside, but the Druid worried about the inner scars that the girl would bear perhaps for the rest of her life. *What have I done to her?* He felt a deep sadness settle in his heart, because he knew that if this world were threatened again, he would find her.

"You haven't heard a word I've said."

Startled, he realized that Miranda was talking to him.

"I beg your pardon. I was lost in thought."

"What were you thinking about?"

Naim smiled, shaking his head. "My dear girl. Laurel gave strict orders that I am not to excite you." But, seeing that Miranda would not rest until she had the full story, he told her how the Elven Prince had followed her into the cave with the Bloodstones and found her fleeing from the Serpents.

"Fire Serpents will not go near water," he said. "Elester remembered that from his studies of the reptiles. When he found you, he carried you to an underground stream and, eventually, made his way back to the mouth of the cave."

"Where is he?" asked Miranda anxiously. "Is he OK? And what about my friends? Are they OK? Are they here? Are they—?"

The Druid threw his hands in the air. "I can do many things, my young friend, but answering six questions at once is not one of them." He looked so rattled that Miranda burst out laughing.

"You asked about Elester. I am happy to say that he has recovered from his wounds."

"What do you mean? What wounds? What happened? How did we get here?"

"Be patient. I am trying to answer your questions," said the Druid. He told her how the THUGS had attacked the moment they saw the Elf emerge from the cave. "Elester suffered deep wounds from the THUG's claws. I saw this as I was battling its companion. I knew the Prince was losing too much blood and I feared for his life, but then, the Dragon made a choice."

"Typhon?"

"Yes, Typhon. The Dragon took us away from the THUGS and brought us here," he said, purposely forgetting to mention the Dragon's grisly snack. "He saved Elester's life, the Elven Ministers did the rest."

"Thank goodness," breathed Miranda. "Where is he? I want to see him."

"He is not here," answered the Druid.

"You're hiding something," cried Miranda. "What is it?"

"If you must know, Elester is away on the King's business. Does that satisfy you?"

Miranda nodded. "I'm just glad he's OK. And I'm glad we got here in time, and I'm glad we got the Egg, and I'm glad Typhon's on our side." She grinned. "I'd probably jump out of my skin if I saw him again, but I kind of like him too."

When the First Minister came to check on Miranda, she was surprised to find the girl awake and showing no signs of exhaustion.

"She should be resting," Laurel said, eyeing the Druid sternly.

"I'm perfectly fine. I don't need any more rest," said Miranda. "Where are my friends? I want to see them. I want to go back to the villa!"

Laurel looked at her in wonder. The girl was right, there really was nothing wrong with her. "You must remain here tonight, but I will let you see your friends if you promise not to stay up half the night."

"I promise," said Miranda, who would have promised to paint the sky green in order to be with her companions. But she had no intention of sharing that with Laurel.

At that moment, the door flew open and Arabella bounced into the room and hopped onto the bed beside Miranda. Next came Nicholas, who gave the Druid a dark look and moved as far away from him as he could. Miranda wondered what was eating him this time. The last one to arrive was Penelope, who acted as if she were terrified to enter the room. She stood in the doorway, looking everywhere but at Miranda and squeezing Muffy so tightly the animal could scarcely breathe. Finally, the poodle wriggled out of Penelope's arms and leaped to the floor, racing from one bed to another, barking furiously before peeing on the terra-cotta floor. There was complete silence and then everybody broke into laughter.

"I will leave you now," said Naim, getting up and walking slowly toward the door. "Even Druids need their rest."

When he had gone, Nicholas flopped into the chair and glared at the door. "I really hate that guy," he said.

"Don't say that," snapped Miranda. "You don't mean it."

"How would you react if he turned you into a tree stump?" muttered Nicholas. "And then had the gall to sit on you."

"He what?" asked Miranda, trying not to laugh in the boy's face and failing.

"I gave you fair warning," said the Druid, peering through the open door. He looked at Penelope and pointed at the puddle on the floor. "And clean that up." Then he disappeared, pulling the door shut behind him.

Penelope was horrified. "He heard what you said."

"Do I look like I care?" snapped the boy. "'Fair warning!' Right! 'I'm going to turn you into a tree stump.' Poof! I'm a tree stump. You call that fair?"

Miranda laughed. "You're lucky it wasn't something worse."

"Like what?" asked Nicholas.

"He could have turned you into a toilet," laughed Arabella.

"Or a bowl of Dragon spit," said Miranda, looking at Penelope and turning red before the words were out of her mouth.

"How did you find out?" asked Penelope, turning even redder.

Miranda felt terrible. "I'm sorry. Naim told us. But I wasn't mocking you. It just slipped out."

"That was so mean of him," said Penelope, blinking back tears, and wondering what else the Druid had told them.

"Don't blame him," said Arabella. "Why shouldn't he tell us?"

"He only told us because I panicked thinking that the Dragon was going to have you for dinner." Miranda hopped off the bed and put her arms about the miserable girl. "Naim made us promise never to tell anyone and we won't," she lied.

"What are you talking about?" asked Nicholas, totally bewildered.

"Dragon spit! What is this?"

"SHUT UP!" yelled the three girls.

Later, Miranda sat with her Ottawa friends in a circle on the floor, listening contentedly as Nick and Arabella talked excitedly about all that had happened to them since the foursome had last been together.

"I saw the Demon," whispered Arabella, suddenly afraid to say the name out loud. "I was never so scared in my life."

At the mention of the Demon, Penelope turned as white as snow but she remained silent, eyes darting restlessly about the room.

Arabella told the others how she had raced to Indolent's Castle to warn Miranda about Hate and how the Demon had brought the Castle down upon her. "Lucky for me, the Riders weren't far behind. They got me out in the nick of time. We just made it through the door when the rest of the place went."

"What about the wizard?" asked Nicholas. "Did you run into him?"

"No. He's probably under the stones, dead as a dodo."

"Did you see my sword?" asked Nicholas.

"No," said Arabella. "I'm sorry you lost it though."

"How did you get here?" asked Miranda.

"The same way you did," said Arabella. "Typhon. He found Noble and Avatar in the woods with Penelope and then we came along so he took me and Marigold, too. The Riders went to Dundurum."

Miranda knew that the Druid had told the others about her adventures in the Serpents' Cave, and she was glad that she didn't have to relive the experience by the telling of it.

Penelope sat with the others, but she didn't join in the conversation. Whenever Miranda spoke to her, she flinched as if she were evading a slap. Miranda wondered what was making the girl so jumpy.

A few minutes after her friends left, Miranda heard a light tapping sound at the door. It was Penelope, squeezing Muffy in a death grip and looking furtively over her shoulders.

"I won't sleep if I don't do this now," she said, pushing past

Miranda into the room.

"What?" asked Miranda.

"Nothing," said Penelope, miserably. "I can't do this."

Miranda, more puzzled than ever, planted herself in front of the door and folded her arms across her chest. "What's going on, Penelope? You've been as jumpy as a grasshopper all night."

"Get out of my way."

"No," said Miranda. "You're not leaving until you tell me what's going on."

"You can't keep me here. That's false imprisonment and it's against the law."

"So, sue me," snapped Miranda.

At that, Penelope threw herself on the unoccupied bed next to Miranda's and started crying. Muffy wriggled free and, thinking Miranda was the cause of her mistress's tears, backed the girl towards the door, snarling and snapping at her ankles.

"NO, MUFFY! BAD DOG!" Miranda pressed her body against the door, glaring at the toy fury and feeling an irresistible urge to giggle. "GET HER OFF ME!"

Penelope stopped crying and gathered the poodle in her arms. "It's OK, Muffers." She shot a guilty look at Miranda. "Sorry, she gets crazy sometimes . . . sort of like me. I'm the reason you almost died in the Serpent's Cave. You didn't lose the Bloodstones, Mir. I took them."

Miranda was speechless. When she finally found her voice all she could say was, "But why?"

"Remember how the wizard put this spell on Muffs. I thought I could use them to take the spell away."

"But they wouldn't work for you."

"I didn't know that and anyway I didn't get a chance to try. When Naim defeated Indolent, the spell was broken." Penelope bowed her head and slipped past Miranda, her hand reaching for the doorknob. "What I did put you in a lot a danger. It was wrong and I'll understand if you don't want to be friends anymore."

Miranda moved away from the door and slumped on the edge of the nearest bed. Part of her wanted to scream at Penelope for being so stupid but a greater part recognized that the girl really was sorry for what she'd done. "It's over. . . ."

A tear rolled down Penelope's cheek as she turned away. "I sort of thought you'd feel that way."

"No, no," said Miranda. "*We're* not over. I got the Egg without the Stones and I survived the Serpent bite. That's over. So let's just forget it."

"You mean it?"

"I mean it. Who knows, maybe if Muffy were my dog and you had the stones, I would have done the same thing. Now get out of here, I'm beat."

Early the next morning, hours before her friends stirred, Miranda said good-bye to the Ministers, but, instead of going to her temporary home, she climbed the flight of steps carved into the face of the steep cliff behind the villa. When she reached the top, she turned her face into the stiff breeze blowing off the lake, and peered down at the roof of her house, letting her eyes roam through the park to the Hall and out to where the city met Lake Leanora. Bethany wasn't like any city she had ever seen or imagined. Instead of office towers, tall green trees dominated the landscape. There were no cars, or traffic lights, or paved streets. She wondered how the Elves got to school or work.

She turned in a circle, expecting to see the sapphire blue lake surrounding her. When she had first seen Ellesmere Island from Parliament Hill, it was a mere dot in the middle of a lake bigger than the Great Lakes of North America put together. She was totally unprepared for the sight that met her eyes. The city of Bethany went on forever, farther than her eyes could see. It was a vast, green ocean and the roofs of the houses small white waves breaking on its surface.

The beauty of the Elven capital, the city where her father and mother were born, was almost too much for the girl. Miranda turned away, and looked down into the park, her eyes following, but not seeing, a large group of people moving across the grass. Then, something about the group caught her attention. A long black cloak billowed out for an instant. Only one person wore a cloak like that. Naim! She studied the group now. They were headed toward the Hall. Why at sunrise? And, why were they in such a hurry?

"Something's wrong," Miranda said as she raced down the stone steps. She didn't have a plan, but she knew she was going to be at that meeting, no matter what.

CHAPTER THIRTY-FIVE
THE DREAM

iranda stood outside the Hall, huffing and puffing after her fast sprint through the park, and staring at the closed door. How was she going to get into the meeting without the Druid spotting her? The thought of getting caught hiding under the table like Nicholas, gave her a funny feeling. No, there had to be another way. But what?

"This is not a place for children, this morning." The voice came from behind. Miranda spun about, and almost died of embarrassment when she found herself face to face with Ruthar, King of the Elves. He was escorted by a dozen Guards dressed completely in black and wearing black berets with a silver oak leaf pinned to the front.

"I-I'm s-sorry," she stammered, wishing an oak tree would fall on her.

"Is that you, Miranda?" asked the King in surprise, coming closer and taking the girl's hands.

Once again, she felt the magic coursing through this good, gentle man with the clear green eyes. Those eyes were looking at her now and she saw both pleasure and concern written there.

"My son told me of your courage," he said. "We owe you more

than you can possibly know, Elven girl. Your father would be proud. But tell me, what are you doing here?"

"I think I've earned the right to know what's going on, Sir," she said, her voice little more than a whisper.

Ruthar looked at her for a long moment. And then he nodded solemnly. "You have indeed. More than any other. Come. We will attend the meeting together."

And so, Miranda walked into the Hall on the arm of the King of all the Elves. The Erudicia and hardened Commanders of the Elven military gazed at her in wonder, for they knew that this was the girl from another world, who went among the Serpents, and came through fire carrying the Golden Egg.

The Druid's eyebrows rose sharply when he saw Miranda enter the Hall beside the King. But, when she was seated next to him, he patted her hand as if he were glad to see her there.

This time, all forty chairs around the long table in the large airy room were occupied. Miranda looked at each place, hoping to see Elester, but his friendly face was not among the grim company. The King raised his right hand and a hush fell over the room instantly. His opening words almost knocked Miranda out of her chair.

"My friends, I would not have asked you here at such an early hour if it were not of the utmost urgency. Last evening, I sent my son with five thousand fighters to help defend Dundurum against the Demon. During the night, I learned that Hate's army of half-dead creatures breached the walls at the base of the mountain and entered King Gregor's country. She has taken the lower cities and the streets are awash with Dwarf blood."

"B-but I thought—" gasped Miranda, before she realized she had spoken out loud.

"You thought it was finished," said the Druid quietly. "But for many, it has just begun."

"I don't understand," cried Miranda. "I thought if we captured the Egg, and used its magic, Hate would be defeated."

The old King tilted his head toward the girl. "I wish it were that simple. Capturing the Egg was the most important undertaking in our war against the Demon. Thanks to you, we have the power to seal the rift. But, to use our magic to force Hate into the Place with No Name, we must drive her away from Dundurum or it, too, will vanish along with the evil ones."

"In other words," said the Druid. "We won the battle, but we still have to fight the war."

Miranda fell silent. She was grief-stricken over the Dwarves who were dying in the lower cities. She thought of the young girl in DunNaith who had waved at her, and she felt a terrible rage growing inside her. She slipped the Bloodstones into her hand and clenched her fist until her knuckles were white. A shiver ran down her back as her anger exploded into the Stones. "Be afraid, Demon!" she commanded, in a voice she didn't recognize. "I am coming for you. I am coming to seize your black stake and drive it through your evil heart. Fear me, for I am coming." Miranda was shaking. *That wasn't me*, she thought, horrified. But if not, who was using her to talk with the Demon?

Suddenly, the Druid leaned over and whispered in her ear. "You got yourself invited to this meeting. At least *look* interested."

Miranda's face burned from the rebuke. She had to admit the Druid was right though. She hadn't been listening. But he was wrong if he thought she didn't care.

King Ruthar looked at the members of the Erudicia, studying each face as if he were saying good-bye. They were the wisest men and women on Ellesmere Island, but they had no wisdom to share with him this morning. Except for the usual border skirmishes and run-ins with the Simurghs, the Bog Trolls, and the Giants of Vark, the Elves had known peace for a thousand years. He touched the large green gemstone he wore about his neck, wondering, not for the first time, what fuelled the Demon? Is Hate, the Destroyer of all living things, necessary for good to thrive? He did not know the answer and probably never would. Sighing, the King shook his head as if to chase away such conundrums.

"Within the hour, I leave for Dundurum along with the Riders and an additional five thousand fighters to stand with the King of the Dwarves against an unspeakable evil—an evil that has not darkened our lands for a thousand years." The King looked at Naim. "We are fortunate to count you among those who will stand with us."

Miranda grabbed the Druid's arm. "You must take me with you," she whispered.

Naim looked at her curiously. "You have done enough, girl. More than enough," he said. "Have you not been listening? Dundurum is at war. It is not a place for children."

"And the Serpent's Cave was?" asked Miranda bitterly.

The Druid stared at her without speaking, and when Miranda saw the pain and guilt etched into his face, she desperately wished that she could take back the harsh words. When Naim finally spoke, his face wore its usual stern expression. "Tell me why you are so set on going to Dundurum?"

"I don't *want* to go," cried Miranda. "Something's calling me there."

"The Demon?" asked the Druid sharply.

"No. Whatever it is, it hates the Demon," said the girl quietly.

The Druid tensed. "Go and gather what you need. Be back here in half an hour." He rose to his feet. "And say nothing to the others," he cautioned before turning away.

When they arrived at the harbour, it seemed to Miranda that the entire City had turned out to see their King sail away to the land of the Dwarves. But then she saw that every man, woman, and child carried a makeshift weapon, anything from brooms and pitchforks to slingshots. *They're here to volunteer,* she thought, amazed. She could see that the King was deeply touched. He walked among the people as if he had all the time in the world, examining their weapons seriously, greeting them as if he knew each one personally, and bending over to talk to the children. He thanked them for coming and then he told them to go home and tend the Kingdom until he returned.

Within the hour, five jumbo hovercrafts, each carrying one thousand Elven troops, slipped out of Bethany Harbour and headed North on a course that would take them to Dundurum. Powered by cold fusion, the Elven ships planed over the waters of Lake Leanora at speeds of over two hundred knots and left no signs of their passing. A number of smaller vessels, equally fast, accompanied the huge troop carriers. Miranda and the Druid travelled with Ruthar's party aboard the ES *Peridot*, a sleek "J" class cruiser. The Elven nation was at war with the Demon.

Miranda went to her cabin. It was a ten-hour trip to Dundurum. For once, she was glad because she needed time to think about what had happened the last time she held the Bloodstones. She smiled as she looked about the cubicle. It was the tiniest room she had ever seen but, like everything Elven, it was beautiful in its simplicity. The brass on the two round portholes was polished to a soft pinkish gold. Antique maps lined the walls. Except for a hammock and a large built-in cupboard, presumably for stowing clothes, boots, and other gear, the cabin was bare. The bathroom, called the Head, was in the passageway outside her cabin.

Miranda crawled into the hammock and removed the Bloodstones from the silver pouch, marveling at their cool smoothness. She poured them from one hand to the other. The cold, hate-filled voice had come from the stones. She was sure of it. Who or what was it? Elester had said that she was the only one who could use them. They were useless to anybody else. Had she uttered that terrible threat? Or did it have something to do with the sixth stone? The room was warm and the girl's eyes closed.

The dream came instantly. It was night and Miranda was running along one of the great arched boulevards in Dundurum. She ran like the wind, faster than her legs would carry her. She heard the Demon close behind, its clawed feet grating on the smooth rock surface. Soon she would feel the creature's putrid breath on the back of her neck. It was pitch-black but that didn't slow her. *I'm using the sight Stone*, thought the part of her that knew she was dreaming.

Suddenly, Miranda slipped out of her body and hovered above the fleeing girl. It happened so abruptly she thought that the evil one had pierced her body with its wicked iron stake, and killed her. But, no. She was still running for her life, gasping for air. Wait! *That's not me*, she thought, trying to see the girl's face. Then who?

The girl in the dream looked like Miranda. She had the same golden hair, but was shorter than the Ottawa girl. As in the recurring dream, she suddenly threw something on the street. It was the silver pouch. "The Bloodstones!" screamed Miranda. But the girl did not react to her frantic cry. Then, to Miranda's horror, the girl came to a stop and looked directly into her eyes and smiled, before turning to face the terrible blackness that was coming at her as surely as Death.

The Demon stalked forward purposefully, a hideous looming blackness that reeked as it came. She stopped thirty feet from the girl and waited, savouring the thrill that ran along her scaly hide. The creature raked one clawed limb across her chest. Blood as black and syrupy as oil trickled down her body, driving the serpents about her middle into a frenzy. Then she dipped her monstrous hands in the blood and smeared the filthy secretion over her neck and under the black hood, her red unblinking glare fixed on the girl the whole time.

The girl waited alone, the sound of her ragged breathing drowned out by the ghastly hissing coming from the Demon. In a flash, Hate came at the girl.

Miranda was rigid with terror. She couldn't bear to watch, but the dream was out of her control and her eyes were glued to the nightmare below. The girl smiled coldly as the Demon advanced. Then she extended her right fist toward the creature and opened her palm. Miranda couldn't believe her eyes when she saw the Bloodstones nestled in the girl's hand. The next instant, the girl was gone, but what appeared in her place turned Miranda's blood to ice.

Hate, the Demon, shrieked in fear and rage before hurling the sharp black stake into the air, straight at Miranda.

"NO!" Miranda screamed, ducking and twisting to escape being impaled on Hate's evil weapon.

CHAPTER THIRTY-SIX

THE SIXTH STONE

"ir! Stop it! Wake up!"

Miranda opened her eyes, arms up to deflect the wicked stake. Instead, she found herself blinking at Nicholas, who was leaning over her, tense and alarmed. She sat up and looked about. What on earth was she doing on the cabin floor?

"At first it sounded like you were fighting with someone, but when I looked, I thought you were having a seizure," said Nicholas. "You were thrashing about like crazy."

"I was dreaming," mumbled Miranda, rubbing her head where she had bumped it on the floor. "Mom was right. It's not my dream."

"What are you talking about?" said Arabella, suddenly appearing out of the cupboard.

Miranda seemed to notice her friends for the first time. "Nick! Bell! What are you doing here? How did you—?"

"You thought you were so clever, but I knew something was up, the way you were sneaking around the Villa trying to avoid us," said Arabella. "So I found Nick, and he told me that the Riders were leaving for Dundurum immediately, and the Druid was sailing with King Ruthar."

Nicholas picked up the story. "We were pretty sure you were

going with them. When we got to the harbour, we saw you and the Druid with the King. It wasn't hard to find the King's boat, with all the Guards around. They didn't even stop us. Bell said we were travelling with you and they just waved us aboard. One of the mates, or whatever they're called, showed us your cabin. The rest was easy."

Miranda stared at her friends dumbfounded. Then she broke into a grin. "You were in the cupboard all this time?"

Her companions nodded. "We couldn't come out until we were far enough away from Bethany they couldn't take us back," said Arabella. "Then you started shouting and we thought you were being attacked."

"Where's Penelope?" asked Miranda.

"Probably still in bed," said Arabella. "I left a note."

"What's this about a dream?" asked Nicholas.

Miranda was heartened at the sight of her friends. She told them about the dream she'd been having for months back home. "Don't laugh, but Mom said it's possible to inherit a direct ancestor's memory." She looked at her friends, but they weren't laughing. They were listening intently. "I think Mom was right. Just now, when I was dreaming, it wasn't about me. It was another girl. I got everything wrong. I always thought the dream would end with the Monster catching me and clawing me to death. Or something. But the girl in my dream knew she was going to defeat the Demon. I saw it in her face. She was actually smiling when she fought Hate."

"That's horrible!" cried Arabella. "You should have told me. I knew something was going on the last time we were at your house."

"Yeah," said Miranda. "For a while, I thought I was going out of my mind."

"What I want to know is how the girl in the dream defeated the Demon?" asked Nicholas.

"It's about the Bloodstones, but it's not something I can tell, it's something I have to do," said Miranda quietly.

Nicholas and Arabella exchanged looks. Then Nicholas slung an arm about Miranda's shoulders. "Whatever you have to do, Mir, we're coming with you," he said.

Miranda's eyes filled with tears of gratitude. "Thanks, I'm not looking forward to facing the Demon alone. But I can't take you with me. I haven't got the right to put you in danger or maybe get you both killed."

"Shut up," said Arabella. "We're coming, and that's that."

"The only place you are going, is back to Bethany," said an angry voice from the doorway.

The Druid paced back and forth, wearing a path in the polished wood floor of the tiny cabin, and muttering angrily to himself. Facing him in a row on the hammock were the three companions, eyes downcast, faces flushed with guilt. "I expected more from you," he growled. Then he glared at Miranda. "And especially from you."

"Miranda had nothing to do with it," said Nicholas hotly. "The question is, what happens now? You can't send us back!"

"I have a good mind to turn you into chum and feed you to the fish." said the Druid.

"You're certainly good at turning people into things," snapped the boy. But when he met the Druid's cold eyes, he looked away quickly, remembering how it felt to be a tree stump.

Miranda stood and went to the angry Druid. She touched his arm gently. "Naim, once you asked me to trust you, and I did. Now I'm asking you to trust me. You know in your heart that it's the only chance we have to defeat the Demon."

"It is too dangerous. King Ruthar cannot spare a hundred Guards to protect you."

"No. We can't take Guards. Don't you see? If the King sends a hundred Guards with us, the Demon will see through it." She waited for the man's reaction before continuing. "If it's just me and my friends—three kids, she won't suspect anything. She'll think we got lost or ran away. I don't have the Egg anymore, so I'm not a threat to her."

"You are placing a lot of faith in a dream, girl," said the Druid softly. He bent over and gripped Miranda's shoulders. "Are you absolutely sure about this?"

Miranda shrugged. "No, I'm not sure. But I believe that the dream is true. I mean the things in the dream really happened to that girl. And somehow, I ended up with part of her memory." But she felt the hairs on her neck stir as she recalled the girl's green eyes meeting hers purposely.

"What if the memory's missing something important?" asked Arabella.

"Or what if it's the Demon planting those dreams to get you alone?" said Nicholas.

"Enough," said the Druid, silencing the others immediately. "We can 'what if' until the sun comes up in the west and not be satisfied." He turned back to Miranda. "If you do this thing, you will be in great peril."

"I know," she replied. "But you do see that I have to try?"

The Druid nodded slowly. "Come with me to the King. We must lay our plans carefully."

After their session with the King of the Elves, the Druid led the companions to the stern, where he peered into the air and then raised his arm and pointed toward the western sky. "There!" he shouted, a rare smile softening his grim features. The three friends followed his outstretched arm and saw a brilliant flash swiftly approaching the boat.

Miranda's eyes sparkled. "Is that what I think it is?" she asked, matching the Druid's smile with one of her own.

"Yes. Charlemagne," he answered, his gaze fixed on the huge bird.

"What's that?" asked Nicholas, his eyes growing wider by the second. His question was answered by the sudden whistle of wind in a pair of giant wings as the two-headed, golden Eagle descended from the sky and landed gracefully on the deck.

Miranda and her friends could not tear their eyes away from the awesome creature. The Eagle stood a head taller than the Druid. Its black wing feathers were tipped with gold and its chest was speckled mahogany and bronze. The great bird shone with a dazzling light from the crown of its heads to its huge gold talons. Its sharp, unblinking eyes were riveted on the Druid's young companions, as the man and the Eagle bowed to one another.

"It is a pleasure to see you again," said the Druid, after the formalities were finished. "What is the news from Dundurum?"

Miranda stared in astonishment as the long hooked beak on one of the creature's heads opened and the Eagle spoke.

"The pleasure is mine, Old One," replied the giant bird, its voice filling Miranda's head with thoughts of autumn leaves rustling in the wind. "But the news I bring from the land of the Dwarves lessens the pleasure."

"Tell me," pressed the Druid.

Before answering, the Eagle tilted one head toward Miranda. "You must be the Elven girl who captured the Serpent's Egg?"

Miranda bowed before the creature. "Yes, sir," she answered. "But I had a lot of help."

The head nodded and swung back to the Druid. "Is the Egg on board?"

"Heavily guarded and well-cushioned. Now tell me what is happening in Dundurum?"

"The three lower cities are under the Demon's control. The Dwarves still hold the upper cities, but they face certain defeat. I delivered your message. The King did not take it kindly at first. In fact he said some rather unpleasant things about you. But after a lot of stomping and swearing, he started evacuating the upper cities." The Eagle bowed its heads. "It is a sad day for the world, Old One."

"A very sad day," agreed the Druid. "But for you and me, the day is not over yet, my friend. There is one last thing I must ask you to do."

"If it is within my power, it will be done," said the Eagle.

The Druid leaned closer and told the bird about Miranda's plan. Charlemagne listened intently. When the Druid finally stepped back, the Eagle turned to the three friends. "It is a daring plan," he said. "And that is why it may succeed." He looked back at the Druid. "Where is this rare Egg?"

When the Guards had delivered the golden Egg, Charlemagne hopped onto the flat roof of the pilot house, spread its broad wings and hovered just over the deck long enough to pluck the Egg from the Druid's outstretched hands. Then the mighty bird soared into the sky.

"How fast does this boat go?" asked Nicholas, staring after the golden arrow until it was lost to sight.

"Charlemagne can outfly lightning when he must," answered the Druid.

Dundurum was a shambles. The companions stood on the deck of the ES *Peridot*, leaning over the rail, oblivious to the tears of sadness mixed with anger that filled their eyes and rolled down their cheeks. They didn't speak, because there were no words to describe the ruin that had once been the land of the Dwarves. Black smoke, as thick as clouds, hid the sunset and most of the mountain, and wrapped about the young friends like a living thing. Nicholas gazed at the carnage, banging his fist on the railing, his face white and drawn. Arabella sobbed and wiped at her eyes with shaking hands, her lips moving silently.

Miranda boiled. She had never hated anyone in her life, until this moment. The black emotion possessed her now, and she welcomed it. She ached to lose herself in its madness—to use its power to lash out—to rip the Demon's hide with her fingernails—to tear the creature's arms off. . . . And then, suddenly, the hatred was yanked from her mind. She actually felt the physical pull as it left her and was absorbed into the Bloodstones. No! Not the Stones—the *sixth* Stone.

In an instant, the young girl understood the power of the dreadful force that consumed and drove the Demon. When the Demon became Hate, she *really* became Hate—a totally different creature from the one who had been known as Taog. They might look alike, but the similarities ended there. Miranda shuddered. She remembered all the times she had said "I hate so and so," or "I hate that." The word had always slipped off her tongue so easily—so thoughtlessly. She shuddered, overwhelmed by her terrible knowledge, knowing that it had changed her forever.

They were met at the docks by a phalanx of Dwarf soldiers, sturdy, sombre men and women, who escorted them through the rubble to the King of the Dwarves. Miranda smiled grimly when she spotted Gregor's familiar shape in the midst of a group of battle-weary troops, bushy head bowed over a map. At their approach, he looked up and raised a hand in greeting. Miranda was shocked at his appearance. Gregor's eyes were red from fatigue, crisscrossed with more lines than the map he had been studying. He looked as if he hadn't slept in a year. His beard was knotted and straggly, and his clothing was torn and bloodstained. He barked orders to the troops and marched toward the Druid.

"Glad you're here. Need your fire. Vermin crawling all over. Like rats." The Dwarf spat in the dirt before he reached out and patted Miranda roughly on the back. "Good work, girl. Worried. Couldn't be there." He stomped the ground and cleared his throat. "Heard about your plan. Eagle told me. It's risky. Bold though. What do you need?"

"I need to get inside Dundurum so I can call the Demon," said Miranda, feeling the colour drain from her face as doubts filled her head. Was she out of her mind? What had she been thinking? There was no way on earth she could face Hate alone.

Her hand sought and found the Bloodstones and she felt a sudden calm wash through her. "You will not be alone," she thought they said.

CHAPTER THIRTY-SEVEN
CALLING THE DEMON

n the gloomy half-light, Gregor led the companions away from the gaping black hole that had once been the main gateway into his mountain kingdom. Miranda felt her heart break as she stepped over great chunks of sculpted stonework. "It's all gone," she whispered, her fist closing tightly over the Bloodstones.

She ran through the plan in her mind. Suddenly it seemed like a stupid idea. What if she were wrong? What if Arabella were right and there was something missing in the dream or, as Nicholas said, what if the Demon planted the dream to get her inside the mountain? No! That didn't make sense. The Demon had no interest in her now that the Egg was in the hands of the Elves. *I'm the last person Hate'll be worried about.*

The King of the Dwarves stopped in front of a rough section of the black mountain. "Can't post guards. Demon eyes everywhere." He slid his hand into a thin crevice and worked his fingers over the uneven surface. Then he moved away and stared at the section of black rock. Miranda and the others waited anxiously, but nothing happened. "Hate knows there's a secret entrance. But can't find it," said the Dwarf.

"I don't see anything," said Miranda, baffled. She noticed, from the looks on her friends' faces, that they were as bewildered as she.

"It's open," muttered the Dwarf. "Wouldn't be secret if you could see it."

"This is where we leave you," said the Druid quietly to the Elven girl.

Miranda gulped. She tried to take a step, but her legs turned to rubber. Naim bent over and placed his hands on her shoulders. His dark eyes searched her face. "No one will think less of you if you turn away now, girl," he said.

Miranda shook her head, unable to speak. Suddenly, from the shadows behind, a familiar voice spoke her name and she felt new strength blossom within. "Elester!" she cried, turning toward the Elven Prince and racing to him with both arms outstretched.

Elester knelt on the rough stony ground and caught the girl in his strong arms. "What kept you?" Miranda demanded, but her eyes shone with happiness.

The young Prince laughed, and the sound of Elven laughter in that terrible place of death ignited a flame of hope in the hearts of all who heard. For the first time since the Demon laid siege to Dundurum, a faint light was visible at the end of the long dark tunnel.

"I am with you now," said Elester, holding the girl at arms' length. "You will not face the Demon alone." Then he rose and joined the others. "Nicholas, I have something for you," he said, handing him the Elven blade that Indolent had filched from the boy.

Nicholas broke into a grin. "All right!" he said, taking the sword and turning it over in his hand before carefully sheathing it in the leather scabbard at his side. "Thanks, Elester. I never thought I'd see it again."

"Do not thank me," said the Elf. "Thank Laury when you see him. He found it on the ground behind Indolent's Castle, or what was left standing after the Demon made a surprise visit. The wizard must have dropped it when he was fleeing for his life."

"You mean he got away?" asked Nicholas, crossing his arms to ward off the icy fingers that walked across his flesh. "It would've served him right if she'd caught him."

"The wizard can do no more harm," said the Druid. "I stripped him of his powers."

Elester looked at Miranda. "Are you ready?"

Miranda managed a weak smile and nodded slowly.

"I might have known you'd try to sneak off without me," said Penelope, elbowing her way through the group and grabbing Arabella's arm.

"Oh, no!" groaned Miranda, Nicholas, and Arabella with one voice.

"WHAT ARE YOU DOING HERE?" roared the Druid.

"It's a free country," snapped Penelope. She wagged her finger at Arabella. "If she gets to go, I can go too."

"I thought you were asleep," said Arabella, yanking her arm free. "Really."

"Did you bother looking? Did you think about asking me to come with you? NO!"

"Where's the Muffrat?" asked Nicholas, dreading the answer.

Penelope glared at the boy. "Where do you think?" she asked, her voice harsh with sarcasm. Then she patted the front of her jacket. "MUFFY is right here, of course."

"Oh, no!" sighed the girl's friends, again.

The Druid shook his head as if nothing would surprise him. "How did you get here?" he demanded.

Penelope giggled. "It was so easy. I followed Bell from the villa and saw her and Nick sneak onto one of the boats. But, just as I got there, they raised the gangplank. So I started crying and went over to this nice woman who was a soldier or something. Anyway, she asked me what was wrong, and I told her I was supposed to be travelling with King Ruthar but I lost my way and now the ship was gone. She took me on one of the big hovercraft. It was excellent.

And everybody thought Muffers was so cute."

Nicholas and Arabella gaped at each other, remembering the hours they spent huddled in the cupboard in Miranda's cabin. When they shifted their eyes to Penelope, they looked as if they wanted to murder her.

"So," said Penelope, brightly. "Where are we going?"

Before the Druid exploded, Miranda acted. "I'm glad you're coming with us," she said, putting her arm about the girl's shoulders. "One more person might make all the difference when we fight the Demon."

Penelope choked. "Y-you're g-going t-to f-fight t-the D-demon?" She looked about at the others. "J-just t-the s-six o-of y-you?"

"Not that many," said Miranda. "Naim and Gregor aren't coming. So we'll be five, counting you."

Penelope looked about wildly, like a trapped rabbit. Miranda could almost hear the wheels going round in her head. "Oh, dear," the girl cried, finally. "Muffy! What about Muffs?"

"You could tie her to a tree," suggested Nicholas innocently.

"NOT!" snapped Penelope. She grasped Miranda hand. "I can't leave Muffers."

Miranda patted the girl's hand. "It's OK. I understand. But would you do one thing for us?"

"What?" Suspiciously.

Miranda looked at Naim. "Give her the flare." Then she turned back to Penelope. "When you hear us coming, light the flare and wave it back and forth over your head. Can you do that?"

"Sure," said Penelope. "Is that all?"

"That's it," said Miranda.

"Let us go," said Elester. "Time is running out."

I can't walk through a mountain, Miranda thought, extending her arms in front to take the brunt of the impact when she hit the solid rock. But, to her astonishment, both hands disappeared into the stone. Then the rest of her followed.

"That was so weird," breathed Arabella, appearing out of the wall.

"Awesome!" said Nicholas, on her heels.

The last thing the companions heard as Elester led them along the tunnel was the harsh voice of the Druid threatening to turn Penelope into a lizard and feed her to Muffy if she so much as blinked during her watch.

The tunnel had been built to accommodate Dwarves. Elester ran crouched low, and even Nicholas kept his head down. Miranda was surprised to find that the secret passageway was not pitch black like the Serpents' Cave. Some sort of lighting, concealed in the stone walls, cast a dim bluish glow over the companions as they hurried toward the main boulevard in the lower city of DunNaith, the same city where the Trust had feasted on sauerkraut, and sausages, and Boot Beer, only days before. It was the first of the lower cities to fall to the Demon.

As they ran in silence through the long narrow tunnel, Miranda fought to control the pounding of her heart. She suddenly wanted nothing more than to go home—to be with her mother and watch TV—and stop being afraid.

The tunnel ended abruptly at another solid rock wall. Quickly, Elester knelt and felt along the uneven surface, searching for the triggering device that would reveal the opening. "Where is it?" he muttered in frustration. "It should be right here."

Miranda and her friends joined in the search, running their hands over the stone.

"Eureka!" cried Arabella, moving aside as Elester worked his hand into the narrow crack and pressed his long fingers into a series of indentations in the stone. Then he stepped back and spoke to Arabella and Nicholas.

"This is as far as you go. Do you understand what you must do?"

Nicholas nodded. "As soon as we hear you or Mir, I run outside and alert Penelope to wave the flare."

"And I wait here to show Mir the way out, in case she's alone," said Arabella, squeezing Miranda's hands tightly. Both pairs of hands were like ice.

Elester touched their shoulders. "The Demon has powerful magic but even she cannot see through stone. You will be safe here. Arabella, if you hear Miranda whistle, do not jump out at her. Call her name until she knows you. That is very important. And then run away from here. Do you understand?"

Arabella's dark face glowed blue in the dim light. She bit her lip to stop the quivering and nodded. The Elf took Miranda's hand and they disappeared into the rock.

It was so black that Miranda thought they were still inside the stone wall, between the blue tunnel and the wide streets of Dundurum, until Elester whispered. "Can you see?"

"No," answered the girl.

"Take the Stones," said the Elf. "Trust the Stones, Miranda."

Miranda fumbled for the silver pouch, terrified that she'd drop one of the Bloodstones on the black surface. If that happened, she'd never find it again. Carefully, she poured them into her cupped palm and quickly closed her hand. Almost instantly, the darkness began to fade. Soon she could see Elester's familiar shape.

"They're working! I can see you!" she breathed. "It's incredible! Everything's getting clearer by the second."

"Good," said Elester. "I can see well enough. Tell me where you are going and I will run ahead and hide myself."

"Where are we?" asked the girl, looking about, totally lost.

Elester pointed. "Down there. If we turn right at that street, we will end up in DunNaith. If we follow it through the town, we will come to the main gates." He looked at the girl. "Wherever we go, we must be careful not to get trapped between the Demon and our escape route."

"The Demon will come by the main gates," said Miranda, wondering how she knew that. "We have to go through DunNaith and wait on the other side of the town."

"Come then," said the Elf. "And pay attention so that you can find your way back to the tunnel."

"But you'll be here."

"I will be here," said Elester. "But if something goes wrong . . . if we get separated . . . you must get away as quickly as you can. Do not wait for me."

Miranda nodded, suddenly terrified that the entire plan could go wrong.

As they started out, Elester put his hand on her shoulder and looked at her sadly. "There is one more thing I must tell you before we go any farther. This is not the Dundurum you remember, Miranda. It is now a tomb—a place where the Demon has committed horrible crimes against the Dwarves and our people." He paused for a second. "You will see things that will make your soul weep."

"I know," answered the girl, feeling sick. "But nothing will make me give up. It'll only make me stronger."

The Elven Prince grimaced and then he and the girl jogged along the deserted street, not speaking until they reached the town of DunNaith.

"From here on, we must move carefully," Elester whispered. "Hate would not leave the town unguarded. Watch out for Trolls and worse things."

As they passed through the town, Miranda fought to keep from screaming. Hate had flattened the town to rubble. The wide boulevard had been blasted apart as if a bomb had gone off. The beautifully carved walls were gone, smashed to fragments. Miranda kicked over a slab of stone and saw a group of eight or ten Dwarves posed in front of a vast cavern. They were grinning and in their raised hands they held steins of Boot or some other beverage. She wondered what they had been celebrating. Perhaps they had just completed a new street or a new town. Sadly, she bent and turned the stone over on its face. For thousands of years the Dwarves had meticulously carved their history onto the walls. And then Hate came and, in a second, it was gone—turned to dust for all time. "I can't bear it," she whispered, as tears blinded her for a moment.

But then she saw the bodies, and her world went black.

Elester caught the girl and clamped his strong hand over her mouth. "I know you want to scream, but I have to stop you. Look at the bodies, Miranda. They are not Dwarves." He did not tell her that the Hellhags had already dragged the slain Dwarves away for their own evil purposes. "Look at them. And be sad for them if you must. But remember, they went to the Demon willingly." Slowly he removed his hand from the girl's mouth.

"I'm OK," Miranda gasped, knowing that she was anything but OK. "I didn't expect . . . I didn't think. . . ." She bowed her head and burst into tears.

"I am sorry that you have had to see things that no ten-year-old should ever have to see," said Elester, brushing away the girl's tears with his hands.

Miranda sniffled. "It's not your fault. I watch the news on TV at home and I know that things like this happen to kids. I see babies so skinny they look like skeletons. Even in my country horrible things happen, but . . . oh, I don't know. I just think it's worse not to know."

"And I think you are a credit to our race, Elven girl," said Elester softly.

Miranda blushed fiercely. Then she took a deep breath, steeling herself to face the horrors of war. "Let's go. I'll be OK."

"We can go back now," said the Elf.

"No, not after this." She waved her arm toward the dead creatures.

"Give me time to get out of sight," said the Elf.

Miranda wiped her eyes with her fists. She felt the Bloodstones talking to her, urging her to hurry. "For Dundurum," she said quietly as she ran toward the main gates. About a hundred yards from the gates, she stopped. "Now. I'm ready." But she was totally unprepared for the horrible sound that issued from her throat as she called the Demon.

CHAPTER THIRTY-EIGHT

HATE

n the filthy air above Dundurum, Hate the Demon circled lazily, gripping the iron stake in two outstretched hands. Her red eyes pierced the smoke and focused on the activity below. The sight of her half-dead creatures crawling over the mountain, like ants on a dying insect, filled her with pleasure. The Dwarves were finished, but she was not finished with them. Oh, no! Now she would enter the land of the swill-eaters and unleash thousands of THUGS to wipe the stinking race from the face of the earth.

For a second, Hate thought of the two THUGS who had failed to kill the girl, letting her escape with the magic Egg. The Dragon, Typhon, had dealt with one of them. She had lived the creature's fear as the Dragon's teeth clamped down upon it, feeling every bone-splintering, organ-crushing bite as if it had been her own body. Yes, and a part of her had died in the Dragon's belly when the light had finally winked out in the THUG's eyes. She had punished the other one, leaving its bloody, maimed carcass in the woods that separated the Swampgrass from Dundurum. And it would rot there until she was good and ready to forgive the creature for its failure.

Suddenly, the Demon's black heart skipped a beat. What? What? She stopped circling, her body rigid, her mind alert to the danger signals that tingled up her scaly back. Something was down there— inside the mountain. She sensed its presence like a bad odour. And then she felt it probe her mind—taunting her, laughing at her. Filled with rage as red and hot as fresh blood, Hate dropped from the sky.

High above the Demon, Charlemagne, the two-headed Eagle, saw the creature streaking toward Dundurum. Abruptly, he opened his twin beaks and screamed—a long, piercing cry that filled the sky and echoed down the mountain to where the Druid and the King of the Elves stood beside Gregor, locked in battle with a large host of Hate's army. The men exchanged quick glances as they heard the Eagle's warning call.

The huge Demon landed in the midst of the chaos. Shrieking and hissing, she raised the iron stake. Fire blazed along its length, turning it red hot and setting the skull's empty eye sockets aflame. Then, the creature stretched out her long arm and pointed the wicked stake at the yawning black hole where Dundurum's main gates had once stood open in welcome. The red Demon-fire exploded into all those who stood between Hate and the opening—igniting her own evil creatures, who ran amok, arms flailing wildly, and like living torches, set others ablaze, including a young Elf and two Dwarves. Raw inhuman screams, coming from the throats of the burning, dying creatures, split the air, drowning out the hard sounds of battle. When the voices finally went silent, the Demon stormed along the wide blackened path toward the entrance to the Mountain.

Just as Hate was about to disappear into the blackness of Dundurum, she turned and fixed her red gaze on the battle raging about her. Something was amiss. She couldn't quite put her claws on it, but there was something. . . . Why wasn't the enemy attacking? Why were they content to simply defend their positions? She had expected to find the ground littered with filthy Dwarf bodies.

She knew the stubborn creatures. They would never give up. They would fight to the last man and woman to protect their precious country. So where were the bodies? Surely the Hellhags would wait until after the fighting to feast. Looking about, the Demon saw that most of the dead belonged to her. Puzzled by the enemy's uncharacteristic behaviour, she kicked the body of a large Troll out of the way, and scanned the battle site one last time.

Her blood simmered when she spotted the Druid. Then she recognized the tall figure of Ruthar, her true enemy, and the simmer became a rolling boil. "YOU!" she hissed, grabbing one of the serpents and pulling it from the tangled knot about her middle. Quick as thought, she raised her arm and flung the poisonous viper toward the small group of men. "*DIE!*" Then the Demon whipped her long tongue across her lips and hissed again with pleasure, as the deadly reptile shot through the air—a living arrow, its jaws wide.

The Druid tried to keep one eye on the Demon and the other on the band of Trolls and a pack of Hellhags pressing in from three sides. Again and again, the staff went up and white fire tore into the front ranks, but others took their places immediately, trampling over the bodies of their dead comrades. There was no end to the creatures. Black circles shadowed Naim's eyes and lines of exhaustion creased his face. He knew he could not evoke the Druid-fire much longer. He glanced quickly toward the Demon just in time to see her hurl something at him.

"GET DOWN!" he yelled, swinging his cloak up to shield Ruthar and Gregor. But he was a fraction of a second too late. As the venomous serpent hit the King of the Elves in the chest, its head was already flashing toward the exposed flesh on Ruthar's neck. The King swatted the snake aside but not before its sharp fangs found their mark and released the deadly toxin.

Gregor went after the creature, stomping the ground with his heavy boots to crush the life out of it. But the wily reptile slithered under a huge boulder and from there, found safety in the thick brush that fronted the forest.

Roaring in anger, the Druid brought up the staff and sent a great wall of white fire raging through the enemy lines. In the confusion, he lifted the dazed King and, cradling the old man as if he were a baby, ran through the smoke.

While the Elves raced after their fallen leader, Gregor signaled the remaining Dwarf troops. They came to him instantly. For a second, they stared at the ruined gates to their beloved country, then they turned their backs on their homes and followed their King away from that place of death.

Deep in the mountain, in the middle of the wide demolished street, Miranda fingered the Bloodstones and waited, watching and listening intently. *Maybe she's not coming,* she thought, hating herself for hoping that the Demon wouldn't answer the call. The more she thought about facing Hate, the greater her fear grew. "Stop it!" she scolded, looking back toward the town where Elester was hiding. She couldn't see him, but just knowing he was near kept her from running away. She couldn't believe that she had planned to come here alone. Now, the thought made her weak. "Trust the Stones," she whispered. "Trust the Stones."

Suddenly, a foul stench filled the cavern. It came from the Demon, who stood motionless at the end of the street, her eyes burning with a mixture of rage and amusement as she studied the small human girl who stared back boldly.

Miranda felt the Bloodstones pulling at her as she spat the stink of the Demon from her mouth. But she resisted and screamed at the Monster, knowing that she had no control over her voice. "I KNOW WHAT YOU ARE! I KNOW YOUR POWER!" Then she turned and ran toward the town. She didn't have to look back. She heard the Demon coming after her, its clawed feet rasping on the hard stone surface.

The girl peered ahead, suddenly panicked when she saw the rubble of DunNaith in the distance. She hadn't realized she had come this far. How fast was the Demon? "Fast!" she breathed. "I'll never make it."

This time the dream was real. Miranda ran until her lungs screamed for air and her heart felt as if it would burst. She ran like the wind, waiting for the creature's sharp claws to rip into her back. Frantically, she clutched the metallic pouch. The clasp broke and the pouch slipped through her fingers and fell to the ground. As a sob escaped from her lips, she realized that she held the Bloodstones tightly in her hand. And then she was leaping over chunks of rock that had once been the town and the Bloodstones came alive. Miranda skidded to a stop and spun toward the Demon.

"Let go! Let go!" cried the Stones.

As in the dream, the Demon slowed and stopped about thirty feet from Miranda, relishing the inevitable kill. She hissed and raked the air with her claws, teasing the girl, torturing her with the manner of her death.

"Let go! Let go!" The Stones were screaming now. But Miranda was paralyzed with terror, her wide eyes locked on the huge looming black creature. Her mind screamed louder than the Stones and the message was clear. *Run! Escape!* The reason she had risked everything to face the Demon no longer mattered. The only thing that mattered was the need for her to get away.

Hate hissed again, a grisly echo in the deathly tomb, and the sound fell on the girl like ice water. White with fear, she blinked, breaking eye contact for a second. That's when she saw the THUGS —hundreds of the red-eyed creatures moving silently along the street behind their Mistress. She reached toward Hate with one tightly clenched fist—the Stones throbbing against her palm.

Hate lunged at the girl, closing the distance between them in three giant strides. Miranda tried to open her hand but it wouldn't respond. Fear turned her courage to ashes. Despair washed over her. To have come this far only to fail. She thought of all those who were going to die because of her. And, after Hate slaughtered the peoples of this world, she'd find her way back to Canada, and then, the killing would start there. Her mother would die, as surely as the sun rose each morning. She couldn't bear the thought of losing her mother and Naim and her friends. But what could she do? After all, she was just a kid. Shoulders drooping in defeat, Miranda dropped her eyes and backed away from the Demon.

She had only taken a few steps when she felt something cold touch her hand. And suddenly, through the mist of fear coating her eyes, she recognized Arabella, the girl's hand covering her own. Without looking, she knew that Nicholas was there too, behind and just to her right. Once again, her friends had risked life and limb to come to her rescue.

Gently, she pushed Arabella's hand away and waved an arm for her friends to stand back. She heard the sound of their boots as they moved into the shadows behind her. Miranda raised her head and glared at the Demon. Slowly, she opened her hand.

The Bloodstones glowed with a dull light. For the first time since Naim had placed the metallic pouch in her hand, she trusted the Stones, answering the pull by letting them draw her into their cool softness. And then, she was gone. But the creature that rose in her place sent the Demon reeling back as terror clobbered her like a sledgehammer.

Just as the sixth Bloodstone had absorbed the hate Miranda felt when she looked upon the devastation of Dundurum, it now drained hate from the Demon, sucking her dry as hay. Before Hate could react, the Stone amassed all of the malice it had soaked up over millions of years and formed the insane emotion into a fearsome creature. Then, it unleashed the abomination at the Demon.

The creature towered over Hate. In the blackness beneath its hood, two eyes glowed red. In one of its four clawed hands, it gripped a black iron stake with a human skull impaled near the sharp end. It was the Demon's worst nightmare—a creature like herself, only much, much worse, turned loose on her.

Too late, Hate saw the trap. Instantly, she remembered that this scene had been played out once before, a thousand years ago, in this same place. It was a girl who had tricked her then, allowing the enemy to drive her into the arid waste and imprison her in the Place with No Name. No wonder the miserable Dwarves and Elves hadn't bothered to attack. They had the girl and they had used her as bait.

The Demon quickly raised three arms to ward off the approaching menace. The fourth hand pointed the iron stake at the black hate-filled creature. But, the creature brushed aside the Demon-fire and ripped the feeble weapon from Hate's grasp. In one great hand, it bent the iron stake as easily as if it were a blade of grass. Almost casually, it tossed the twisted bit of metal on the ground and reached for the Demon with two arms, steel claws biting through the thick scales into Hate's flesh as she hissed and screeched. A third hand grabbed hold of Demon's long protruding tongue, and pulled.

From his hiding place, Elester watched in horror as Arabella and Nicholas darted from the shadows and placed themselves on either side of Miranda. He saw Arabella touch the girl's hand. Then they were moving away and, before he could react, Miranda stretched out her hand.

A loathsome creature burst from the Elven girl and towered over the cringing Demon. Elester's mind raced as he struggled to understand what had happened. Had Miranda transformed into the Monster, or was it the work of the Stones? If the Stones released the beast, where was the girl? And the others? And then he saw them, supporting Miranda between them, as they backed slowly away from the huge creatures. Elester ran to Miranda and caught her by the arm, dragging her into the deeper shadows. He crouched and looked into her pale, frightened face.

"I think I did it, Elester. I disappeared," she said, her voice flat, as if her spirit had fled from her body.

Elester nodded, too overcome by what had just happened, to find words for the girl. He barely found the strength to take her icy-cold hand and lead her through the desolation that had once been home to thousands of Dwarf families. Nicholas and Arabella raced ahead to locate the exit tunnel and Miranda stumbled along beside the Elf like an old woman, lost within herself. She still clutched the Bloodstones, but she was unable to open her mind to them.

The showdown with the Demon kept replaying over and over in her head. She couldn't have explained it, but she thought she understood something of the power of the sixth stone. It was like a magnifying glass. It took things and enlarged them, and made them worse. It stole the force that gave the Demon life and sent a blown up image back to her, showing her what she thought she was. Or had the image come from her? She wondered if she'd ever know for sure.

For a second, she thought she saw the girl in the dream, a shy grin spreading across her face. Then the girl raised her arm and vanished. Miranda made one leg move and then the other as she tried to keep up with Elester. They saw no one. They met no one. When they finally turned into the side street that led to the tunnel, the prince gathered Miranda in his arms and sprinted down the passageway.

Nicholas heard them coming and reacted instantly, bolting along the tunnel and through the rock to where Penelope waited anxiously in the darkness. "They're coming. Light the flare."

Penelope jumped, staring at Nicholas as if he were a ghost. Her hands shook so badly, she dropped the flare. "I'm sorry," she wailed. "Oh, Nick! I never thought I'd see any of you again. Is Mir—?"

"She's OK," said Nicholas, dropping to his knees and scrabbling in the dirt until his hand closed over the flare. Quickly, he pulled the tab and the stick burst into a green flame. "Here," he said, passing it to Penelope. "You do it."

Inside the tunnel, Arabella wrung her hands and tried to peer into her friend's face in the darkness. "Is she going to be all right?"

"I do not know," replied Elester.

"Of course, I'm going to be all right," snapped Miranda. "Put me down, Elester. And let's get out of here."

Arabella giggled. "It must be the company you keep. You're starting to sound just like the Druid."

Charlemagne the golden Eagle saw the flare and dropped like a thunderbolt, clutching the Serpent's Egg in his strong claws. The Eagle's fierce cry cut through the night air and reached the ears of the great Dragon, Typhon, who was perched on top of the fifteen-thousand-foot mountain known as Dundurum, the land of the Dwarves. The huge, solitary beast unfurled its mighty wings and plummeted toward the ground just as Elester pushed through the rock wall with Miranda and Arabella.

"What *is* that?" cried Nicholas, peering up into the black sky.

"It should be the Dragon," answered Elester.

Penelope turned white. "What does it want? I gave them all back."

Arabella snickered and nudged Miranda.

"A real Dragon!" said Nicholas in awe.

"Typhon has come to take us to my father," said the Elf. "It is time to send the Demon back to the Place with No Name."

The colossal flying reptile swooped low over the companions and gently gathered them up in its giant claws. Then the creature flapped its wings and lifted into the air, creating a fierce gale that sent boulders tumbling over the ground like giant marbles. It seemed that they were aloft only seconds before Typhon descended and landed heavily in a clump of thorny bushes. He opened his great claws and released the passengers.

"That was amazing!" cried Nicholas, beaming happily. "A Dragon! A real Dragon!"

The huge creature snorted contemptuously, a stream of fire gushing from its cavernous nostrils.

"Thank you, Dragon," said Elester. "Once again, we are in your debt."

"IN THAT CASE," roared the Dragon. "PERHAPS I CAN HAVE THE BOY."

Nicholas paled and shrank back in fear. But Typhon only chuckled, his massive tail thumping the ground, knocking over several small trees. Then the creature stomped into the darkness. "YOU OWE ME NOTHING, ELF."

"Elester! Over here! Quickly!"

As Miranda and her friends turned at the sound of the Druid's voice, Elester was already running toward the dark figure whose hand glowed with a white flame.

"What is it?" cried Elester. "Where is my father?"

Naim laid his arm about the young Elf's shoulder. "Your father was struck down by one of the Demon's evil ones."

"What? Is he—?"

"I am sorry," said the Druid quietly. "It was poison and very fast."

"My father is dead?" He grabbed the Druid's cloak in his fists. "Where is he? I must go to him."

"No!" said the Druid sharply. "There is nothing you can do for him, who was also my dearest friend." He caught Elester's wrists and gripped them tightly. "You will be King of the Elves soon, and it rests with you to finish what we came here to do."

Miranda and the others were struck dumb by the terrible news of Ruthar's death. The girl's heart wept for the kind gentle man who had promised to tell her about her father. The Demon just kept on winning and hurting and destroying. *Yes*, she thought fiercely. *She must be stopped.* She walked over to the Druid. "I am an Elf," she said. "Give me the Egg and tell me what to do."

The girl's words cut through the young King's shock. He shook his head. "No, Miranda. I know what must be done and the duty is mine alone." Face wet with tears, he took the girl's hand. "But come! You and your friends can watch a miracle." Then he walked a short distance away to a small rock cavern and knelt on the ground.

Naim took the Serpent's Egg from Charlemagne's outstretched claw, unwrapped it, and passed it carefully to the bereaved Elven Prince. Elester held the pulsing golden oval in both hands. He uttered words in a language that Miranda had never heard, but knew as if she had spoken it all of her life. They were Elven words of creation—of beginnings and endings—of life and death. Then the Elf tapped the shell against a sharp rock. The Egg cracked. Elester placed it on the floor of the cavern and took a step back.

Miranda stared at the Egg as the crack spread around the shell. Then, to her amazement, a tiny black head with an amber mark in the shape of a crown on the flat top, poked from crack. A Fire Serpent, the size of her little finger, wriggled onto the ground. Suddenly, the hard surface beneath her feet trembled and a split appeared in the black Agni, the rock that formed Dundurum. Fire flickered from the crack along with a fierce heat that drove the humans back. But the infant Fire Serpent slithered toward the fire and disappeared into the earth. The ground shivered as the edges of the crack came together, and total silence fell over the land.

For a second no one spoke, and then, realizing that they had been holding their breaths, the companions, the Druid, and the Dwarves and Elves exhaled and the sound filled the darkness. And then Nicholas was shouting and pointing. "Look! Look!"

Miranda and the others raised their eyes and peered toward the dark looming mass of Dundurum. The land of the Dwarves was gone—sucked into the void along with the Demon and the rest of her evil creatures at the exact instant the earth closed about the infant serpent.

In the dark woods surrounding the place where the mountain had once stood, Hate's poisonous snake found the dying THUG.

The reptile wormed over the creature's wounds, slathering them with a frothy green secretion. As the serpent worked its vile magic, the pale spark in the THUG's eyes became a red flame. Satisfied, the nasty serpent slithered toward the harbour and hid among the gear that was being loaded onto the Elven ships for the return trip to Ellesmere Island.

EPILOGUE

"ow did my father die?"

It was over—exactly nine days after Miranda and her friends had fled from Ottawa with the Druid. The Trust's return to Ellesmere, after Miranda had snared the Demon and Elester had used the magic of the Serpent's Egg to drive her back into the Place with No Name, had been bittersweet. There were no parades, no victory celebration. Instead of wild cheering, tears streaked the faces of the hundreds and thousands of Elven men, women and children who lined the streets for a last glimpse of their beloved King.

Elester, leading Noble, had walked alone behind the body of his father, head bowed in sorrow. Miranda, Arabella and Penelope, walking beside the Druid, cried openly, their eyes on Elester's back. The King's Guards followed the companions, right fists pressed over their hearts. And behind them came Laury at the head of a thousand Riders and their horses—Nicholas among them, leading Fetch.

Now it was time for the Ottawans to go home, but first, Miranda was determined to learn more about her father. That's why she had left the others at the villa and gone in search of the Druid, finally running him to earth in the Council Chamber of the Hall.

Outside in the park, Miranda made for the bench she had found on her first trip to Bethany when she ran from the Hall after learning about her Elven heritage. Her face still burned whenever she thought of that night.

"How did my father die?" she repeated. "You promised. . . ."

The Druid settled himself on the soft grass, his back pressed against the slender trunk of an oleander tree. "And I shall keep my promise." He leaned his head back and closed his eyes.

Miranda waited, noticing the deep lines in his face and the dark shadows around his eyes. When he didn't move for a long minute, Miranda wondered if he had fallen asleep. But then he was speaking.

"You heard King Ruthar mention the Bog Trolls who inhabit the Swampgrass?"

Miranda nodded.

"They have been a thorn in the side of the Elves, Dwarves and other races for hundreds of years. In the first battle with the Demon, the one that resulted in the Elves creating the Place with No Name, the Bog Trolls joined the evil one because she promised to give them all the lands from Dundurum to Vark."

"After she killed all the Dwarves and Elves," prompted Miranda.

"That is true," answered the Druid. "They never for a minute considered what would happen if the Demon lost the war."

"But she *did lose* the war."

"Yes, she lost the war. You know that and I know that. But the Bog Trolls refused to believe that the Demon could be defeated. 'She is coming' has been their doomsday slogan for a thousand years."

"But surely now, these Bogs—"

"No, Miranda. They do not believe that we had anything to do with the Demon's sudden disappearance. They see that Dundurum has been destroyed and they attribute that to the power of the Demon."

"That's insane," cried Miranda.

"The Bogs, as you call them, are insane. In fact, they are so insane that their reasoning is flawless. Remember, for a thousand years they have been awaiting the return of the Demon. Meanwhile we have been arguing that she is locked away for all time in a horrible place from which she can never escape. Then suddenly, she is free. She has returned just as the Bogs said she would." He shook his head in frustration.

"About ten years ago, your father convinced King Ruthar to allow him to try and negotiate a lasting peace with the Bog Trolls. He said that he could show them proof that the Demon had been defeated once and for all time—proof that not even their warped logic could withstand. Ruthar agreed. I agreed. Every year, dozens of Elven soldiers die in the border skirmishes with the Bogs. And many more dozens of Trolls die as well. Garrett's plan promised to finally put an end to hostilities. Emissaries went back and forth between Ellesmere and the Swampgrass and a meeting was set. The Trolls insisted that your father attend alone. 'To demonstrate good faith' was how they put it." The Druid paused and ran his hand over his forehead as if to brush away painful memories.

"What happened?" asked Miranda, suddenly feeling cold in the warm sunlight.

"It was a trap," said the Druid. "I went with your father, along with a contingent of Riders. He left us and went to the meeting alone. He would not break his word. He left the Bloodstones in my care—to be held by Ruthar for his unborn daughter if he did not return." He looked at Miranda and took her hand. "He did not return."

"And nobody knows what happened to him? Maybe he's still alive?"

"Miranda, do not do this to yourself. Your father went to the Trolls and he did not return. Like the Demon, the Bog Trolls do not take prisoners."

Miranda's limbs felt heavy with sorrow, but she didn't cry. "I don't even know what he looks like. He never even knew about me."

"Your mother was pregnant with you. He knew that."

"Why did my mother run away? She *did* run away, didn't she?"

"A month after your father disappeared, King Ruthar received a message in which the Bog Trolls claimed responsibility for his death. They falsely accused him of treachery and swore that they would murder your mother and her 'unborn spawn.' Their words exactly. Your mother left her home and all that she knew to keep you safe."

"Oh. . . ." Miranda wished she could scream or cry—anything to take away the awful, dead feeling.

Naim gently squeezed her hand. "I am sorry."

Miranda nodded. "Don't be sorry. Knowing is better than always wondering."

"COME ON, MIR!"

She looked over her shoulder at Nicholas and her friends. They stood together under a large oak tree, surrounded by the Riders who had come to say their farewells. Nicholas unbuckled the leather belt that held the Elven short sword and held it out to Laury. Miranda saw the boy smile bravely, but he could not hide the sadness in his eyes. She went to join them. For a moment, the Druid remained where he was and then he pushed himself up and slowly followed.

"The sword belongs to you, Nicholas," said Laury. "You have earned it."

Nicholas grinned foolishly and rebuckled the belt about his waist. "Most of the time I felt pretty useless. I didn't do anything except get myself captured by Indolent."

"No, Nicholas," said the Druid quietly. "You showed courage beyond your years when you made the decision to accompany Miranda, and after, when you faced the Hellhags at The Devil's Fork. And, when you followed the poodle, you did not think of your own safety, you thought your friends were in danger and so you did not hesitate."

"If I was so great, then why did you have to go and turn me into a tree stump?"

"I did not say you were great, young man. I said you were

brave." Naim chuckled. "Turning you into a tree stump was the only way I could ensure that you did not die at the hands of the THUGS." He held out his hand to the boy.

Nicholas flushed but he shook the Druid's hand. Naim turned to the other companions. "What I said to Nicholas, about bravery and loyalty, I now say to you. Arabella, do not change. You are indeed a terrier. Once you get your teeth into something, you do not let go. Time and again, you proved what true friendship means."

"It was nothing," mumbled Arabella. "Once I stopped being afraid for myself."

"You don't have to say anything about me," said Penelope, scuffing her boot on the ground. "I know I did some pretty stupid things."

"And you will do lots of stupid things before you are done," said the Druid. "But your heart is in the right place and you, also, showed great courage. In fact, if the three of you had not accompanied Miranda, I do not think the Trust would have succeeded."

The companions exchanged happy grins.

"But now, we've got to go home," sobbed Penelope loudly, hugging Muffy to death. Finally, the little dog wriggled out of her grasp and ran in circles through the grass, barking happily.

"I don't know why she's crying," whispered Arabella, feeling tears fill her eyes and wiping them away on her sleeve. "I thought all she wanted to do was sue somebody or *steal* something."

"Come on Bell. That's not fair," said Miranda. "She found the Pearl plant and tried to rescue us from the Wobbles. And, remember, she paid for stealing. Dragon spit, you know."

"I guess," admitted Arabella, starting to cry again. "Can we ever come back here?"

"No," answered the Druid, coming up behind them. "The gateways from your world are closed."

"But, why?" sniffed Arabella, glaring at the Druid. "It's not fair. Whose dumb idea was it to seal off your world from ours?"

"Do not look at me like that, young lady," snapped the Druid. "If you are not happy with the way things are, take it up with the Elves. They are the ones who split the worlds. *And* they did it because your people wanted it that way." He took Miranda's arm and led her away from the others.

"I had hoped to accompany you and visit with your mother for a while, but Elester has taken his father's death very hard. And with the coronation in three months, my place is here."

"I'm never going to see you again, am I?" asked Miranda. The thought hurt like a stomachache. "And I didn't even get to say good-bye to Gregor."

"Gregor is busy with the Dragon working on plans for DunMorrow."

"I still can't believe Typhon just gave the Dwarves Oranono."

"Dragons never just give anything. There were some conditions attached."

"What sort of conditions?"

"Typhon stays and the Dwarves must redo his haunt."

Miranda grinned. "That sounds fair. I only wish I could see the new home of the Dwarves."

The Druid patted the girl's shoulder, his eyes twinkling. "I said that the ways into this world from your country were sealed, but I did not say that it worked the same from here into your world. You can pass into this land if, for example, I were to visit Ottawa and accompany you to Ellesmere."

"You mean . . . I can . . . you will . . . when?"

Naim chuckled. "I do not know, but I give you my word that I will come for you."

Miranda's green eyes shone with happiness. "I know you don't have e-mail or stuff like that, but there must be some way I can reach you."

"You can write," answered the Druid. "Charlemagne visits your world frequently. Just leave the letter on your doorstep and he will deliver it to me."

"Can you write in my language?"

"I can," said the Druid, his dark eyes twinkling. "But now that you claim to have found our alphabet, perhaps every now and then I will revert to the language of your ancestors."

Before Miranda could reply, she heard a commotion and saw a group of Dwarves coming toward them through the park. At first she thought Gregor had changed his mind, but she did not recognize his familiar shape among the others. The short, sturdy mountain folk stopped in front of the girl and one stout fellow stepped forward. "Gregor's apologies, Miss. He can't be here, but he sent us instead."

"Please thank your King," said Miranda. "And tell him I am glad that—"

The Dwarves exchanged looks, stomped their boots on the ground and burst out laughing. "We'll thank him in about two years," said the speaker. "He sent us to accompany you back to your home so we can patch up the damage caused by the Demon on Parliament Hill."

"Really?" gasped Miranda, wondering how she was going to explain the presence of a dozen Dwarves to the neighbours, not to mention the prime minister.

"I know what you're thinking," laughed the stout Dwarf. "But we'll be more comfortable making our temporary homes in the fine limestone caves under the Hill and working at night when the building's vacant. No one'll even know we're there."

"Cool!" cried Nicholas. "The workers are going to go out of their minds when they arrive every morning and find more work done."

"You were right and I was wrong, Miranda," said Elester quietly. "It appears that Gregor's people were in your country."

"Elester! I-I m-mean Y-Your M-Majesty," stammered Miranda, turning red.

"My name is still Elester," said the Elf, taking Miranda's hands. "I am sorry to see you go, Elven girl." He looked at the others. "And you also, my friends." Then he kissed Miranda's forehead and released her hands. "Neither I nor our people will ever forget what you did for us." He bowed his head and Miranda saw the clouds in his green eyes. Her heart ached for the grieving young man as he turned and walked away.

"MUFFY!" yelled Penelope. "HERE, MUFFS!"

"BAD DOG!" yelled her companions, breaking into giggles and startling the Dwarves as the toy poodle bounced out of the bushes and raced toward her mistress.

"What's she got in her mouth?" asked Nicholas, staring at the growling poodle.

"IT'S A SNAKE!" screamed Arabella. "Go away, Muffy!"

"There are no snakes on Ellesmere Island," said the Druid, as if it were something everybody should know.

"Either it's a snake or I'm a dinosaur," snapped Nicholas. "And I'm not a dinosaur." He thought for a second. "That reminds me . . . I didn't get to see a dinosaur."

Muffy chased the screaming girls through the park, the limp serpent dangling from its mouth. When the dog finally cornered Penelope, it dropped the ugly reptile on the ground by the girl's feet and stared at its mistress, tail wagging, as if to say. "I brought you a present."

Nicholas bent, arm reaching to pick up the dead snake.

"DON'T TOUCH IT!" roared Naim, racing across the grass, the wooden staff raised high.

Nicholas fell back as if he had been pricked by a thorn, shocked at the alarm in the Druid's voice. He drew his sword and chopped at the grass where the snake had been, but when he examined the ground, it was gone. Muffy barked and raced in circles, her black nose pressed to the ground. But she could not find the Demon's creature. Naim ordered the Guards to search the Island and destroy the serpent.

In the midst of the chaos, it was time for the young Ottawa

friends to go home. They said their final tearful good-byes to the Druid and, with the dozen Dwarves close on their heels, they took a step under a plain archway built between two massive oak trees. Before they could blink, they found themselves completing the step in a long dark tunnel.

"We're home!" cried Arabella.

"At least we didn't have to fly up here in one of those nasty fish bubbles," said Nicholas.

"I'm going to take a taxi home and start writing my fantasy novel," said Penelope. "What're you guys up to?"

Nicholas brushed the hair out of his eyes. "I'm going to walk home, very slowly, and hope that my dad doesn't kill me for taking the car."

Arabella grabbed Miranda's arm. "I know one thing I'm not going to do," she said.

"What?" asked her friends.

"Copy the phone book," she answered.

Penelope and Nicholas looked at her as if she were crazy. "Never mind," she said. "It'd take too long to explain."

Miranda giggled. "I think it's time I gave Stubby a little demonstration with the Bloodstones."

"Make his zipper keep coming undone in class," said Nicholas.

"Make all his teeth fall out," said Arabella.

"Seriously, what are you going to do, Mir?" asked Penelope.

"Me? I'm going to go home and have a long talk with Mom about my father and the girl in my dream, then I'm going to rent a movie, order a pizza and veg." She looked at the others and held out her hand. "I'm lucky to have you guys as friends. I couldn't have done it without you."

Arabella placed her hand on Miranda's. "Together!"

Penelope and Nicholas added their hands on top of Arabella's. "TOGETHER!"

The Dwarves stared at the companions, nudging each other and tapping their heads knowingly. Then they hitched up their backpacks, stomped their heavy boots, and faded into the nearest side-tunnel.

Back on Ellesmere Island, the dying serpent squirmed under the door and made its slow, painful way toward a table at the far end of the room, upon which rested an open casket. Inside the casket, the body of Ruthar, the late King of the Elves, lay in state. The serpent twined about the legs of the table and slithered up until it reached the casket. Hissing softly, it slipped onto the King's chest and raised its head as it studied the dead Elf through red, hate-filled eyes. Then it slid into the King's mouth and disappeared. Within a few minutes, the creature curled into a tight coil in the Elf's abdomen and died there. But not before it had laid five round eggs, as black as Hate.

Celtic Ogham Alphabet

Use the following alphabet to decipher Miranda's letter found on page 33.

A =	+		N =	▥
B =	⊤		O =	✚
C =	⊞		P =	⧣
D =	⏊		Q =	▥
E =	⧻		R =	⧼
F =	⊤⊤		S =	▥
G =	⧸		T =	⏊
H =	⊥		U =	⧺
I =	⧼		V =	
J =			W =	
K =			X =	
L =	⊤⊤		Y =	⧸ *
M =	⧸		Z =	⧼

Author's creation